Suicide Squeeze

Also by Victor Gischler

Gun Monkeys
Pistol Poets

SUICIDE SQUEEZE

VICTOR GISCHLER

DELACORTE PRESS

SUICIDE SQUEEZE
A Delacorte Book / April 2005

Published by
Bantam Dell
A Division of Random House, Inc.
New York, New York

Book design by Glen Edelstein

Delacorte Press is a registered trademark of Random House, Inc., and
the colophon is a trademark of Random House, Inc.

Library of Congress Cataloging in Publication Data
Gischler, Victor
Suicide squeeze / Victor Gischler.
p. cm.
ISBN 0-385-33725-6
1. DiMaggio, Joe, 1914–1999—Collectibles—Fiction. 2. Baseball
cards—Collectors and collecting—Fiction. 3. Boats and boating—
Fiction. 4. Bounty hunters—Fiction. 5. Repossession—Fiction.
6. Pensacola (Fla.)—Fiction. 7. Suspense fiction.
PS3607.I48 S85 2005
0504   2004065520

Printed in the United States of America
Published simultaneously in Canada

www.bantamdell.com

10 9 8 7 6 5 4 3 2 1
BVG

For Jackie

"Some people are so fond of bad luck they run half way to meet it."
—Douglas William Jerrold

"A stout heart breaks bad luck."
—Miguel de Cervantes Saavedra

Suicide Squeeze

Prologue:

Anatomy of a Collectible

NEW YORK CITY, 1954

Horace Folger didn't have time for bullshit. He couldn't take the evening off from the hardware store for just anything. But for his son, Teddy, Horace would make the time. He put his thick hand on Teddy's shoulder, drew him close. He didn't want to lose his son in the big crowd that had gathered to watch the movie people.

But those movie people didn't seem to know their ass from a hole in the ground. The director guy kept yelling "cut" and everybody would stop what they were doing, then they'd go back and he'd yell "action" and everyone would do the exact same shit over again. The director seemed bothered by the big crowd, which was mostly men.

They all wanted to see the blonde.

And Jesus Christ what a blonde. She kept standing over this subway grille, then there'd be this whoosh of air, blowing her white dress up, and everyone got an eyeful. Whenever that dress went up, Horace's knees turned watery. *I'd never, ever cheat on Mildred, but if that blonde ever came knocking on my door late one night . . .*

Horace nudged the guy next to him. "Hey, Mac, who's the dish?"

"Are you pulling my leg?" said the guy. "That's Marilyn Monroe. What, you been lost on a desert island or something?"

"Yeah, yeah." Everyone was a goddamn wiseass.

Horace scanned the crowd, searched each face. And there he was, Joe DiMaggio. Now, here was a real man and a hell of a ballplayer. Word had flashed up and down the streets, into the little neighborhood a few blocks away where Horace ran his hardware store. DiMaggio! Horace didn't have to think twice about it. He ran up to their apartment above the store, snatched up his boy Teddy, and took him down to get a look at the greatest ballplayer who'd ever lived.

And Horace was looking right at him. DiMaggio was less than a hundred yards away, standing with some people. Some working the lights, others with clipboards, microphones, everybody running around like decapitated chickens.

Except Jolting Joe. He made fists and stared at the blonde. He seemed pissed royal. Now Horace remembered. DiMaggio was married to the blonde. Ha. No wonder Joe was so bent out of shape. Horace wouldn't want a crowd of sweaty gorillas gawking at his wife either.

"Come on, Teddy." He hoisted his son up on his shoulders, pointed at the pissed ballplayer. "That's Joe DiMaggio, son. That's the greatest man in the sport of baseball." In Horace's mind, he might as well have been pointing at the president or the pope or Frank Sinatra.

Teddy didn't say anything, just held on to Dad's head, taking in the spectacle with big brown eyes.

The kid made Horace nervous. He almost never spoke, clung to his mother's dress. Wouldn't look strangers in the eye. Mildred just said he was quiet and shy. Horace didn't care to hear that. His cousin Leo had been "quiet and shy" and now he cut women's hair in the Village. So he brought Teddy to see what a man looked like.

The director yelled "action," and Monroe's skirt flew up again. DiMaggio looked like he could spit nails.

Horace loved his son, but he worried like lots of fathers worried. All the kid seemed to do was read Superman comics. Teddy wouldn't play with the ball and bat Horace had gotten him for Christmas. But he loved the Buck Rogers ray gun. The kid took it to bed at night, clutching it to his chest like a stuffed animal.

And then one day Horace came upstairs from the store and found Teddy on the floor in front of the big radio. He was arranging little rectangular cardboard cards with pictures on them. Horace had knelt next to his son, seen they were baseball cards. Baseball! Now, this was more like it. And right in the middle was a Joe DiMaggio card. Teddy had sorted them all by team, lining them up on the knotted rug. That weekend, Horace had taken the kid to a Yankees game. Teddy had been bored.

At least the kid wasn't playing with dolls.

Horace watched the director throw up his hands and tell everyone to take five. Monroe went to her husband on the sidelines. It looked like they were having words. Horace edged closer, found himself in a milling crowd, some leaving, others trying to edge in and get a look at the starlet.

If Horace hurried, he could get the autograph. Maybe DiMaggio would shake Teddy's hand. It might make all the difference, make some kind of important, lasting impression on the kid.

Somebody held up a hand, big guy, maybe a teamster, halted Horace in his tracks. "Not through here."

"I wanted my son to meet—"

The teamster shook his head. "Trying to shoot a picture here, pal. Got to keep everyone back."

Then the sailors. Three of them, reeking like a brewery, tried to surge past the line. The teamster caught one, grabbed at the others, yelled, "Jesus, Pauley, get over here. We got some wise guys."

Another teamster the size of a battleship leapt in front of the sailors. They wrestled, the sailors cursing and throwing feeble punches, one calling for "Marilyn, baby."

Horace saw his chance, slipped around the fracas, Teddy still bobbing on his shoulders and holding on to his hair.

Horace beelined for DiMaggio and Monroe. Monroe had turned away from the ballplayer, but Joe latched on to her wrist, pulled her back. Horace winced. It was obviously a private moment, and it wasn't like Horace to stick his nose in where it didn't belong. But he'd come too far to turn back. His son was going to meet Joe DiMaggio and that was all there was to it. He pressed on, got within five feet of the couple.

DiMaggio looked up abruptly, released Monroe, and put his hands in his pockets. Horace stood right in front of them now. He was nervous, but knew he couldn't stand there all day staring at the man.

"Mr. DiMaggio, I'm a big fan." He put out his hand, and DiMaggio shook it.

"Thanks," DiMaggio said.

"My son too." He pushed Teddy forward. "Shake the man's hand, son."

Teddy raised his hand like a zombie. He seemed to be in some kind of trance, eyes not quite focusing on DiMaggio.

DiMaggio managed to summon half a smile, took the kid's hand. "How're you doing, slugger?"

Teddy's mouth hung open slightly. He pulled his hand back.

Horace touched his son on the shoulder. "Give it to him. Go on."

In his other hand, Teddy held the Joe DiMaggio card. He handed it to the ballplayer, who looked at it and laughed.

"I remember sitting for this one." DiMaggio patted his jacket pockets, looking for a pen.

Horace was ready. He handed DiMaggio a fountain pen, watched as DiMaggio signed his name right under his face. Horace realized he was far more excited about the whole situation than his son was. DiMaggio handed the card back to Teddy, who took it quietly. But he wasn't looking at the ballplayer, seemed not even to realize he'd gotten the autograph.

Teddy stared with wide-eyed awe at Monroe. The movie lights

lit her hair up like a blond halo. She seemed to glow—white skin, lips wet and red.

Monroe saw she was now the object of the child's attention. Her face transformed, smile suddenly warm and gleaming. "Well, hello, honey. How's my little man?"

Teddy stepped forward, a hazy, lopsided grin turning up the corners of his mouth. Inexplicably, he handed Monroe the Joe DiMaggio card.

Monroe took it, then snatched the fountain pen, which was still in DiMaggio's hand. "I'll sign this too, okay?" She shot DiMaggio a sideways glance before turning up the volume on her smile and looking Teddy in the eyes. "Joe doesn't mind. That's because he knows we're a team, right, Joe?"

"Sure."

Monroe signed her name right under DiMaggio's.

Horace said, "We don't want to take any more of your time."

"Nonsense," Monroe said. "Joe and I love to visit with the people. Don't we, Joe?"

DiMaggio frowned. Teddy continued to gawk at the starlet, naked worship on his face.

Horace felt uncomfortable now. "We'd really better be going. My wife probably had supper ready an hour ago and—"

The director came over, took Marilyn by the elbow. "We're ready to start again. Up for another take?"

Monroe said, "Oh, Billy, we're all signing one of Joe's cards for this charming young man. Here, you sign too."

The director signed "Billy Wilder" underneath Monroe's name, then handed the card back to Teddy.

DiMaggio's face was the color of a stoplight. Furious.

"I can see you need to get back to work," Horace said. "Thanks a lot, folks." Horace scooped Teddy up under his arm and retreated quickly. The chaos of the movie shoot resumed behind them.

When they'd made it through the crowd, Horace set his son on the sidewalk. Strolled back toward the hardware store. Teddy held the baseball card delicately, took special care not to smudge the ink. The encounter had not gone quite as Horace had planned, but Teddy seemed to have enjoyed it.

"Daddy, what was that lady's name?"

Horace stopped walking, blinked at his son. It was the first thing the kid had said in five hours. "Marilyn Monroe. She's in pictures."

"Marilyn Monroe," Teddy repeated with wonder, like the words to a magic spell. Like a prayer.

MARCH 11, 1962

Dear Miss Monroe,

My name is Teddy Folger, and I am your biggest fan. Ha. I have to laugh because I just bet every letter you get starts out with some guy saying he's your biggest fan. Well, for me it happens to be true. I don't know if you remember me, but I met you when I was six years old while you were doing *The Seven Year Itch*. My dad took me to see Joe DiMaggio and you were there too and you signed my DiMaggio card. I will never forget that day. I have seen every one of your pictures ten times. I think you are the most beautiful woman in the world. I don't mean that in a dirty way or like a come-on. You probably get lots of fellows writing you with some kind of pitch. I'm not like that. I'm just a fan who thinks you're about the greatest movie star that ever lived.

Three days ago I went to my dad's funeral. He was hit by a cab. I don't know why I'm telling you this. I think my dad wanted me to be different than I am. He never said anything. He never got mad at me, but I could tell he wanted me to be different. He always took me to your movies.

Usually a matinee. I just wanted you to know that my dad was the greatest. He wanted me to be happy, so he took me to every one of your movies even though I don't think he really cared about movies too much. I hope you have a new movie coming out soon.

Your biggest fan,

Teddy Folger

JULY 30, 1962

Dear Teddy,

I'm sorry it took me so long to write back. I get so many letters, and I'm just so very busy. Of course I remember you, honey. I'm so happy that you find my films so enjoyable. It makes my heart happy to hear it. To tell the truth, I've been a little blue, so your letter was a much-needed pick-me-up.

I can't tell you how sorry I am to hear about your father. People are funny. They all want us and expect us to be a certain way. Sometimes people never know the real us. It sounds like your father knew you pretty well. He might have had some very different expectations from you, but I'm sure he loved and accepted you just how you are. You seem a special and sensitive young man. Thanks so much for your letter.

Love,

Marilyn Monroe

NEW ORLEANS, 2002

"Welcome back to *Antiques Road Show*," said the host. "This week, we're in New Orleans, the Big Easy, and we have another amazing assortment of antiques and collectibles. Let's continue now with Arlo Watts, curator of the San Diego Museum of Pop Culture. He's looking at an item that combines baseball and Hollywood. Arlo."

The camera switched to Arlo, a middle-aged man decked out in tweed, little half glasses. He stood next to a stout man with gray hair, midfifties. On the table between them was a large picture frame.

Arlo said, "We're here with Teddy Folger, who's driven from Pensacola to show us this piece of not only baseball memorabilia, but also an extraordinary piece of Hollywood history. Mr. Folger, tell us how you came to possess such a special item."

"It all started when my father wanted me to meet Joe DiMaggio." Folger told the tale succinctly, all facts, no embellishments. The story was already good. It needed no exaggeration. Folger finished the story, then said, "And if you want to see this wonderful treasure of American history, I'll have it on display at my store, Pan-Galactic Comics & Collectibles on Davis Highway, in Pensacola, Florida." Folger waved at the camera.

Arlo ignored the plug and dove into a lengthy and tedious story about the filming of *The Seven Year Itch*. Folger smiled, tried to appear patient and interested, but what he really wanted to hear—what *everyone* wanted to hear on this show—was all about how much the damn thing was worth. *Get to the money, egghead!*

Now Arlo was yakking on and on about Monroe's marriage to DiMaggio. Folger knew all this already. He supposed the TV audience found it interesting. In the last forty years, Folger had read every word written on the subject. He'd even written a short book on Monroe, but twenty New York agents had turned it down, claiming the subject was exhausted.

Finally, Arlo asked the golden question. "Mr. Folger, do you have any idea what this item is worth?"

Folger had seen the show many times, knew what he was supposed to say. "Oh, I really have no idea. Its sentimental value is more important as far as I'm concerned." *A million dollars. Say it. It's worth a million if it's worth a penny. Say it, you nerd.*

"First, let's review what we have here," Arlo said. "The presentation is very nice. You've taken a full-size *Seven Year Itch* film poster and framed it nicely in glass. The poster features Marilyn in her famous pose, the skirt flying up. On either side of Marilyn, you've encased the two artifacts. Individually, each artifact would probably bring a nice price, but the letter and the card are connected by a personal story. This all adds value."

Get on with it, thought Folger. He felt sweat under his arms.

"The card," Arlo continued, "is a wonderful example of an Apex brand Joe DiMaggio baseball card in mint condition. Signed by Joe DiMaggio, Marilyn Monroe, and film director Billy Wilder. These are the key players in one of Hollywood's great stories. Really the quintessential American marriage between one of the nation's great baseball athletes and perhaps the nation's greatest movie star. It all comes together on this one baseball card."

Folger nodded along with Arlo's lecture, but in his mind, he was spending money.

Arlo said, "Then we have the letter. It goes without saying that Monroe got millions of fan letters, so the fact you received a return letter is in itself pretty amazing. But notice the date." He pointed to the corner of the letter. "This letter was written less than a week before Monroe was tragically found dead in her home. I haven't had a chance to check this yet, but it may very well be the last letter she ever sent. Certainly *one* of the last."

Arlo scratched his chin. Folger held his breath.

Arlo said, "Unfortunately . . ."

Folger's heart stopped.

". . . it's difficult to predict how much such an item would fetch at auction," Arlo said. "It all depends how eager collectors would be to get their hands on such an item. Certainly the rarity and importance of the item would drive the price up a good bit, but one never can tell."

Folger felt sick. His fake smile hurt so much, he was afraid his face was going to detach and fall on the floor. He cleared his throat. "Well . . . that's interesting."

"It is an irreplaceable item," Arlo said. "For obvious reasons. For insurance purposes, I'd value the card and the letter together at close to a hundred thousand dollars. At auction, it would be anyone's guess, but I'd certainly get this insured without delay."

"Thanks," Folger said. "I'll look into some insurance right away."

TOKYO, TODAY

Ahira Kurisaka was a fat billionaire in a leather jacket. Kurisaka stood in front of a full-length mirror, turning from side to side, admiring himself even though the jacket was clearly five sizes too small.

Billy Moto watched, trying to suppress the disgust he felt. It was sometimes difficult to maintain respect for his employer. The newspapers were kind in merely referring to him as eccentric, but Billy knew Kurisaka more completely than perhaps any other person in the world. Ahira Kurisaka was one of the strangest, most paranoid people Moto had ever met.

"How does it look?" Kurisaka asked.

"It's too small." There was no point in lying. His boss would know. Lying wasn't something Billy Moto would do anyway.

"Perhaps," Kurisaka said. "And this was actually worn by Fonzie during the television series?"

"Our sources are positive. The Smithsonian would not sell us the one they have on display, but it was simple enough to contact the studio people and purchase another."

Kurisaka looked in the mirror, slicked back his hair, and stuck his thumbs out. "Aaayyy."

In the past five years, Billy Moto had performed a variety of services for his master. The most trivial of which, in Billy's opinion, was his overseeing of various purchases of . . . well . . . nonsense. One of John Wayne's saddles, a Joe Namath football helmet, a speedboat owned by the Kennedy family. Fingernail clippings from Elvis (of dubious authenticity, Billy thought). Just a few of the recent acquisitions. Ahira Kurisaka was one of the richest men in Japan, yet on any given day, Billy could find the man stuffing his face with Big Macs and Chicken McNuggets. Billy's boss was obsessed with American culture.

Billy's grandfather had been an American G.I. In spite of Billy's impressive qualifications, he strongly suspected Kurisaka had hired him simply because he liked the name Billy.

"What of the card?" asked Kurisaka.

Billy cleared his throat. "There have been complications."

"I want the DiMaggio card," Kurisaka said. "Hyatta will turn green with envy."

Kurisaka maintained a semifriendly (meaning semiunfriendly) rivalry with fellow billionaire and Americana collector Hito Hyatta. Hyatta continually one-upped Kurisaka at every opportunity. One time, Kurisaka had bragged about his recent purchase of an autographed picture of General Douglas MacArthur. It was a good photograph, the general wading ashore upon his return to the Philippines. Hyatta had congratulated Kurisaka on his purchase before casually mentioning he had a signed, first-draft manuscript copy of the general's memoirs. It seemed Hyatta's acquisitions were nearly always more expensive and more rare than Kurisaka's. Moto believed if Kurisaka had JFK's underwear, Hyatta would produce the former president's brain in a jar.

Moto said, "There have been conflicting reports. Our eBay bid of twenty-five thousand dollars was clearly in the lead, but it turns out the card has been destroyed."

Kurisaka gasped, eyes growing wide.

"One of our underground sources reports an offer coming through a third party. Apparently, someone is offering the card for sale at one million dollars."

"And how can this be possible if the card has been destroyed?"

Billy shrugged. "Perhaps the card is a counterfeit. I'm only guessing, Mr. Kurisaka."

Kurisaka slipped off his Fonzie jacket, hung it carefully on a hanger. He paced the floor for several minutes before taking his plush chair behind a gigantic oaken desk. Both chair and desk had belonged to Ulysses S. Grant. Kurisaka picked up an Etch-A-Sketch and began drawing random lines, deep in thought. "The man's name in Florida? The one who owns the card?"

"Teddy Folger."

"It's him," Kurisaka said. "The card has not been destroyed. Folger has some scheme to drive up the price."

"Perhaps." Billy could really give a shit.

Kurisaka scratched his chin, glanced at his watch. "I'll be late for my lunch with Hyatta. Find out what you can about Folger. I don't like being tricked, Billy. I didn't get where I am today by allowing myself to be screwed."

High atop Tokyo's Mitsubishi Building, in a window seat of an elegant restaurant, Ahira Kurisaka ignored the breathtaking view of the city and instead contemplated a gigantic platter of shrimp. After thirty minutes of waiting for Hyatta, Kurisaka had decided to order. He didn't enjoy being stood up. Was it a deliberate snub? Should he be insulted? He was so upset, he almost lost his appetite.

Almost.

He shoved shrimp into his mouth.

Kurisaka had come up the hard way, working his way from street tough, up through the Yakuza ranks until he was one of the most powerful crime bosses in Japan. He took his ill-gotten gains and began investing legitimately, buying out corporations, reinventing himself as an upstanding member of the community. But it was sometimes difficult. Although he now ran in mostly legitimate circles, he often felt his peers were whispering about him behind his back. Rumors of his former underworld life circulated.

And so now, when Hyatta had failed to show for a routine luncheon, Kurisaka had to wonder. Was Hyatta weary of associating with him? Was Kurisaka not fitting into the upper echelons of Japanese society as he'd hoped?

Indeed, Kurisaka's Yakuza past refused to vanish completely. He'd made many enemies. Two or three assassination attempts a year were to be expected. There were many who wanted revenge, and many more still who would benefit from the power vacuum should Kurisaka be killed. And it wasn't just his criminal past that engendered these attempts on his life. A few of his corporate competitors would be delighted at his demise.

Kurisaka still retained many of his connections. One never really retired from the Yakuza, and many of Kurisaka's legitimate businesses still laundered money for the syndicate. If need be, Kurisaka could call on those connections at any time. If someone were bad-mouthing him to Hyatta . . . Well, Kurisaka was not the sort of man to sit still for an insult.

Hyatta appeared in the restaurant, spotted Kurisaka, and waved. Kurisaka forced a smile and stood as Hyatta took the chair opposite him.

"I apologize for my lateness," Hyatta said.

"Oh, are you late? I hadn't even noticed," Kurisaka said.

Kurisaka waited politely for Hyatta to give the waiter his order. "And a Jack Daniel's on the rocks," said Hyatta. Both he and Kurisaka drank American whiskey.

Hito Hyatta was a proper, formal Japanese gentleman. He wore a conservative and expensive gray suit, hair white and perfect. There was always an air of royalty about the man. Kurisaka became aware of his own attire. A red sports jacket the size of a circus tent, jade buttons on his black silk shirt—more suitable for a Las Vegas casino. Too many rings. Garish. He made a mental note to call his tailor. Kurisaka was uneasily aware that quiet elegance was something he had yet to master.

"Again, I apologize for being tardy," Hyatta said, "but I was waiting for a special delivery. I hope you don't mind if I boast a little about my latest find, but I knew this would be something you'd appreciate."

Hyatta took a small plastic case out of his jacket pocket, placed it reverently on the table between himself and Kurisaka. He opened the case. A gold coin within.

Kurisaka shoved more shrimp into his mouth, leaned forward to look at the coin. A gold American Double Eagle. Kurisaka was not impressed. He had a few of these coins himself. The US government had started minting them about the time of the gold rush. Kurisaka kept the smile off his face. If Hyatta thought this was worth boasting— Kurisaka spotted the date on the coin. His mouth fell open. Shrimp dropped out.

"Is that a 1933?" he asked.

Hyatta smiled and nodded.

"But I can't—it must be a replica," Kurisaka sputtered. "Roosevelt had them all melted down. The Secret Service tracked down the ones that were stolen."

"It's genuine," Hyatta said. "An interesting story actually."

Hyatta dove into the story, how the coin had turned up during a renovation of a basement in San Francisco. Hyatta had good contacts with dealers throughout the United States. When the construction worker who'd found the coin sold it for five hundred dollars to a dealer in Oakland, the shop owner had immediately recognized what the coin was. But he'd needed to be careful. Otherwise, the US Treasury Department would claim the coin. The shop owner had contacted people who contacted other people until finally Hyatta had arranged to purchase the coin.

Kurisaka barely listened. His eyes were fixed on the coin. A sickening, mixed feeling of admiration and envy settled in his stomach. He desperately wanted to ask Hyatta if he could hold the coin but didn't want to give his rival the satisfaction. He simply said, "Congratulations."

Hyatta offered a modest shrug. "We are fortunate to be men of means. We can afford to pursue our passions. What of you, Ahira? Any new additions to the collection?"

Kurisaka brightened. He knew Hyatta had a special weakness for baseball memorabilia. Now here was his chance to make Hyatta jealous. "I'm negotiating the purchase of a baseball card. It's one of a kind, quite special." He picked up the dropped piece of shrimp, put it back in his mouth.

"What a coincidence. I'm also in the middle of acquiring a baseball card. My people are in contact with a Florida man who claims to have something unique."

Kurisaka choked on the shrimp, went into a coughing fit.

"Are you all right?" asked Hyatta.

Kuriska washed down the shrimp with a glass of water. "I'm fine."

They finished lunch, and Kurisaka returned to his limousine, surrounded by four bodyguards. He sulked in the back as the long black vehicle slid through downtown Tokyo. The thought that Hyatta might get his Joe DiMaggio baseball card made him physically ill.

He picked up the car phone and dialed Billy Moto. "Billy, pack a bag and arrange for one of the company jets. I'm sending you to America."

PART ONE

In which Conner Samson
is Philip Marlowe.

1

Conner Samson bounced a check for a dollar draft in Salty's Saloon and decided it was time to get serious about looking for work.

Sid, the eternally bald and surly bartender, set the draft beer at Conner's elbow and handed him the phone from behind the bar. Sid took Conner's check and frowned at it before crumpling it into a tight wad and tossing it over his shoulder. He wiped the length of the bar with an old rag, muttering in his amiable cranky way.

"Thanks, Sid."

"Yeah, yeah."

Conner looked up again at the TV hanging over the bar to see if the nightmare was true. Maybe the whole thing had been a bad hallucination. The score: Atlanta 6, St. Louis 7, and Chip Carey telling everyone about the outfielder's error, which had cost Conner five hundred bucks.

Hell.

Salty's Saloon was old and dark and filled with quiet regulars who wanted to watch sports, nurse drinks, and be left alone.

Conner's kind of place. Salty's had been through a few transformations: a disco, a Chinese takeout place, a pool hall. A wooden cricket bat still hung on the wall from the brief period Salty's had masqueraded as an English pub. Conner liked the current incarnation. Neon beer signs, a jukebox nobody played, a TV with a ball game always on, and cheap suds. And Sid. A crusty retired Marine, but a good guy who knew the names and life stories of all his regulars.

Sid glanced at the television, shook his head. "You got the worst luck of anybody I've ever known." He was still shaking his head as he stacked clean glasses behind the bar.

Conner drank his beer and looked at the phone.

He didn't want to make the calls yet, so he stalled, paged through the *Wall Street Journal*. DesertTech was up three points. A friend of a pal of a guy somebody knew had suggested the stock a week ago. Conner kept tabs. The stock was going up and up. That would have been great, except Conner hadn't bought any. He'd been trying to put some bets together, get a stake so he could buy a hundred shares. Then the stupid fucking Atlanta Braves . . .

"I guess you ain't a millionaire yet," Sid said.

"Would I be in this dump if I were a millionaire?"

"Yeah, I sorta think you would," Sid said. "My sister owns an alpaca farm in California. Says it's the latest thing."

"No animals."

"They always need guys on the offshore oil rigs."

"I want my money to work for me. Not the other way around."

"Yeah, but it takes money to make money."

"That's clever," Conner said. "I'm going write that down."

"Oh, blow it out your ass."

Conner couldn't stall anymore. He dialed Harvey Sterling at Sterling's Bail Bonds. Harvey sometimes paid well whenever he sent one of his guys to chase down a skip. Conner didn't consider himself a tough guy or anything like that, but he was tall and had some shoulders, and sometimes just the sight of a big guy standing there would keep somebody from running or putting up a fight. Harvey didn't have any work for him. Conner left his number in case anything changed.

Next, Conner dialed Ed Odeski at Gulf Coast Collections. He really didn't want to, but repossessing cars for Odeski was usually worth a couple of bucks. Last time, Conner had to hot-wire a Jaguar. The delinquent owner had caught him in the middle of the job. He hit Conner, and it hurt a lot. Conner hit him back a few times, but it didn't seem to bother the guy. They went on like that for a little while. By the end, Conner had managed to get away with the car. What he got paid for the repo almost covered the cost of his stitches.

"Gulf Coast Collections," said the secretary.

"Tell Ed it's Conner Samson."

"Hold please."

Conner held.

Ed's gutter ball voice came on the line. "You must need work, Samson."

"What? A guy can't call up an old buddy?"

"No."

"Okay, so I need work."

"Ain't got none."

"Come on."

"None."

"Awwwwwww, come on." Sometimes just being pathetic was the best way to get a job out of Ed. He liked to save most of his repo work for a squat little hunk of meat he called his kid brother. "I'm not picky here, buddy. I just need some folding money."

"No. You always bust up the cars. Bring them back all banged." He was from Albania or Lithuania or some kind of ania. Conner always forgot where, but Odeski's accent was thick with spit.

"It was only that one time," Conner said.

"All headlights smashed real good."

"The guy had a tire iron. He was trying to cave in my skull."

"So you hit him with a car."

"The light was green."

"Then you back over him," Ed said. "Smash up taillights and bend the bumper."

"I was going back to see if he was okay. It wasn't my fault, man."

Ed sighed, the sound of a hippo sitting on a beach ball. "You wait. Stay on phone."

Conner waited again, wished for the tenth time he had a cell phone.

Sid brought another draft. Conner waved the checkbook, arched his eyebrows into a question.

"Yeah, right," Sid said. "Don't make me laugh."

Conner mouthed "thanks" at him.

Ed came back on the line. "Okay, I got something. Maybe good for you. You got a pencil?"

Conner reached over the bar for a pen, spread a napkin to write on. "Go ahead."

Odeski told him a phone number. "This man might have work for you, Samson. You call. His name is Derrick James. Okay. You call. Okay?"

"Okay."

"You call," Ed said. "Tell him my name. Ed Odeski."

"I'll tell him," Conner said. "Thanks, Ed."

"Is nothing." He hung up.

Conner called Derrick James next. He had a business in Mobile, boats and marine supplies, etc. James said to drive out and see him the sooner the better.

Conner said he was on his way.

James Boat & Nautical Supply was tucked away at the grimy end of the industrial shipyards in Mobile. Traffic was light, and Conner made the trip on I-10 over the Bay Bridge in just under an hour. James had an office in back of the big, warehouse-size shop. The girl behind the counter directed Conner down an aisle of big nets and winch equipment. He found the door all the way back and knocked.

"Come in."

Conner went in.

"You must be Samson," he said.

"That's me."

"Derrick James." They shook hands, and James motioned Conner to a chair across his sad little desk. The office on the whole looked dark and uninteresting, a five-hundred-year-old computer buzzing its tale of obsolescence. A nautical chart of the Gulf Coast on the wall behind him, yellowing at the edges.

James was so tan and crusty, his face looked like a catcher's mitt. Well-groomed salt-and-pepper hair. Big white horse teeth. He was trim, tall, wore khaki shorts and a Hawaiian shirt with too many buttons undone. He sported a nifty shark-tooth necklace. Somehow, he was making believe he wasn't at the tail end of his forties, maybe fifty.

Conner became aware he might be looking at himself in twenty years. Conner was just as tall, not quite as tan but almost. He'd picked a few strands of premature gray out of his black hair just two days ago. He ran a hand along his angular jaw and frowned. James had shaved more recently than he had.

"I know Ed Odeski pretty well," James said. "I trust his judgment." He opened his top desk drawer and fished out a manila folder. "He said you were the man for the job."

"I'm your man."

James opened the folder and slid a color picture of a sailboat across his desk. It wasn't a real picture. Printed on computer paper, but it was clear, and Conner could see the boat fine. A nice sloop, maybe five years old, thirty-six feet, one mast and a spinnaker. Nice lines. An athletic blonde sat in the cockpit and waved, a bright and happy Sunday sailor. She had nice lines too. Conner tossed the picture back on the desk.

"That's the *Electric Jenny*," James said. "Good-looking vessel, huh?"

Conner agreed she was a good-looking vessel.

"And she's got the works," he said. "New radar, GPS, depth finders. Hell, she's even got that new state-of-the-art air-conditioning. You know how hard it is to keep a boat's air-conditioning up and running with the salt air and everything?"

"I know."

"Sleeps seven, no problem."

"Nice." *Get on with it.*

He shuffled papers again, came out with a statement, columns of numbers. "I held the note on fifty-eight thousand dollars. He bought the *Jenny* in March, made five payments but missed his last one August first."

"He's only late on one payment?"

James said, "I took the boat as collateral on a shitload of equipment for some guys who were starting a marina. They went belly-up, and I got stuck with her. I was glad to hold the note as long as somebody was making payments. But I ain't the Federal Reserve. I want my money on time. I got my own bills."

James shoved a stack of papers to one side, revealing an expensive-looking cherrywood humidor. He flipped it open and grabbed a cigar. A Macanudo. He bit off the end and spit it in the trash can, stuck the cigar into his mouth without removing the band. He lit it with a disposable lighter. Conner raised an eyebrow.

James nudged the humidor toward Conner. "Want one?"

"Please." Conner plucked one out of the humidor between thumb and forefinger, bit the end, clamped the cigar gently between his teeth. James lit it, and Conner puffed it to life. *Oh, baby.* Conner's budget had him on Swisher Sweets, the Pabst Blue Ribbon of cigars.

"Thanks," Conner said, and meant it.

James waved away the gratitude. "I probably wouldn't be so hot to sic a repo man on the guy, but circumstances make me think we need to act fast."

"How so?" *Puff-puff.*

"Believe you me, I'd much rather have Folger just pay on time than go through the hassle of taking the boat back. So I had my girl out front call him. A friendly reminder."

"What did he say?"

"He didn't say anything," James said. "That's the trouble. My girl calls him at home, but the number's disconnected. Then she tries the work number. Same story. Now I'm starting to wonder."

"Uh-huh." *Man, this cigar is good. Smooth.* Conner rolled it on his tongue, sucked smoke deep into his lungs.

"So I call around," James said, "and find out his business has gone under. Okay, so the guy has hit the skids. A repossessed boat is the least of his worries, right? He rents a slip at a marina in Gulf Shores. I go down there with a padlock and a photocopy of the finance agreement. I hate to do it to the guy, but I can read the writing on the wall. If he's belly-up, I'll have to take the boat back."

"But when you got to the marina, the boat wasn't there."

"You've heard this story before."

"Variations on a theme."

"I've called disconnected numbers, sent angry letters, and I'm still short one sailboat."

Enter Conner Samson, repo dude, cigar aficionado, washed-up left fielder, and all-around swell guy.

"So here's the deal," James said. "You bring back the boat, and I can pay you four thousand dollars. Call it a bounty or reward or whatever. I've done some arithmetic, and I'm confident I can make that back when I turn around and sell the boat again."

Okay. Here's the tough part. Conner cleared his throat. "I'm going to need half up front."

"Screw that."

"I've done this kind of work before, Mr. James. If it were just a matter of sneaking into some guy's yard and stealing a Chevy with the spare key, that would be one thing, but you don't know where the sloop is. You don't know where Folger is. All you know for sure is that you got a big, expensive, missing boat."

"I know this already."

"It'll cost to look for the boat. Expenses. I need something up front."

"I gave you a cigar."

"That won't fill my gas tank." The fumes left in Conner's Plymouth Fury wouldn't even get him back over the bridge.

James sighed, leaned in his seat, and pulled a wallet from his back pocket. He fished out five hundred-dollar bills and gave them to Conner like he was handing over a testicle.

"That's not half," Conner pointed out.

"That's what you get."

"Deal." Conner shoved the bills into his pants pocket before James could change his mind.

"You get thirty-five hundred more when you bring in the *Jenny*. And I mean in one piece."

"I understand."

"I hope you do. I don't fork over five bills to every Tom, Dick, and Harry. Only because I know Ed Odeski."

Yeah, Ed's church folk. "Can your girl photocopy Folger's file for me? It'll help."

"Sure. Sit tight. Hands off the cigars."

Conner pulled into his shabby apartment complex and spotted Fat Otis's banana yellow 1979 Lincoln Continental parked outside of his building. He turned around quick and left. Fat Otis was a four-hundred-pound, six-five black man with a shaved head and a talent for turning strong, healthy men into little, mashed-up heaps of bone and flesh.

Otis wouldn't do that to me. Not yet anyway. He was a collector for Rocky Big, Pensacola's premier bookie, fence, badass, and super-pimp. The fact that Otis had parked in plain sight meant Conner was still within the grace period. Otis had come to collect but not to bust kneecaps. Conner wasn't too worried. He and Otis went back a long way, but Conner wasn't really in the mood to explain himself or fork over the money James had given him.

Note to self: The Atlanta Braves suck.

So Conner headed up Scenic Highway with the idea he'd stop in to see Tyranny. It had been a few days, and he conjured her image in his head. It was early afternoon. Maybe he'd catch her out by the pool—taut, thin body stretched in a lounge chair, string bikini. She'd smile that crooked smile at him from behind her starlet sunglasses. Conner was never sure what to expect from Tyranny. She was a mystery. But he wanted to see her, and maybe today would be the day something good happened.

But only if her husband wasn't home.

2

Tyranny Jones didn't answer the door in a bikini. She wore jeans, sneakers, one of her husband's oversized T-shirts smeared with paint. She had another very picturesque smudge of bright red across the bridge of her nose. Conner took her face in his hands, drew a thumb down the length of her slightly too-pointed nose, and showed her the paint.

She pulled away, laughing gently. "I've been in the studio."

"Working again?"

"Trying."

"Show me."

She smiled, took him by the hand, and led him through the house and into the breakfast nook just off the kitchen. She called it her studio, and Conner indulged her by not pointing out it was really just a little patch of tile floor surrounded by big bay windows. She had a huge canvas on the easel, a palette of paints to the side.

Tyranny's current project was a black-red swirl of heavily textured paint with flecks of dark green. It looked more like a diaper load than art. Conner didn't tell her this.

What he said was "nice."

She snorted. "You're a terrible liar, but I love you."

It was the most natural thing in the world to say. *I love you.* Maybe that's why the room turned real quiet all of a sudden. Her hand was still on his. He squeezed, and she squeezed back. The afternoon sun drifted in through the bay windows, washed them in dusty warmth. She leaned into him, bodies touching at the hips. Conner's breath came quick and shallow, heart fluttering.

Tyranny and Conner had taken a long, strange ride together to get to this point. He'd met her during his four-semester attempt at college before he'd blown his baseball scholarship. They'd met in an introductory art class. She was the star pupil. He just wanted to kill an elective. They'd liked each other immediately, but she'd had a boyfriend, some long-haired kid who splashed artistic angst all over himself like it was cheap aftershave. By the time she'd ditched him, Conner was involved with an uncomplicated cover-girl blonde whose sole mission in life seemed to be climbing on top of him. Tyranny and he remained friends.

As a matter of fact, they were such good friends that they couldn't un-friend themselves when they were finally single at the same time. They looked at each other with a mysterious gleam in their eyes, but maybe nobody was brave enough to take that next step.

And maybe another reason they never got together was the fact that they were so obviously wrong for each other, at least that was the way it seemed on the surface. He was a jock. She hung with the art crowd. But it was that difference that kept Conner interested. Tyranny wasn't like the sorority bubbleheads that seemed to find their way so easily into Conner's bed. Tyranny could talk for hours without ever resorting to the subject of her hair or nails or shoes. She intrigued him, and maybe the feeling was mutual, and it wasn't anything he could quite put his finger on, but there was a strange and powerful chemistry whenever they were together. The fact that she was somehow attracted to him, and that it had nothing to do with his tan or his muscles or his straight white teeth, simultaneously excited and worried him.

Tyranny had been accepted to the grad program, and he'd long flunked out to pursue half-assed, get-rich-quick schemes full-time when Professor Dan proposed marriage. Conner hadn't even realized Tyranny was seeing anyone. *I guess it isn't good policy to advertise you're humping one of your teachers.* If it had been a movie, he'd have walked out.

Their friendship cooled after that. Conner got a wedding invitation in the mail and conveniently misplaced it. He supposed it was unreasonable to feel hurt. Being reasonable wasn't one of his hobbies.

Then one long bourbon night, Tyranny called and said it had been a long time, and how had he been, and what had he been doing with himself, and wasn't it silly that they hadn't stayed in touch, and Professor Dan was at a conference in Baltimore, and why didn't he drop in for a visit to catch up on old times?

So Conner had gunned the Plymouth through the pouring rain and three red lights to see her again. She let him in, offered a towel and a drink, and spilled her story. Professor Dan had been good to her, but she'd been getting the itchy, crowded, uncomfortable feeling that the whole thing had been a mistake. Her schoolgirl crush on the older, worldly teacher was perhaps a novelty that wasn't novel anymore.

And so she sat closer, played with Conner's hair. Their lips met, hands found one another. Shirt buttons somehow got themselves unbuttoned. And then suddenly Tyranny panicked or freaked out or God knows what. She said it was all wrong and that he was too important for such a stupid fling.

Conner had insisted he wasn't very important at all, and look, he already had his pants down. No no no no, it was all wrong and Tyranny insisted he leave and she was so sorry but he'd surely understand that this was the right thing to do in the long run.

He'd gone back the next day to talk it out. Something had changed. Of course she wanted Conner, but it just wasn't right. From there, things proceeded in the most frustrating manner. She found excuses to call or drop by his apartment. She insisted they could only be friends. Close and special friends, but no more. Conner was confused, sick at his stomach. Was this a love affair or not?

Now, in the warm glow of her breakfast nook, she melted into him. Her arms slipped around his waist. She tilted her head up, offered her lips. Conner bent and accepted. She undid two of his shirt buttons, her hands darting inside, roaming his chest and belly. He kissed her hard.

She unzipped his pants, pulled him out of his boxers, and pumped. Conner moaned and kissed. His hands found the curve of her butt. She pulled away, looked him in the eyes. A wicked smile.

She reached for the paint palette, scooped an oily handful of bright blue paint, and grabbed Conner's length with it. He started to object, but the gliding friction dissuaded him. Then he took a glob of paint in each hand, found passage beneath Tyranny's T-shirt. He ran oily hands over her small, pert breasts. The nipples hardened, the paint oozing between his fingers. Conner closed his eyes, leaned his head back as Tyranny's fist did its work.

"Oh, my God." She let go of him, grabbed a roll of paper towels.

"What's wrong?" Conner was shamefully aware of the urgency in his voice.

"We can't."

"Yes we can."

Tyranny glanced at the oversized wall clock. "I can't believe the time." She wiped her hands on the paper towels and offered Conner the roll. "Dan will be home any minute!"

And here it was, the bad sequel to the bad movie, but he still never walked out. It was goddamn frustrating.

He took the paper towels, did a sloppy job wiping the paint off his pecker, and zipped up.

"I'll call you. I promise," she said as she pushed him out the door.

•   •   •

Fat Otis wasn't parked in front of the apartment anymore, so Conner went inside and stripped off his clothes. He made the shower hot even though he needed it cold. Conner lathered his dick, wanting to wash off the paint. He couldn't get Tyranny out of his head, so he soaped up good and finished the job she'd started. Relief. Conner knew it was only temporary. He finished showering and walked into the bedroom, drying himself.

He thought he heard some movement in the kitchen and froze. What a burglar might want in his shithole apartment Conner couldn't guess. He'd pawned anything worth more than twenty bucks except for his pistol, unloaded, somewhere in the distant reaches of his closet.

It wasn't a burglar.

Fat Otis walked into Conner's bedroom, a can of Coors in each hand. "Hey, man, how come you always got this shitty, watered-down beer?" Otis's voice was high and Southern, a cross between Mike Tyson and Colonel Sanders. "You should once in a while treat yourself to— Hey, why's your dick blue?"

Conner pulled the towel around himself. "It's a long story. Can I get a minute here, please?"

"No problem, man." He handed Conner one of the beers and left the room.

Conner pulled on jeans and shrugged into a loose Hawaiian shirt with a gaudy palm tree pattern. He shuffled barefoot into the kitchen.

Fat Otis dwarfed the kitchen table. He was a giant, sitting hunched over a box of chicken tenders, dipping them in barbecue sauce and packing them into his mouth like a machine. Conner sat across from him and opened a beer. It went down good and wet.

Fat Otis paused in his systematic demolition of the chicken to lick the sauce off his fingers and consult a small spiral notepad he carried in his shirt pocket. "You owe Rocky Big two hundred fifty dollars."

"I thought it was five hundred."

He shook his head. "You got lucky. The Phillies."

It wasn't all bad news, then. Conner sighed, rose from the table, and went into the bedroom. When he returned, he dropped three Franklins in front of Otis, who made them disappear into his pocket and came back with two twenties and a ten. He shook his empty beer can at Conner, raised his eyebrows.

"Yeah, yeah." Conner fetched two more from the fridge and set one in front of the giant.

Conner never let his gambling get to the point where Otis would be forced to snap a few of his little white-boy bones. Conner vividly remembered being a week late paying off a hundred-dollar bet two years ago. It was the first time he didn't have the money to pay up after losing. And so it was also the first time one of Rocky Big's leg-breakers had shown up at Conner's door. But Conner was surprised to see his old buddy Fat Otis.

Conner and Otis had been on their high school baseball team together. Otis had been the starting catcher, and with his wide body, he did a good job of blocking home plate. But after graduation, they'd taken different paths. Conner's grades were average at best, but he'd managed to squeak out a baseball scholarship to the local university. Otis had been a decent catcher, but he was too big to run the bases very fast. His career as an athlete was over, and he'd ended up working as one of Rocky's trusted henchmen.

Conner and Otis had talked over old times, remembered other buddies from the team, and Otis had looked sheepish when he told Conner he'd have to pay up "or else." It was obvious Fat Otis wasn't eager to bust up his old teammate. So Otis had given Conner an extra week to pay. They'd maintained an odd friendship ever since.

Otis finished his nuggets and wiped his hands on his pants. "Give up the gambling, Conner-man. You're no good at it."

"If I quit everything I was no good at, I wouldn't exist."

"You should come work for Rocky." He looked around the apartment. "Man, you live like shit."

"It's the maid's year off." There were still dishes in the sink from the Reagan administration.

"You need a steady paycheck," Otis said. "Maybe I can get you in with Rocky."

"No thanks." Conner wasn't sure he needed those kinds of favors. "As a matter of fact, I got a job just this morning."

"Congratulations. Gonna steal a Rolls-Royce?"

"No. A boat."

He laughed. "This is the Gulf Coast, Conner-man. You can't swing a dead cat without hitting a boat. Needle in a fucking haystack."

"This one's a thirty-six-footer. The *Electric Jenny.*"

"If I see it, I'll call you."

This reminded Conner he needed something.

"Otis, do you have a pair of good binoculars in the store?"

"Let's take a look."

Conner stepped into his sandals, and they took their beers outside. The "store" was the trunk of Otis's Lincoln. Otis handled select surplus items for a small commission. He opened the trunk, revealing the big, illegal, portable Wal-Mart of hot stuff: cameras, CD players, cell phones, and even a laptop computer. Everything was neatly arranged in wooden dividers in order to maximize the trunk's space. Otis slid one of the trays back, exposing a selection of handguns.

"You need one of these." Otis picked out a formidable silver automatic and held it up for Conner's inspection. "Nine millimeter. Twelve in the clip plus one in the chamber. When you're up against the shit, this is the kind of heat that can get your ass out of the soup."

"I don't need a gun, and I've never heard such a clusterfuck of metaphors."

"I'm not kidding, man," Otis said. "Guy in your line of work needs to watch his back."

"I don't have a line of work, and I already have a gun."

"The antique? Hell."

Otis had a point. The Webley was vintage 1917. Conner's great-uncle Warren had given it to him before he died, claimed it had seen action in the Black Forest. Maybe. Who could say? Originally, it had fired great big .455 caliber shells, but the ammo was hard to get. Some clever monkey handy with tools had filed the gun so it could fire standard .45 dumdums. Conner had to use special metal clips to hold in the shells. It was bulky, awkward, ugly, and huge. Sort of like Uncle Warren himself. Still, it was a solid gun in good shape.

But that wasn't really the point. Conner had never carried a gun, and didn't plan to. Not even when doing a repo in a really rotten gang neighborhood.

It wasn't that he had an ethical problem with guns. *If some guy starts shooting at me, I'm all for shooting back.* No, not an ethical problem. It was the klutz factor that worried him. When Conner Samson held a firearm, the safest place to stand was stock-still right in front of him. He was a lot more likely to shoot himself in the ass.

"Or maybe this." Otis showed Conner a big silver belt buckle like a rodeo cowboy might wear. It was gaudy and enormous.

"I've seen smaller satellite dishes."

Otis said, "It's sneaky like. Ever see one of them canes that's got the sword inside? Same kind of deal." Otis thumbed a hidden latch, and the front of the belt buckle sprung open. Inside was a single-shot derringer. "Thirty-two caliber. Take some motherfucker by complete surprise."

"No guns," Conner said. "Let's see the binoculars."

"Didn't you used to have binoculars?"

"No." Pawned.

Otis slid the gun drawer back and picked out a new pair of binoculars, handed them to Conner. They were midsize. Conner looked through them, and they brought the streetlight at the far end of the complex up close and clear.

"How much?"

Otis scratched his belly. "They run one eighty in the store."

"How much do they run from the back of a Lincoln?"

"Man, you can see flies fuck on the moon with these."

"Otis."

"Fifty bucks."

"How about a discount for your old buddy Conner?"

Otis smiled. "I'll knock off ten bucks if you tell me why your dick is blue."

3

Joellen Becker pushed paper into arbitrary piles, glanced at file folders, tapped at her computer, her brow furrowed as if deep in thought. She had one of those little square offices with glass walls, and to everyone else in the offices of Marvin & Strauss Insurance Company it looked like she was working hard.

She wasn't.

She was sneaking Little Debbie Swiss Rolls from her bottom desk drawer and playing Texas hold 'em poker online. She was up nine bucks.

Becker had trouble taking her job seriously. Just a few years ago, she'd been an elite member of a special ops unit for the National Security Agency. Highly trained in combat and investigations. Things had gone wrong. Mistakes were made. *Jesus, you just shoot a few of the wrong people, and everyone goes apeshit.*

Now she investigated claims for a second-rate insurance company. How the mighty had fallen. It was only temporary, she told herself. Something to pay the bills until the big opportunity came along.

The phone rang just as a heart flush beat her two pair, and she was maybe a little too cranky when she answered. "Yeah?"

"May I speak to Joellen Becker, please?" The voice was formal, crisp, just the hint of an accent.

"Speaking." She cradled the phone between chin and shoulder so she could continue typing at the keyboard. The computer dealt her a jack and a three. She'd stay in and get a look at the flop.

"Ms. Becker, my name is Billy Moto. I understand you are the investigator in charge of the Teddy Folger claim."

"The baseball card thing?" The computer dealt the flop, a queen, a six, and a ten. No help. She folded and logged off.

"Yes," Moto said. "A rare Joe DiMaggio card signed by the player, his wife at the time, Marilyn Monroe, and the film director Billy Wilder."

"We closed the file on that one," Joellen said.

"May I ask you a few questions about it, please?"

"What the hell for?"

Moto cleared his throat. "My employer is most interested. I was hoping we could discuss the claim in detail. I would naturally compensate you for your time."

"Uh-huh. Who's your employer?"

"Ahira Kurisaka."

She made a mental note of the name. "The card burned in a fire." Joellen absently twisted a lock of black hair as she spoke. "I'll tell you that for free. No compensation needed on that one, sport."

"So I've heard," Moto said. "Nevertheless."

"What else?"

"As you say, the file is closed," Moto said. "So it could not possibly be of any consequence for you to divulge to me the information in that file."

"Are you fat?"

A long pause. "What?"

"Are you fat or ugly?"

"What does that have to do with—"

"I want you to buy me dinner, and I don't want to be seen in public with some toad."

"Buy you dinner?"

"I haven't been out in eight weeks. I'll bring a photocopy of everything in the Folger file, but you have to meet me in a restaurant. A nice one with cloth napkins."

Moto cleared his throat on the other end. "I'm authorized to compensate handsomely for your full cooperation and any information—"

"Yeah, we'll get to all that over dinner. Be sure to wear a tie. And I want wine."

"Ms. Becker, this is a most peculiar conversation."

"You want to throw dancing into the bargain, sport? Keep talking."

"Your terms are acceptable."

"Damn right." She told him the time and place, then hung up.

Joellen bit her thumbnail a second, reviewed the Folger case in her mind. A lot of bullshit, kids' stuff, comic books and games and Star Trek crap. And this one crazy expensive Joe DiMaggio baseball card. The card's price tag had sent a red flag through the insurance company's hierarchy of pencil pushers, and Joellen had been dispatched to investigate. She'd had a few mild suspicions, but really she was always suspicious of everyone, so the feeling hadn't meant much. Anyway, a routine look-see had turned up zilch and there was a backlog of case files cluttering her desk. She knew she'd given the case a perfunctory effort at the time.

Now she was curious. She put on some coffee and pulled the Folger file. She meant to give it a close read before her meeting with Billy Moto.

The thought suddenly struck her she should have asked Moto about his teeth. Nothing was more off-putting than a mouth full of yellow, crooked teeth. Oh, well. Too late to worry about that now.

•   •   •

Teddy Folger wondered if anyone was still looking for him.

Probably not, he mused. He sat at the Pensacola Beach Resort Tiki Bar feeling pretty pleased with himself. His master plan was coming together nicely. Still, he looked over his shoulder now and then, half-expecting to see his wife.

The vile and vicious Mrs. Folger wanted Teddy's balls dipped in bronze and mounted on her mantel. *That blood-sucking bitch can kiss my fat white ass.* He was pretty sure she'd given up the chase, and anyway it wasn't like she could afford a private dick to come track him down. He'd cleaned out the account, left her high and fucking dry. Served her right. She'd blindsided him, no doubt. Little gold digger tricked him into popping for a marriage license, and in two seconds flat her legs slammed shut tighter than a clam and Teddy was going bust paying for pedicures twice a week.

Teddy'd thrown the brakes on that shit. His master plan was now in full swing. He had the boat, the cash, and a ton of suntan lotion. His schemes hadn't all gone like clockwork. Not quite. The arson job hadn't produced the insurance payoff like he'd expected. No matter. He'd been trading online for a few years, and selling off all his stock would keep him liquid until he got his asking price for the Joe DiMaggio card. He'd tried to sell it on eBay but was dissatisfied with the bids. This card was his prized possession, and he wouldn't part with it lightly. But he'd made his start. The new Teddy Folger was headed for the Caribbean, and the whole world could just suck on that. His total and complete bliss lacked only one key ingredient.

The blond girl behind the bar eyed him from the taps at the far end. She wasn't in any hurry to come down to Teddy's stool. Considering the circumstances of their last meeting, Teddy wasn't surprised that Misty was a little skittish. Misty. What a perfect name.

And the Tiki Bar was the perfect place for Misty. All the girls wore bikinis. Misty was soft with big curves. Wonderful, golden-age-of-Hollywood starlet curves. None of this emaciated, toothpick, starving stick-girl bullshit that was on the covers of all the fashion magazines. Butter-silk hair, big wet red lips. Perfect skin. When Teddy had first plopped his ass on the stool and glimpsed her pulling drafts for the tourists, his big fat sappy heart skipped a beat. It was as if Marilyn had been reborn.

Almost.

The magic and mystery wasn't quite there in Misty; the strange playful alchemy of seductress and innocent that flicked behind Marilyn's eyes, captured on thousands of feet of celluloid, was absent in Misty's face. Teddy had looked hard for it, had searched her eyes, hoping. Teddy was a sap, but he wasn't dumb. There was no reincarnation of Hollywood's favorite bombshell in Misty, but there were good legs and straight teeth and breasts that stood up for themselves. Her face glowed with youth and eagerness, and there was something pretty okay about that. A simpler Marilyn for more complicated times. And when she laughed—not the fake laugh so the tourists would leave a bigger tip, but a genuine laugh, head thrown back, eyes closed—Teddy could squint and almost see a starlet.

So there he'd been a month ago, slogging back Tecate with lime and waiting for the weekday crowd to thin, and he was drunk and wanted her and struck up a conversation with a pretty girl, which was maybe the bravest thing he'd ever done in his life. And they talked, and Misty told him how hard it was to be a student and that she was behind on every single one of her bills, Visa and MasterCard maxed to the limit and beyond. It was a good little sob story, made even better by the fact Teddy suspected most of it was true. Probably she'd only been fishing for a bigger tip. Teddy doubted she'd been ready for what he'd done next.

Teddy pulled a wad of cash from his front pocket, peeled off ten one-hundred-dollar bills, and spread them on the bar like he was dealing a hand of solitaire. Misty blinked at the bills, looked at Teddy. He told her she was about the greatest thing he'd laid eyes on in a long time and he knew she was a good girl and didn't mean any insult but he'd sure be happy to help her out if only she could help him out a little bit too, and after all Teddy was a man with a man's needs and what could be more human and kind than two people giving each other aid and comfort?

Teddy braced himself for a slap or a scream or a couple of big bouncers tossing him into the Gulf of Mexico. None of that happened. Misty looked at the cash, looked at Teddy, nibbled her lower lip, and wrung her hands.

After shelling out a thousand dollars, Teddy found it odd how much he resented the twenty-nine bucks for the shabby room at the Dixie Winds Motel. Maybe he'd half expected her to ask him back to her place. The dim, dirty, anonymous motel room had almost ruined it. But then the grunting and sweating and heaving, and Teddy groped and thrust and howled and for a split second he'd touched Heaven and it had all been worth it.

All the following month he'd thought about her nearly every minute. It wasn't anything as good as love or as dangerous as obsession, but she lodged herself in his thoughts and he started imagining Misty at his side in the Caribbean, tanning on the deck of the *Electric Jenny* (he'd need to rename the vessel, he reminded himself) with an umbrella drink, cruising the bright waters under the sun, the salt breezes kissing their skin. Yes, Misty completed the picture, a picture Teddy'd been forming in his mind for a long, long time. The new Teddy Folger.

The old Teddy Folger was a dud. A pale comic-book nerd. Teddy'd never had a bad life. Nobody had picked on him in high school. He was not totally out of touch with reality as were many of his peers, the folks who frequented the comic-book and sci-fi conventions. Teddy was an adult. Most of the other people he knew who were into collectibles were also adults. Whenever Teddy told people he ran a comic book/baseball card/sci-fi store, they invariably thought of the quintessential geek with the sinus condition and the pointy Spock ears.

That wasn't Teddy Folger. Neither was Teddy the slick, trim, beach volleyball hunk with the six-pack abs and deepwater tan. The dude who had women climbing all over him. Teddy had always, always, always hated and envied those guys.

So he'd been working on his tan, and had done about ten thousand sit-ups since leaving Jenny in the dust. He'd gotten a really cool haircut and a pair of expensive wraparound sunglasses. A bottle of Polo cologne. A shitload of Tommy Hilfiger and Abercrombie & Fitch clothing.

And a fat, juicy bankbook.

And now if Misty would just muster the courage to talk to him, Teddy could make his pitch.

Finally, she came, replacing ashtrays and wiping the bar with a rag until she was near Teddy. "Uh . . . hi." She wouldn't look at him.

"I've been thinking about you a lot, Misty," Teddy said.

"Uh . . . okay."

This wasn't going to work, Teddy realized. He didn't have a chance in hell and was going to get shot down in flames. Misty had needed the money, needed it quick. She was obviously embarrassed to see him. He decided to forgo the preliminaries and dive right in. Might as well get the rejection over with.

He put a photograph of the *Electric Jenny* on the bar. "This is my boat. I'm headed to the Caribbean."

Her eyes darted briefly to the photo.

"Why don't you quit your job and come with me?" Teddy said.

Misty's eyes flashed from side to side like a trapped animal looking for escape.

Billy Moto spotted Joellen Becker as she crossed the restaurant toward his table. Moto had the semiuseful talent for matching faces with voices he'd heard on the phone. Joellen was almost as he'd pictured her. A little taller. Hair black and thick and cut short and round in the Prince Valiant style. Features dark and hard and Slavic. She wore a charcoal gray pantsuit, tapered to highlight her thin waist. Shoes with no heels. She didn't need any extra height, but something in the way she moved told Moto this woman wanted to be quick on her feet if needed. No rings, necklace, or earrings. A wristwatch with a plain black band.

She arrived at the table. "Moto?"

He stood. "Yes."

She sat, shook open the napkin, and dropped it into her lap. "Where's the waiter?"

Moto took his chair, sat stiffly. He did not know what to expect from this woman. "I asked for a wine list. I didn't know if you'd want white or red, but there's a good pinot noir and—"

"Cancel the wine, sport," Becker said. "I looked over the Folger file again, and it looks like we're going to need to talk business." The waiter wandered near the table, and Joellen grabbed his sleeve so he couldn't escape. "I need a triple Bombay martini with an olive the size of a poodle's head."

The waiter looked at Moto.

"Water with lime, please."

Joellen curled a lip. "Jesus, Moto, order a man's drink."

What was that look on her face? Contempt? Moto felt his cheeks flush. The woman was most vexing. "Johnnie Walker Black. No ice."

Joellen set a thick file folder and a VHS tape on the table. She crossed her arms on the table, leaned in. "Let's talk about what you want, and don't leave out the part about my being handsomely compensated."

"My employer is interested in the DiMaggio card. I'll pay you a reasonable sum for your information. We're simply hoping to ascertain Teddy Folger's whereabouts."

"I told you," Joellen said. "The card burned."

Moto nodded, a slight shrug. "My employer is interested in any other cards of similar value Folger might possess."

"Bullshit."

"Excuse me?"

The drinks arrived, and Joellen took half hers in one gulp. "Here's what I think. I think the card didn't burn. I think Folger collected a juicy insurance check and now wants to unload the card on the sly. One card, two payoffs. I've seen it a dozen times, although it's usually jewelry or something. Folger's gone to ground, ducking his wife probably, and you can't find him."

Moto didn't know what to say. He sipped his drink to buy some time. "You are a clever woman," Moto finally admitted.

"I have my moments. So you went to Princeton, then Oxford, then served five years in Japanese Military Intelligence. Impressive."

"How did you know that?" Moto asked.

"Oh, it's easy enough to look up."

It shouldn't be. Moto had gone to some moderate amount of trouble to conceal his personal information from the general public. A routine background check should not have turned up anything. Either there was more to Becker than met the eye, or American insurance companies were damn strict.

Moto cleared his throat, and said, "Your insurance company's file isn't completely necessary, but it will save me some preliminary steps. How much?"

"Not for sale."

"Ah. You are negotiating, playing hardball."

"How much is your boss willing to pay for the card?" She sipped her martini.

"One million dollars."

Joellen sputtered, sprayed gin all over the table. "How much?"

"It doesn't matter. I only need the folder."

"The card's not worth that much."

"Mr. Kurisaka wants it," Moto said. Also, Kurisaka wanted to preempt any other offers and figured a million dollars would do it. Moto's boss had also sent word to the most prestigious collectibles dealers in America. Kurisaka wanted them to contact him instead of Hyatta if the card should happen to come into their possession.

"A million?" Joellen frowned. "Is he retarded or something?"

Moto pushed his drink away, threw his napkin on the table. "This is pointless. You are a bizarre, annoying woman." She was also completely unfeminine, a fact Moto found oddly disturbing. He stood. "This has been a most unpleasant encounter. I will say good night now."

"Jesus, Moto," Joellen said. "Sit down, will you? Let me make my pitch. You can leave then if you don't like it."

"Please be brief." He sat.

"I already know where Folger is."

Moto's eyes widened. Perhaps this whole baseball card business could be concluded quickly, and he could get back to Japan. "Is he still in Pensacola?"

"What if I had the card? Instead of Folger?"

"If you can put us in contact with Folger, I'm sure a finder's fee—"

She shook her head. "No, you're not hearing what I'm saying. What if I had the card *instead* of Folger?"

Ah. "Then . . . I suppose we would pay *you* the million dollars."

"And how would that work exactly?" asked Joellen.

"I'm not sure I understand."

"There's insurance fraud involved."

"No questions asked," Moto said.

"I've heard that in the movies," Joellen said. "No questions asked. What exactly does that mean?"

"It means do whatever is necessary. Beg, borrow, or steal. This is a private transaction, and legal technicalities concern my employer not at all."

Joellen smiled, nodded. "Beats the shit out of working for the insurance company." She ordered another martini.

4

The next morning at dawn, Conner dropped Otis's bargain binoculars onto the passenger seat of the Plymouth and drove toward the beach. His eyes blurry, stomach coffee-sour, he made the circuit of likely places.

He didn't really know what he was doing.

By noon, he'd worked all of Pensacola Beach and half the places around Mobile, starting at Old Navy Cove and making his way west through marinas small enough for private craft but still big enough for a guy with a boat on the lam to take on fuel and provisions. He scanned the major channels with the binoculars and spotted a few sloops the right size, but none was the *Electric Jenny*.

Conner hadn't told Derrick James that the whole deal was probably a waste of time. Teddy Folger and his unpaid-for boat were probably long gone. If it had been Conner, he'd have hauled ass straight across the Gulf to Mexico by now. He didn't say that to James. Conner wanted to get paid, and there was always the chance

Folger wasn't too bright. He might be catching a suntan on his boat in the next bay or inlet. Sipping a piña colada with a stupid grin on his face like he'd gotten away with something.

So far, he had.

Conner walked to the end of his third fishing pier, scanned the horizon, saw nothing, sat down, and figured he was going about this like a sucker. The Plymouth had guzzled twenty dollars' worth of gas, and all the sailboats began to look alike. Time to shift gears.

He drove to an IHOP, ordered a cup of coffee, and opened the manila file folder James had given him.

On *Rockford Files* reruns, Rockford often got his police buddy to show him the file on a suspect. Rockford would dig through the file and uncover some kind of clue that jump-started the case or nudged him in the right direction. *Where the hell's Rockford when I need him?*

But the package on Teddy Folger failed to produce anything like, say, a map with a big red X labeled *secret boat slip here*. The file was mostly financial information. Naturally, James had wanted to make sure Folger could afford the boat. Conner couldn't say if any of this was helpful or not. He read the file, drank coffee, picked his teeth, looked at the waitress's legs.

He blinked, rubbed his eyes. He was drifting.

The file listed properties Folger owned and how much he paid on them each month. Another wad of papers looked like a stock portfolio. A statement from a Pensacola law firm detailed the monthly alimony payments Folger was supposed to make to his ex-wife and which of his assets she did or didn't have a claim on.

Jenny Folger, the wife.

The boat was one of the disputed items.

Conner tsked and wondered if Teddy Folger had still loved his wife when he'd named the sloop *Electric Jenny*. But Folger had dumped the wife and kept the boat. Marriages end, so divorce lawyers and bartenders and Dr. Laura and third-rate repo men can earn a living too. The circle of life in a modern world.

The file seemed pretty useless. Copies of the boat's insurance policy, copies of the contract, copies of copies. A paper clip.

Conner packed it all up and dropped two bucks on the table for coffee and tip.

He sat in the Plymouth and opened Folger's file again, looked at the insurance agreement. The company was called Allied Nautical and specialized in maritime policies. Conner desperately wanted this information to be helpful somehow. He strained his brain so hard thinking about it, he almost shit his pants.

The paperwork from Allied Nautical had scribbling in the margins, little loops and a crude drawing of a frowny face with the tongue sticking out. Conner imagined Derrick James doodling as he made phone calls, tracked down the same leads Conner was trying to track down. Maybe Conner was spinning his wheels. He needed a new approach.

No epiphany manifested itself. But it did remind him the insurance on the Plymouth was a week late. He hated paying bills. He was bad at it. It seemed to take some kind of Herculean effort to write the check, get a stamp, write his return address on the envelope. . . .

Conner got out of the car and went to the pay phone in front of the IHOP. He dropped in the coins, dialed the number at the top of the insurance company's letterhead, and a young, efficient female voice answered.

"Allied Nautical, this is Maureen."

"Hi, Maureen." All cheerful. "This is Denver Colgate from Southbank Mortgage and Trust. I need to consult you about one of your clients." Fake name number thirty-two from the sneaky dude's handbook.

"How can I help you, Mr. Colgate?" Maureen asked.

"Southbank is purchasing the mortgage on a boat belonging to a Mr. Teddy Folger. Derrick James said you guys wrote the policy on that one, and we just need to make sure it's current before we finalize the transaction."

"Hold just a moment, Mr. Colgate. I'll pull it up on the computer. Do you happen to know the policy number?"

Conner did happen to know, and he read it to her from the file. He waited amid the *cluppety-clup* of her keyboard action on the other end of the phone.

She said, "The policy is still up-to-date, although he is overdue for this month's payment."

Damn.

"Oh, wait. Here we go."

Conner held his breath for the payoff.

"His most recent payment arrived in the mail this morning. It just hasn't been logged yet."

"Everything seems to be in order then," Conner said. "I just need to know the postmark on the envelope."

"The postmark?"

"Yes."

"Why?"

"Routine."

"I've thrown it away," Maureen said.

"Uh-huh. What I'm going to need you to do, Maureen, is poke around in the garbage until you find that envelope. Hopefully it's not out back in the Dumpster yet."

Her end of the phone got real quiet.

"Maureen?"

"Did you say you wanted me to look in the garbage?"

Conner exhaled roughly, an attempt to communicate the appropriate amount of bureaucratic despair. "We need to determine that Mr. Folger's boat remains in American waters. We can't assume the mortgage if he's taken the boat to Mexico or . . . uh . . . Borneo."

"Oh, hold on then. I'll check the trash basket."

He heard her rummage the trash, and when she came back on the line she said, "Got it. Pensacola, Florida. That okay?"

Okay? It was beautiful. Folger was dumb as dirt. *You don't insure something you're stealing, Mr. Folger, you stupid stupid son of a bitch.*

Conner pictured Folger at his desk, stuffing bills into envelopes, not really paying attention. A matter of routine.

"Thanks, Maureen. I owe you a big kiss."

"What?"

Conner hung up, feeling like a genius. Like Philip fucking Marlowe.

5

"**Nymphomania isn't a word we** use, Tyranny," Dr. Goldblatt said. "Sexual addiction. A compulsion. Not a choice. Dealing with your condition is a daily struggle. You mustn't beat yourself up for the occasional lapse."

"Uh-huh." Tyranny Jones wasn't listening. She was imagining Dr. Goldblatt naked, her legs thrown over his shoulders, his bony ass thrusting. These fantasies simultaneously thrilled and repulsed her. She did not find Dr. Goldblatt attractive. In fact, she'd interviewed seven psychiatrists and had intentionally chosen the ugliest one. Goldblatt had a nose like a Vienna sausage, thick glasses, and a comb-over that looked like it was trying to eat his head.

Whether or not she found her therapist attractive wasn't the issue. Fifty minutes a week for eight months had at least taught her that much. Control issues. The warped way she related to men. It had nothing to do with being horny all the time.

Almost nothing.

It had only occurred to Tyranny after five months of therapy that she could have seen a female therapist. She'd often contemplated coming on to Goldblatt, pushing him down, riding him there in the office among the leather-bound books and earth tones, rattling the nonoffensive abstract art off the wall, but he seemed completely professional, detached almost, and probably would have turned her down with a mild rebuke. She couldn't stand the thought of being rejected by somebody so utterly revolting.

"Tyranny, were you listening?" Goldblatt tapped his pencil.

"Sure. What?"

"I asked if you'd been masturbating."

"You're obsessed with my orgasms, aren't you, Dr. G?"

Goldblatt said, "Do you enjoy thinking I'm obsessed with them?"

"What you mean is do I enjoy your obsession more than I enjoy the actual orgasms," Tyranny said. "Yes, Dr. G. That's it exactly. I masturbate just because I know you'll ask about it. Is that what you want to hear?"

"Is it what you think I want to hear?"

"Did *you* masturbate today, Dr. G?"

"Now, Tyranny. We're here to discuss you," Goldblatt said. "Let's pursue another matter."

"Yes. Let's," Tyranny said.

"Something you mentioned in your last session."

"That was so long ago I hardly remember." She wondered if Goldblatt was circumcised. All Jews were, weren't they?

"You said you'd had sex with three different men in one day. None your husband."

"Oh, that's right. I'm a nymphomaniac. I almost forgot."

"There was another man." Goldblatt flipped through his notebook, found the name. "Conner Samson. You didn't have sexual relations with him."

"No."

"Why not?"

Tyranny rolled her eyes. "I'd think you'd be happy. A little restraint."

"This is not about my happiness, Tyranny. We're trying to delve into the root cause of your behavior. You said you were attracted to Conner. Why not him?"

She crossed her arms, sank back into the chair.

Goldblatt waited her out, tapped the pencil.

He's always tapping that pencil. He knows it drives me batshit. Dr. clever-smug-son-of-a— "Look, I am married, after all."

"That didn't stop you from engaging in intercourse with the others," Goldblatt said.

"The others weren't—" She waved her hands, groped for words.

"That's my point. He's different. It might be significant."

"Maybe I was just tired. My vagina was sore. I'm a slut, remember?"

"Nobody's called you that, Tyranny."

"Did you pick out the paintings in this office, Dr. Goldblatt? About as bland as fucking dishwater. You should let me paint you something."

"You're changing the subject, Tyranny."

"That's right."

Goldblatt sighed, squinted at his watch. "We only have a minute left."

"Oh, darn. I was having such a good time."

Goldblatt said, "The next time you masturbate, I want you to use a cucumber. Then chop the cucumber into a salad and eat it. It's important."

"What?"

"I'm afraid our time is up."

Freak.

Tyranny drove home fast. She liked to drive her Beemer fast, weave through the leaden traffic. She liked to punch the accelerator, feel it kick in, the high-pitched hum of the German motor, the feel of it pushing her back in her seat. She drove fast when she was excited or angry or anything.

Dr. Goldblatt had dug into her brain about Conner. Of course Conner was different. She didn't need a shrink to tell her that. But what exactly did Tyranny see in Conner anyway, what was so special about him? She wasn't immediately able to put it into words, had never before had to dissect her feelings for him. Goldblatt obviously wanted her to give it careful thought.

Conner was handsome, but that wasn't it—although it didn't hurt. Conner was different, unpretentious, simple, straightforward. In a time when she'd been surrounded by an overly complex, pseudointellectual, angst-ridden art-school crowd, she'd often taken refuge in Conner Samson's company. To Tyranny, Conner was an open book, and come rain or shine, hell or high water, Conner would always be Conner. His concrete simplicity balanced the beehive of complicated thoughts and feelings that was Tyranny Jones.

She screeched into her driveway, went in the house, threw her purse and car keys on the table. Then to the breakfast nook, hot summer light pouring through the bay windows. She didn't even bother to change clothes, just picked up the palette and began slinging paint on the canvas. Her project: less a painting, more a frustrated bright smear.

It wasn't working.

She was pent up.

She wanted to masturbate. Had Goldblatt predicted this? She was supposed to use a cucumber, then eat it. She didn't know if she was intrigued by the thought or horrified. Goldblatt had always been fond of unorthodox methods, but this was a new extreme. *Stupid fucking psychiatrist weirdo.*

The doorbell. She answered it.

It was the UPS guy with a load of art supplies she'd ordered off the Web. He was short, pale, soft around the middle. He set the packages just inside the door, had her sign his clipboard.

She grabbed his arm as he turned to leave, pulled him inside. "Come in here a minute, will you? I need your help with something." Even as the anticipation mounted, there was also the beginnings of guilt. Shame.

But the alternative was a cucumber.

6

Conner had driven two miles feeling pretty damn pleased with his own cleverness when he realized he didn't know where he was going.

He pulled over.

He went back to the file and found a home address. Hopefully, the divorce had been particularly bitter, and Conner could get Jenny Folger to fink on her ex-husband. Maybe Jenny would get a kick out of taking away hubby's big toy boat. Conner pulled back onto the road and drove.

The address from the file was a nice, three-bedroom, two-bath American apple pie special in a good neighborhood. But a yellow real estate sign sprouted from the overgrown lawn like a middle finger. Conner looked in the windows. The place was empty.

A phone book at a nearby convenience store had nothing to offer, but information had a J. Folger listed in Mobile. Conner scribbled the number on the outside of the Folger file.

Conner called, and she answered. He told her who he was and

that he was looking for her husband. She said her husband could burn in the fiery pits of hell, and wherever he might be it sure wasn't at her apartment. Conner said he wanted to find her husband's boat and take it away from him. She said Conner should get a merit badge. He suggested she might be able to help. She didn't see how but said if Conner held Teddy's arms, she'd punch him in the gut. Conner offered to come by and discuss it. She gave him the address.

Teddy Folger's ex-wife lived way the hell on the west side of Mobile, so Conner had to pass Hank Aaron Stadium to get there. The stadium was where the Bay Bears played.

I would have been a good Bay Bear, Conner thought.

When he'd blown his baseball scholarship at the University of West Florida, he'd tried a few more schools, even some community colleges, to see if he could get on with another team. Nobody was impressed by his 0.5 grade point average, and he'd struck out all around. Conner sat on his thumb for a year, drinking beer and shaking his fist at the world.

Then he'd gotten the bright idea to try out for the triple-A club in Mobile. It was still a long way from the show, but it was professional sports and a steady paycheck. He swung the bat, ran the bases. The coach said he had a good arm, a decent eye in the batter's box, but maybe he should join a gym. He was out of shape and sucking wind. He was told there were a dozen guys in top form who could throw and swing as well as or better than Conner.

What if I got into shape, worked really hard?

Sorry, kid. Maybe next season.

He spent the next few months doing sit-ups and running three miles a day, but somehow when tryouts rolled around again, his heart wasn't in it. His heart wasn't in much of anything. He earned a buck here and there with repos and the occasional gambling score.

But it was more than a simple lack of willpower that kept him from tryouts, something worse and deeper. Fear. He was scared. It was that simple. What if he worked hard, did his best, gave it everything he had, and yet he still failed? Could he handle that? Would he be able to stand the knowledge that he was exactly as useless as he suspected he might be? It was easier for him not to try than to give it his best only to crash and burn.

Conner had failed at college, failed in his attempts to win Tyranny. Life had been so easy for him for so long, and now life was calling in all its markers. Growing up was unpleasant and uncomfortable.

He put baseball and Tyranny out of his mind. Today he was looking for a boat, and that was all.

Jenny Folger's apartment complex rivaled Conner's own in drab efficiency and unimaginative landscaping. He climbed a flight of steps and knocked. She let him in and directed him to a sofa that was a little too nice for the apartment.

"It's early, but would you like a beer?" she asked.

"There's no such thing as too early."

She came back with a Labatt's Blue, and Conner stopped her before she poured it into a glass. "Straight from the bottle is fine."

She took hers from the bottle too, sat in the matching chair across from him. They drank beer and took each other in for a second.

Jenny Folger looked like she'd once been a sunny, stunning blonde. Hourglass shape, long hair pulled tight into a butter-silk topknot. Athletically thick, broad back, built for action. She was just into middle age. Bouncy, sun-kissed youth had left her behind but reluctantly, and she was just divorced. Jenny sent out a vibe of broken-winged desperation that stirred the predator in men. Conner sensed it filling the room between them, thick like perfume that was a little too sweet. He could see it in her eyes as she searched his face.

"I told you I was looking for the boat," Conner said.

"Yes. Teddy's little plaything."

"Do you have any idea where he might have stashed it?"

"Not the faintest," she said. "Believe me, if I did, I'd have my lawyer on him in a second. I was supposed to get a big, fat settlement. I haven't seen a dime or I wouldn't be here." She waved her bottle at the apartment.

Conner sipped beer, shrugged. "It's not so bad."

"It's not so good either."

"Can I ask what happened?"

"The divorce?"

"Yeah."

She frowned, took a hit off the beer. "The same thing that happened to the first Mrs. Folger. Teddy found somebody he liked better."

Oh, yeah. Conner had heard this one before.

"I suppose I'm some kind of idiot," Jenny said. "When he left his wife for me, I thought I was hot stuff. It never occurred to me I could get older and sag and sprout crow's-feet."

"You look okay."

"Gee, you're sweeping me off my feet. Anyway, he found this woman in Pensacola, tends bar at one of the beach places. Half Teddy's age. It's ridiculous."

"How old is Teddy?"

She nibbled the inside of her lip. "Let's see. Next month he'll be fifty-six. He's a motherfucker. He sold everything, cleaned out the checking account, and took off. He hadn't made a mortgage payment on the house in five months. Bastard. I had to get the most hideous job as a receptionist downtown."

"You didn't get *anything*?"

"There was nothing left to get." She finished the beer and lit a thin cigarette, exhaled gray smoke, her head back against the chair. "I got a lawyer, of course, tried to grab back what I could, but it was no good."

Conner opened the file on Folger. "It says here he had some properties. You couldn't claim any of that?"

"It was just one property."

He rechecked the file. "It says a tanning salon, a comic-book shop, a Blimpie—"

"No." She shook her head, puffed the cigarette. "It was all one property. A strip plaza in Pensacola. It burned down."

"The whole plaza?"

"The insurance investigators were all over his ass," Jenny said. "Nobody could prove anything."

"Did he do it?"

"Of course he did. The new mall was killing him. He didn't confess it to me, but you bet he torched the plaza."

He asked, "You couldn't claim any of the insurance money?"

She shook her head, mashed out the cigarette in an amber glass ashtray. "The banks were faster than I was. The plaza was mortgaged up the ass, and the insurance barely paid everything off."

All Conner could think was that Teddy Folger was a dumb fucking asshole. He'd pulled off the most useless insurance scam in history, burning down his own property only to lose the payoff to his creditors. How could he sail off to Costa Rica or the Dominican Republic without a stash of cash?

Conner opened the file again, scanned all the same stuff, hoping it would look more useful this time. It didn't.

Jenny lit another cigarette, nodded at the file. "Can I see that?"

Conner handed it to her.

She started reading, flipping pages, the cigarette dancing between her lips with nervous puffs. She scrunched her eyes severely as she read. Too vain for glasses maybe.

Conner turned the Labatt's bottle around in his hands. He was pretty sad about how empty it was.

"Son of a bitch." She flipped pages rapidly. "Son of a fucking bitch bastard!"

"What's the matter?"

"I married a shit. That's what's the matter."

She dropped the file folder on the coffee table. Pages spilled out. She stood, crossed the room to the front window, arms folded, her foot tapping away pent-up anger. She let her cigarette ash fall on the carpet. Her shoulders bunched tight, knotting in frustration.

Conner let her stew for a minute, then said, "You might as well tell me. Maybe I can help."

She thought about it a moment, spun, looked hard at him. "You said you were looking for the boat."

"That's right."

"How would you find it?"

Conner said, "Systematic investigative techniques."

"You don't have a fucking clue, do you?"

"Nope."

"That's why you came to me," Jenny said. "You thought I might know where Teddy went."

"I'm new at this," Conner admitted. "Usually someone hands me a name and an address and says to go get the car. There's no mystery about it. I wait until it's dark or the guy's at work, then jump in the car and take off."

"You hot-wire it?"

"Sometimes I have an extra key. Most of the work is done with tow trucks nowadays."

"Same with the boat?" Jenny asked. "When you find it, you're going to steal it back?"

"It's not stealing, but yeah. I'd just as soon never meet Mr. Folger. Better I grab it while he's napping or on the crapper. It'll be a problem if he's hauled it out of the water. I don't have a trailer or a hitch."

The tendons along her hand twitched. Her jaw muscles tightened. She was thinking something, and it was giving her trouble. She said, "What if I could show you where the boat is?"

"That would completely kick ass."

"I mean, what's in it for me?"

"The satisfaction of knowing you've thwarted your husband's evil schemes."

"Get real."

Conner sighed. "Mrs. Folger—"

"Jenny."

"Jenny, I'm not being paid a lot to do this. Cutting you in for even a small chunk makes the job more trouble than it's worth."

She dropped the cigarette butt into the ashtray with the others. It looked like she was trying to build a little fort. She snatched up the pack, pulled another out, and lit it. Conner had her figured at about three packs a day.

"I know Teddy. That rat-fuck, little turd. He has money. Something. He was always squirreling it away. Stocks and things. It's half mine. I'm not going to get screwed on this, goddammit!"

"I'm just supposed to get the boat."

"He probably sold all the stock or something," Jenny said. "And I want to see his face when we steal the boat out from under him."

"What's this *we* shit?"

"I'm going with you."

"No."

"Yes, or fuck you. I know where he's got the boat. I *think* I do."

"Fine." *Who cares?* "Where?"

Jenny grabbed the file, tucking the loose pages back into the folder. She sat next to Conner on the couch, smelling like coconut oil and Pall Malls. She opened the file and showed him a listing for some property in Pensacola.

"So what?"

"He owned this property before we were married," Jenny said. "It was just a lot, weeds and grass. He told me he sold it."

"Didn't he?"

"Look, see what it says there?"

He read the document. "It says there's a house on the property."

"That sorry bastard built it."

"You're a very angry person."

"He said he was going to sell the lot, but instead he built a little bungalow. Fucker. He didn't even tell me. It's probably where he screwed his little whore." Jenny lit another cigarette, forgetting she already had one in the ashtray.

Conner let her get a lungful, then asked, "What's this got to do with the sailboat?"

"The property is on a canal," she said. "Big enough for the *Electric Jenny*, no problem. It's probably sitting there right now. You'd be pulling your pud another week looking for it if I hadn't told you." She grabbed her purse, fished out a jingly collection of keys, picked one out, and showed him. "Also, I have the other key."

She looked at him. He looked back.

Conner held up the empty Labatt's bottle. "So can I have another beer or not?"

7

Billy Moto was still numb from his encounter with Joellen Becker. She had rattled him. Japanese women were not like that. At no point during the dinner did Moto ever have control of the conversation. He felt steamrolled. Bludgeoned. She was out there somewhere shaking Pensacola by the lapels in search of a small rectangle of cardboard that probably still smelled faintly of stale bubble gum.

At least he'd had the presence of mind to insist on a copy of the file. He refused to leave the investigation in this woman's hands and fully intended to pursue the matter independently. Moto went back to his room at the Airport Hilton and pored over the information. The VHS tape was of Folger showing the card to some expert on a public television show. Moto watched the tape. He studied Folger's facial expressions as the expert appraised the card for insurance purposes. Moto watched Folger's body language as the expert described the best way to maintain the card and prevent corrosion.

Based on Folger's brief television appearance, Moto decided he did not like the man. Folger was impatient and selfish and a little weak it seemed. He'd expected the card to be worth more and felt slighted by the expert's low appraisal. At heart, Folger was a spoiled child and a bit of a sissy. Five minutes was a very short amount of time to sum up a man's heart and soul, and Moto realized he could be way off in his estimate. But Moto was seldom wrong in such matters.

Moto's cell phone played Darth Vader's theme from *Star Wars*. He flipped open the little phone. "I'm here, Mr. Kurisaka."

"Billy, I sent you a package by FedEx. It should have been delivered to your room."

Moto looked around, saw the box in the middle of the desk. "It's here."

"Open it."

Moto opened it. A heavy-duty metal attaché case.

"Use it to transport the card," Kurisaka said. "I had it specially made. It can survive one hundred fathoms or a fall from twenty thousand feet. Fireproof. Also a small homing beacon built into the lining."

"Mr. Kurisaka, I'm just not sure all of this is necessary."

"I want the card well protected."

Moto hesitated a moment, then said, "Mr. Kurisaka, things are going a bit more slowly than anticipated. I'm having trouble locating Folger. He's seems to have gone missing and has taken the card with him."

A long pause. "You don't think he's selling the card to . . . someone else?"

"I couldn't say," Moto admitted. "I just wanted to make you aware this may take a few days. But as soon as I find him, I will make your offer. A million dollars is much more than the appraised value of the card. I'm sure he won't refuse."

Moto had no trouble interpreting Kurisaka's silence. He was displeased.

Kurisaka said, "Billy, do what you must. Find him. And if a million dollars isn't good enough, then convince Folger it is in his best interest to part with the card. Do you understand what I mean?"

"I understand."

"Good-bye, Billy." He hung up.

Moto considered Kurisaka's words. Moto knew when he started working for the billionaire that he would be asked to do difficult things. A man like Kurisaka did not need another administrative assistant. He needed a right-hand man, and he expected results from Billy Moto. Yes, Kurisaka was willing to pay a million dollars, but he wouldn't hesitate to get what he wanted by less scrupulous means.

Moto searched himself and wondered how far he'd go to get Kurisaka what he wanted.

The conversation with Billy Moto lingered in Kurisaka's mind, distracted him. He flipped on his hundred-inch, flat-screen television and put in the DVD of *Pillow Talk*, which always calmed him down and let him think. Doris Day's voice was like creamy butter.

But he barely watched the film, was hardly aware of Doris Day at all. His mind raced. It should have been so simple. Kurisaka had sent Moto to America to expedite the purchase of the DiMaggio card. Why should there be complications? Unless . . . Unless . . . Something was going on behind his back. His old Yakuza instincts bubbled to the surface. Hito Hyatta had agents everywhere, men who labored to make Hyatta aware of rare and valuable collectibles that came on the market. And Kurisaka knew Hyatta's passion for their shared hobby. He knew Hyatta would spare no expense if he wanted the DiMaggio card for himself. Hyatta had practically admitted it at lunch. He was after a highly collectible card in Florida. What else could it be but the DiMaggio card?

Kurisaka would not be thwarted again by Hyatta! He was tired of playing second fiddle to his rival. This time he would get the card and rub it in Hyatta's face. Let Hyatta sit and seethe with envy. This time Kurisaka would be the one to gloat over his new prize.

But Billy Moto was usually very competent. Moto's lack of progress was most troubling. Could it be . . . no . . . was it possible that Moto would betray him? Had Hyatta gotten to Moto, made him a better offer for retrieving the card? Yes, of course it was possible. Anyone could be bribed or threatened. A lesson from Kurisaka's Yakuza days he'd almost forgotten. Kurisaka had become complacent. He felt ashamed and lost. As a Yakuza boss he'd been feared and respected. As a legitimate businessman he was mocked and ridiculed. Men like Hyatta laughed behind his back. Damn them! Damn them all. He would show them. He would not be toyed with. He would—

A red flashing beacon in the corner of the TV screen and a harsh *beep* made Kurisaka jump. Kurisaka thumbed the remote, paused the film, and the face of one of his employees filled the screen.

"Mr. Kurisaka, there's been another attempt on your life."

Kurisaka raised an eyebrow. "Tell me."

"A man outside your offices. A routine security screening found he had a bomb. We think he was going to try to sneak in disguised as a custodial worker. Probably plant the bomb in your office. Shall we turn him over to Tokyo Police?"

"No. Question him. Find out who hired him."

"It shall be done. But if he proves as resistant to interrogation as the others . . ."

"Make sure no remains are found." He had not *completely* forgotten the Yakuza ways.

"*Hai.*" The man's face disappeared from the screen.

Enemies. All around him there were enemies. Enemies and traitors. Kurisaka needed someone he could trust. No one in his current organization would suffice. He needed somebody from the old days. He picked up his phone, dialed a number he knew by heart.

"Hello?"

"Cousin Toshi," Kurisaka said. "It has been too long. How would you like to go to America?"

•   •   •

Joellen Becker had opened her mouth and puked lies until she'd convinced Billy Moto she practically had Teddy Folger in her back pocket.

Moto's call to her office had intrigued her. She'd done a very specific Internet search. You can find some surprising information on the Web if you know where to look and how to read between the lines. An hour on Mercenary.com and a visit to Bountyhunterand-rewards.com confirmed her suspicions. She also made several calls to some folks she knew from her old NSA days.

Her investigation had turned up a few interesting things about the billionaire Ahira Kurisaka. Things she could exploit although she would need to first confirm a few details. Later.

After dinner, she went home and opened the gun chest in the bedroom closet, took out the Smith & Wesson .380 auto and two extra clips, snapped them into the lightweight nylon shoulder holster. She did not delve into the metal chests containing her array of special equipment. Keepsakes from her government days.

Becker had names and addresses and some other good information from Folger's file, including where the man's ex-wife lived. She'd go to the man's places, follow the trail, sniff him out. She was an investigator. This was her specialty.

She shrugged into the holster rig, snapped it tight. She strapped the .25 automatic to her ankle. A million bucks for a baseball card? Yes, that was a lot of money. But to Joellen Becker, the card was merely bait for a much bigger fish.

8

When early man had formed the notion of real estate, it had been decided by all involved that land near water would be more expensive. A lot more expensive.

Still, oceanfront property wasn't always a good idea. Every few years a grumpy hurricane shuffled through Pensacola and kicked over all the beachfront houses. People rebuilt. Insurance rates soared, but snowbirds and carpetbaggers flocked to the sunny coast, bought up the beachfront property, then the beach-access property, plunked down big wads of cash into cookie-cutter time-shares. Or they bought houses on canals that in turn led to the sea.

Anything to be on or near or in view of the ocean.

Conner figured Teddy Folger had caught on late. Folger's sad plot of land was on a narrow canal which connected to a small river that emptied into a bay which opened into the Gulf of Mexico. It wasn't much, but it was there, the distant connection to wide-open seas. Maybe Teddy could even feel it, standing on his back porch with a beer in his fist. Maybe he looked at the muddy dribble of a canal but felt and heard the salty roar of the ocean. Conner could only guess.

Jenny Folger and Conner Samson watched the house and the sailboat from a rented canoe two hundred yards away. He looked through his new binoculars. No signs of life. The boat was squeezed into the canal pretty tight, less than two feet to spare on each side. There was a spacious, green backyard and then the bungalow. They'd passed half a dozen houses after turning off the river. Then they'd passed two construction sites. Then about a mile of empty lots, and they thought they had the wrong canal, but they rounded a bend and there it was. Teddy Folger's house was the very last one at the end of the canal, the sailboat backed in, stern away from them.

Conner handed the binoculars to Jenny.

"That's it all right," she said. "You can't see where it says *Electric Jenny* from here, but that's it."

Jenny had changed into an American-flag bikini top and denim shorts. She was tan just short of leathery, breasts nearly overflowing the stars and stripes. Conner worried she'd catch him sneaking peeks.

He dipped the paddle into the water and began turning the canoe around.

"What are you doing?" Jenny asked.

"Leaving."

"The boat's right there, for Christ's sake. Let's just get it."

"It'll be dark in a few hours. Does Teddy have a gun or anything? Is he violent?"

She bit her lower lip, looked back at the boat and the bungalow. "Probably not."

"I don't think I'll risk it," Conner said. "We'll come back when he's asleep, scull the boat out with a paddle or push it out with the boat hook. Then crank the engine and take off when we're a safe distance away."

"What if he leaves in the meantime?"

Good point. "Okay. The bait place where we rented the canoe

has a little motel. We'll get a room facing the water and keep watch. We'll get some sandwiches."

They paddled back. (Actually, Conner noticed he did most of the paddling. Jenny rubbed suntan oil over her body.) He paid the rental guy to keep the canoe until the next morning. The motel rooms were not fancy. They'd been designed for boaters and fishermen, and the motel's main feature was that it was right on the water. Conner paid the forty-eight bucks and went to the room while Jenny hit the bait shop.

The room was clean but dismal, cheap wood paneling, two shabby chairs. Conner flipped on the air-conditioning, a small window unit, and it rattled and coughed out something akin to cool air. He pulled back the drapes so he could see the river. They were into the long days of summer, so even though it was past dinnertime, they still had a good two hours to kill until dark.

Jenny knocked once, then walked in with a paper bag under her arm. She looked the room over. "Not exactly the Plaza, is it?"

Yeah, but I'm the one who paid for it. Conner sat on the bed and flipped on the TV, looking for a ball game. No cable. He switched it off. The money Derrick James had given him was running low. He was glad they'd found the sailboat. Conner reluctantly admitted he owed Jenny some gratitude. He didn't admit it out loud.

She pulled a six-pack of Bud and two sandwiches out of the bag. "Not much of a selection. Egg salad or tuna salad."

"I'll take the tuna."

She frowned. "There's also egg salad."

"Fine." Conner could take a hint.

They chewed sandwiches, sipped beer, watched the window.

The sun faded to dirty orange, and the boats made their way down the river—speedboats, party barges, and the occasional sailboat. Some pulled into the bait shop for gas or a last-minute six-pack. College kids, families, old men buying bait for night fishing.

Some boats were coming up the river, back to waterfront homes after a long day of fishing. There weren't many sailboats. They all had to get in before the County Road 25 bridge—

"Aw, crap," Conner said.

Jenny looked up from her beer. "What?"

"The bridge," he said. "The operator knocks off at seven. We won't be able to get past it until morning. The *Jenny*'s mast is too tall." It was one of those old, swing-to-the-side bridges that hadn't quite fallen apart yet. Sooner or later the county would probably hand it over to the state, then the state would tear it down and build a higher bridge so the boats could fit underneath. Conner cursed himself for forgetting about the damn bridge.

Jenny said, "I *told* you we should have done it while we were there."

"Shut up a second and let me think."

She pouted, lit a cigarette.

"Here's what we do," Conner announced. "We'll grab the *Jenny* tonight as planned, sail her downriver. There are a dozen places I can pull in, little branches and hidey-holes. We'll stash the boat, come back in a day or maybe two and get her then."

"Fine." She smoked, propped her feet up on the bed next to Conner. Her legs were tan and firm. She'd unbuttoned the top of her denim shorts, the zipper halfway down.

She might've caught Conner looking again, so he decided to start some conversation.

"So . . ." That was about all he had.

"You look in shape," she said. "You work out?"

"I used to play a little ball."

"I go to the gym almost every day," she said. "That's one of the reasons I'm so pissed. I kept in good shape, you know? He didn't need another girl."

"It doesn't work that way," Conner said. "That's not how men decide things about women."

"How do men decide?"

"I don't know, but not like that."

She lifted one of her legs. "Feel that calf. It's as good as a twenty-year-old's."

He took her ankle in one hand, felt her calf with the other. Taut. Good tone. "Nice."

"Damn right." She swigged beer, stood up, and shimmied out of her shorts. She wore the bottom half of the American-flag bikini underneath, cut high on the hips. "The good thing about the bridge being closed is we don't have to keep watch." She turned to close the curtains, showed Conner the backside of her bikini, a thong. Firm and tan all over.

Conner began feeling a little twitchy.

She came back to him on the bed, straddled him. She rubbed his places. He rubbed her places in return. Then their places started bumping against one another. She peeled Conner out of his clothes. He untied her bikini top. Tan lines, stark white triangles around pink nipples.

Conner thought of Tyranny, how she kept working him into a frenzy until he was crazy, then pulling away, leaving him hot and bothered. So he swung Jenny underneath him, entered her hard, pounded, fucking her angry, her grunts and moans working into a steady rhythm, her nails digging into his back, ankles locked behind his knees. Conner clenched his teeth as he thrust. Like it was some kind of punishment.

She squealed, and Conner was right behind her. They collapsed into a pile of sweat and beer breath and coconut oil.

After, they lay there under the sheets in the dark, both awake but not talking.

Finally, she asked, "Was that . . . did you like it?"

"Of course." He might not have liked it the way she wanted him to, maybe it wasn't so much to do with her, but he'd needed it.

"Then why—" Her voice caught. "I thought I hated Teddy so much. I thought . . . what did I do wrong? Why did this happen?"

Conner thought she might be crying, but in the dark, he wasn't sure. He tried to think of something to say, but nothing seemed helpful, so he moved in close, draped an arm over her. Soon her breathing was easy and regular like she was asleep. Then he drifted off too.

9

The cab dropped Teddy Folger in front of his bungalow. He went inside, a little tipsy and a lot depressed. The depression segued to a grumpy, simmering, insulted anger. He'd been rudely and abruptly rebuffed by Misty, and now that he'd stocked the *Jenny*, there was nothing to keep him in Pensacola. It was late, but he could flop into bed and get a few good hours of sleep. Then it was up early to catch the morning tide to a bright new future.

Teddy flipped the light switch in the living room. The two guys in dark suits sitting on his rattan furniture startled him. He squeaked surprise and fear, started backing toward the door.

"Mr. Folger," said the one with the long sideburns. "I represent a party interested in your Joe DiMaggio baseball card."

So that was it. Teddy looked more closely at the two men. The one guy had spoken with a thick accent. "You're not from around here."

"We flew in from Tokyo. My name is Toshi."

Toshi looked lean and wicked and had a hard dark gleam in his eye that might have been a warning not to mess with him if Teddy hadn't been slightly drunk.

Teddy said, "Well, I don't know how they do things in Tokyo, but around here people don't go into each other's homes without an invitation. It's pretty damn rude."

"We're not here to be polite," Toshi said. "We're here for the card."

Good, thought Teddy. *Time to drive up the price.* "I already have a very good offer. You're going to have to pay top dollar if you want it."

"I don't think you understand." Toshi and his associate stood, advanced toward Teddy.

"What the hell is this?"

They jumped on him, punched him in the stomach. He tried to talk but couldn't catch his breath. Toshi landed a punch to the side of his head. Lights exploded. Teddy's head buzzed. He tried to talk, but he was too rattled.

"Let me be clear," Toshi said. "We want the card, and we're prepared to offer you the bargain price of your life."

Teddy barely heard them, was barely even conscious he was being dragged across the floor.

The alarm went off at midnight. Conner splashed water in his face. Jenny spent ten minutes in the bathroom. They dressed, cleared out of the motel. They pushed the canoe into the deep water, paddled upriver against the weak current.

A thin, clinging fog lay low on the river. It was too dark. Conner hadn't thought to bring a flashlight, but occasional dock lights or flood lamps from a riverfront home kept them on course.

It was silent work, paddling in rhythm with their heavy breathing, muscles just a little sore from yesterday's canoe trip. They didn't want to talk anyway. Conner thought maybe they were finished with each other. They'd gotten what they'd needed from a moment in a certain time and place. There was left only the business of the sailboat.

They turned the canoe into Folger's canal, passed the houses into the dark, deserted stretch, paddled a little faster, and emerged into the fuzzy light spilling from the bungalow's windows across the yard. Conner motioned for Jenny to quit paddling. They glided along the quiet, glass-topped canal, not even the obligatory screech of a night bird.

Which was good because the screech of nearly anything would have scared the shit out of Conner. Conner didn't like any of this. Not one damn bit. He'd never repossessed anything as clumsy and slow as a sailboat. Should he paddle it out like he'd told Jenny, or should he crank the engine and make a run for it? His arms were already too sore from the canoe trip, but he hated the thought of the engine not turning over. He pictured Folger barging out of the bungalow in a bathrobe, a shotgun in his hands. Conner had spent some time with boats. He knew the engine might crank, make a racket, then sputter out.

And Jenny. When Conner made a repo he usually didn't have a sidekick. Worrying about her would only be a distraction.

Jenny leaned close, her hot whisper on his ear. "Why did we stop paddling?"

"I'm thinking how to do it," Conner whispered. "Drop me off, then take the canoe to the *Jenny*. Tie up the canoe. We'll tow it. I'm going to peek in his windows. If there's nobody home, we'll start the engine and do this the easy way."

"What do you want me to do?"

"Cast off the lines. Be ready to leave in a hurry."

"Right."

She paddled him to the edge of the canal, and he hoisted himself up and into Folger's backyard. He paused a second to watch Jenny paddle toward the sailboat. What would he do if somebody came out of the house? Jump in the canal maybe. Start swimming. Conner decided not to think about it.

He jogged toward the bungalow, keeping low in war-movie

crouch. One of Folger's windows glowed from a lamp inside, but the yard was dark, no outside floods. Some houses had lights that kicked on when motion detectors were tripped. Maybe Folger had a dog. A hundred things could go wrong.

Conner let that thought drift away with a shrug. The lights would either blaze or they wouldn't. Dogs would bark or not. Teddy Folger would pepper his ass with buckshot or he wouldn't. Nothing to do now but go for it.

He ran toward the house, ducked and rolled on arrival, landing under the windowsill where the lamp within cast weak yellow light. Deep breaths. He waited, listened. *I hate this shit.* When he heard nothing, he lifted his head slowly, peered through the window.

Inside. Bare beige walls, fake bamboo furniture, cushions with a tropical pattern. Tile floor. Ceiling fan. Conner thought it looked like his great-aunt's retirement villa in Boca.

Conner watched for a minute. Three minutes. Five. Nothing. Maybe he'd sneak around the front of the house. If the driveway was empty, he could safely assume nobody was home. This wouldn't be so tough after all.

Then a figure wearing a dark suit came into the room. He talked over his shoulder to somebody else out of sight. The man was medium height, black hair, Asian features. Conner watched as the man lit a cigarette, paced with his free hand in his pants pocket. More chatter from the other room. The Asian guy nodded and went to join his accomplice.

Who was he? Not Teddy Folger. Conner looked back at the sail-boat, brass fittings shining with moonlight. He strained his eyes to see if he could catch sight of Jenny's silhouette, but the boat was dark, no movement. She should have been aboard by now. He thought about tiptoeing back, telling her they'd have to call it off. Strangers in Folger's house, too many variables.

He wanted more information.

Conner circled the bungalow, found another window lit from within. The kitchen. He looked inside. He blinked at what he saw. His mouth fell open.

The guy tied to the kitchen chair must've been Teddy Folger. He was about the right age and the only white guy in the room. The other two were Asian. Teddy didn't look good. A split lip, a black eye, hair disheveled. Folger's Hawaiian shirt was ripped.

Conner smelled cigarette smoke and realized the window was open. Smoke and sound carried through the screen. Conner froze. He didn't want to sneeze or snap a twig. Whatever the hell was happening to Folger was none of Conner's business.

One of the Asian guys backhanded Folger in the face, and the sharp crack of skin on skin made Conner jump.

"Okay. That's good," said one of the others. "I think maybe Mr. Folger want to cooperate now. That okaydokey with you, Mr. Folger?" The man's accent was heavy. Folger's name came out *Mistah Folgah*.

Folger nodded. "Water. A drink." Folger spit, a gooey strand of blood and saliva hanging from his chin.

"Get him water," the guy in charge said. The other opened a cabinet, found a glass, and filled it in the sink.

Conner had seen enough. He'd tell Jenny the deal was off, and if she didn't like it, he'd toss her in the canal and paddle the canoe the hell out of there full steam ahead. Conner wasn't interested in getting his ass kung-fu'd.

Conner took a deep breath, tensed for gingerly steps away from the window. All he had to do was sneak away and—

From the backyard, the hot cough of a boat engine startled sleeping birds. It sputtered, rumbled, and petered out. It cranked again, turned over, revved into a high idle.

The Asian guys and Teddy Folger all turned their heads at once.

Conner's heart beat up into his throat. *Oh shit oh shit oh shit—*

The Asian guy in charge screamed something to his pal, who took off through the kitchen toward the back door. Conner was already running.

He rounded the house and sprinted toward the boat. He heard the back door slam open, footfalls galloping behind him. A flash and gunshots, bullets whizzing. Yelling in a language Conner didn't know.

Ahead of him the *Electric Jenny* was already under way, slowly gliding through the canal, a Jenny-shaped bulk stirring the darkness in the cockpit. At the first gunshot, the engine revved and moved faster.

Conner angled, ran an intercept course, hit the edge of the canal, and launched himself. He landed on the bow, tumbled, rolled onto the anchor, and howled bloody murder.

His pursuer leapt too, landed on his feet near Conner, and pulled a pistol from his jacket. Conner didn't wait for him to take aim or get his sea legs. He kicked out as hard as he could, slammed his heel into the guy's ankle. The guy didn't make a sound, but he tilted left and hit the deck, the pistol clattering over the side. Conner struggled to his feet, took up a boxer's stance.

The Asian guy sprang up, seemed to be unhurt. Conner threw an overhand punch, but the guy wasn't there. Conner felt a punch to the ribs, something hit his face. He threw another punch just to feel involved, but nobody paid any attention.

Another rapid series of blows to Conner's ribs took his breath away. A hit on the ear. A bloody lip. Conner was getting his ass kicked by a blur.

His world tilted, a streak of moonlight and a slam to the back as he hit the deck. He blinked his eyes open. He was flat on his back, the Asian kneeling over him, preparing to deliver a killer blow to Conner's throat.

Then the sound of glass shattering. The Asian fell across Conner, lay there without moving. The smell of rum.

Long seconds. Nobody moved.

A voice. "Conner." Jenny.

Conner rolled the guy off him, stretching, groaning. Conner didn't have enough hands to rub all the places that hurt. He looked at Jenny. She came into focus. She held the broken end of a Captain Morgan's bottle.

"I had to get him off you," she said.

"Thanks."

She bent over, looked the guy up and down. "Who the hell is this?"

"Who's driving the boat?" Conner asked.

"Hell." She ran back to the cockpit, took the wheel.

They were into the main part of the river now. Jenny had been smart enough not to turn on the running lights. Or maybe she just hadn't thought of it.

"I need a flashlight," Conner said.

Jenny found one under the pilot's seat, gave it to Conner. He flipped it on, used it to sort through the items in the Asian guy's pocket. He found a passport. Japanese.

"Dump him over the side," Jenny called from the cockpit.

Conner ignored her, examined the guy's head and pulse. He'd be okay, but he'd also be out for a while.

Conner remembered Jenny had started the boat, nearly got him killed. "Why the hell didn't you wait for me?"

"I wanted Teddy to know he was getting his boat taken away," she said. "I wanted to see the stunned look on that fat fucker's face."

Conner didn't say anything, but he remembered Folger's split lip and black eye, wondered if that would be stunned enough to satisfy the former Mrs. Folger.

10

Neither Conner nor Jenny was eager for the Japanese guy to wake up and resume his whirlwind frenzy of karate death. Jenny's suggestion to dump the guy over the side was surprisingly cold-blooded. Then again, the guy had been trying to beat Conner's brains out.

Still, it just wasn't Conner's style.

They put him in the canoe and set him adrift. Without the paddle.

Conner would make up some lie for the canoe rental place. You could blame rowdy teenagers for almost anything nowadays.

Conner took the helm, kept the boat slow ahead and in the middle of the river. Without the running lights, they could run up on a sandbar or plow into a cluster of downed trees if he hugged the shoreline too closely. As soon as Conner had the wheel in his hands, Jenny disappeared belowdecks. Within ten seconds he heard cabinet doors slamming, the sounds of an angry woman rummaging for loot.

Conner gripped the wheel so tight his knuckles turned white. He eased up, took deep gulps of night air into his lungs, held them, and then exhaled raggedly. He had been shot at. Actually, it wasn't the first time, but somehow this was different. Scary.

The adrenaline rush melted away, and the pain seeped in, face and limbs sore and raw from the pasting the little Japanese guy had given him. Conner's ear throbbed hot, the corner of his mouth was sticky with dried blood. He didn't even want to think about the pounding his ribs had taken.

Conner replayed the scene in Folger's kitchen. Folger was in deep shit with more than just his wife. Seemed like he was pissing off people on an international level. Maybe that would work to Conner's advantage. Folger had bigger worries than a missing sailboat.

Still, Conner didn't want to get taken by surprise. He did a little math in his head. This caused a dull ache behind his eyes. He switched from math to half-assed guesses. It would take somebody driving fast at least thirty minutes to get from Folger's bungalow to the swing-out bridge. The road didn't run alongside the river, so no chance he could be spotted that way. And there wasn't anyplace to rent a boat at this hour, so nobody could follow him on the water. As long as he found a branch or an inlet and stashed the *Jenny* before sunup, Conner figured he was in the clear.

The boat glided over the dark water, and with the danger behind them, Conner indulged a brief fantasy. The helm felt good in his hands. He could go places with a vessel like this, maybe follow Florida's Gulf curve down to the Keys. Tyranny. He could take her, leave everything behind, the repossession gig, Tyranny's husband. It was all new and possible over the distant sea-green horizon.

Could he convince her to leave Professor Dan? She was too used to nice things, and her husband had been hot shit in the art community in the late eighties. A big Dutch corporation had paid him a two-million-dollar commission for a steel and glass sculpture that decorated the lobby of the corporate headquarters. The sculpture had put him into the international spotlight and three more quick commissions followed, all in the seven-figure range. Now in the cool autumn of his career, he coasted on his past reputation and lived easy in his big house by the bay, a cushy professorship supplying him with coeds.

Until Tyranny. He'd married her. Conner might have been able to stomach a quick affair. For some reason women like Tyranny always had to dabble with older men. What was it? Some kind of Freudian father thing? Just kicks? But it wasn't a quick fling. It was a wedding.

Conner shouldn't have been surprised. Professor Dan could give her what she wanted. He was plugged into the art scene. He knew the chic, important people in New York or LA or Mars or wherever. He could talk the talk and walk the walk of the cultured and educated. Conner knew a good place to get oysters. On a good day, he could hit a curveball. It wasn't the same.

What would Conner do for money, to be somebody important, to have whatever he wanted at his fingertips? Conner felt a fleeting kinship with Teddy Folger.

The cabin hatch slid open and white light blinded him.

"Jesus," barked Conner. "Put that lamp out!"

"Sorry." Jenny switched off the lamp, and everything went back to dark.

Conner had lost his night vision, blinked until the spots were gone from his eyes. Soon the moon and stars came back into focus. "What were you doing down there?"

"Looking."

"Find anything?"

"No." Fatigue in her voice, or maybe just a pout.

"You're going to have to go forward with the flashlight," Conner said. "I think there might be a place up here we can put her out of sight, but it's too dark. Don't turn on the light until I tell you."

"Right." She took the flashlight, felt her way the length of the boat until she was leaning over the bow.

Conner throttled the *Electric Jenny* back just short of stalling as he approached the riverbank. Several likely places turned out to be too narrow or obscured by low-hanging branches. Jenny snapped the flashlight on or off whenever Conner signaled. On one attempt, they tangled badly in low-hanging cypress branches. It took both Conner and Jenny to shove free, but the effort was painful. Conner felt something pull along his bruised ribs.

Finally, they passed a narrow gap in the trees. They'd already motored halfway past when Conner caught a glimpse of moonlight on water. He reversed the boat, told Jenny to scan the water with a flashlight. He hadn't come this far only to hang the boat up on a submerged log.

"It's clear," Jenny said.

"Hold on," Conner said. "This'll be tight."

The screech of tree branches on fiberglass launched a shriek of flapping swamp birds. Once through the branches, the passage opened up a little and doglegged left. Conner eased the boat in as far as he could. It was well hidden but not completely. Somebody sailing within twenty feet might catch a glimpse of the stern, but the vessel was more or less out of sight.

Once Conner had snugged the boat in as tight as possible, he and Jenny tied it off. They went below, made sure all the ports were covered, curtains drawn before switching on the galley lights over the sink.

Conner had to look twice at Jenny. In the unforgiving wash of fluorescent light, she looked haggard, dark circles under the eyes, hair limp and matted. It had been a long night. She'd been through the wringer. They both had.

Conner went into the cramped head, squinted at his reflection in the small mirror over the toilet. He looked worse than Jenny. Swollen lip, a shiner under his left eye. The weight of the world sank into his bones. He leaned against the sink, splashed cold water on his face. His heart sank at the sudden knowledge they had no way to get back to the little riverfront motel. They'd set the canoe adrift with the Japanese guy. He started laughing uncontrollably. It was so ridiculous. The whole night. What was he doing here?

He thought about Teddy Folger tied to a kitchen chair and stopped laughing.

Back in the main cabin, he found a mess. Contents spilled from cabinets. Drawers left open, clothes tossed and scattered. He heard Jenny in the master sleeping cabin, presumably searching in the same haphazard manner. Conner didn't know how to feel about her, didn't have the energy to care. As soon as he found a way back to his Plymouth Fury, he'd take something from the boat back to Derrick James, prove he'd successfully made the repossession. Maybe he could find the *Jenny*'s registration.

He opened the galley's little refrigerator and was delighted to find a six-pack of Tecate. But the fridge was off, the beer warm. Instead, Conner found a new bottle of Maker's Mark. He broke the seal and swallowed; it burned a hot trail down his throat and set his gut on fire. The egg salad sandwich seemed like a long, long time ago. He heard broken glass and cursing from the forward cabin. He shook his head, took another hit of whiskey. How did Jenny still have the energy?

He cast about the cabin, took in the interior of the boat. She was a good craft, sloppy now from Jenny's search, but a good vessel, new, nice upholstery. The framed print over the dining table stood out for being so ugly. Seabirds gliding over a beach landscape. It looked like something from the lobby of a cheap beachfront motel. Conner supposed having lots of money didn't automatically confer good taste. Conner was no kind of art expert, but he knew ugly when he saw it. Tyranny would have been able to articulate why the painting sucked in highbrow art-class jargon.

Conner thought about Tyranny again, frowned, decided he was unhappy, and took two big gulps of the Maker's Mark.

Jenny returned, slid into one of the bench seats at the dining table. She put her elbows on the table, rested her chin in her hands. "There's nothing," she said. "He must have all his money stashed in the bungalow. Damn. I wanted to clean him out *sooooo* badly. I wanted him to fucking squirm."

Jenny's petty revenge didn't interest Conner. "We don't have the canoe anymore."

"So what?" She reached across the table, took the bottle out of Conner's hands. She tipped it back, swallowed. She sputtered, coughed, wiped her chin.

"How are we supposed to get back?"

Her eyes widened, mouth lolling open. "Oh, shit."

"Yeah."

She snapped her fingers, face brightening. "There's an inflatable dinghy in the forward storage area."

"If you tell me I have to blow it up, I'll cry."

When Jenny fetched the box with the canvas hanging over the sides, Conner was relieved to see it came with a foot pump. There was also a two-stroke outboard motor with a pull-cord starter. It was small, resembled an overgrown blender with a tiny propeller at the end of a long, rusty shaft. No amount of coaxing could make the thing turn over. Conner shook his head over the worthless chunk of machinery. "Can't catch a break."

They pumped up the dinghy and lowered it over the side. It was a tight fit for the two of them and precarious. They settled in and began paddling, arms moving in numb routine. *Keep stroking*, Conner told himself. *Just keep going. Breathe in, breathe out. Get back and you can go home and collapse into bed.*

"Only thing I don't get," Jenny said. "Who the heck were those Jap guys? Teddy has a lot of goofy friends but nobody like that."

And Conner realized she didn't know. Why should she? She hadn't seen into Teddy's kitchen, didn't know what kind of hot water he was in. What would her reaction be? Conner didn't say anything, not a word. He dipped the paddle into the water, put his back into it, pointed the little boat toward home, and kept his mouth shut.

11

They left the inflatable dinghy on the riverbank and parted ways. Neither Conner nor Jenny had the energy to pretend anything special had happened between them. Conner had the *Electric Jenny*'s registration tucked into his pants pocket. He'd exchange it for the rest of his repo fee. Maybe Jenny got some kind of satisfaction from stealing her ex-husband's boat out from under him.

Jenny was sour and unhappy and mad at the world, and Conner already had enough of that to go around. She was a little bit sad and a lot pathetic, and that made Conner hope things would turn around for her, but not so much that he wanted to get into her up to his eyeballs.

The sun was just yawning and stretching over the horizon when Conner parked the Plymouth, shuffled into his apartment, and fell on his bed. Sleep mugged him, pulled him down into his pillow with his clothes on. He dreamed about bullets and blondes and drowning in the dark.

•   •   •

Conner pried his eyes open at noon, showered, drank four cups of black coffee, and swallowed three aspirin. If he'd had health insurance, he'd have gone to the emergency room. His ribs blazed, roared pain whenever he turned or bent over. He prodded his side, took deep, experimental breaths. He didn't think anything vital had been punctured.

The day was hot and bright, and the sun glittered on the bay like a picture postcard. Conner's Plymouth sailed over the bridge into Mobile and he found Derrick James's shop and parked. He folded the *Electric Jenny*'s registration and shoved it in the front pocket of his khaki shorts. He hoped showing James the boat's location on a river chart would be good enough. He didn't feel like paddling back out there and bringing the boat back by sea.

As Conner approached the shop, he noticed the police cars. The front door stood open. Inside, three uniformed cops poked around. He went back to the office, found another cop standing over James's dead body.

Hell.

James sprawled on the floor, arms awkwardly beneath his own body, legs twisted, with the knees pointing at one another, mouth slack, eyes glassy and lifeless. A pool of blood the size of a pizza spread from his head.

The cop noticed Conner standing in the doorway. "Hey, you can't come in here." He seemed young and nervous. He herded Conner out of the office, whipped out a pen and notepad. "Don't step on anything, for Christ's sake. The crime scene guys will go nuts."

"Sorry."

"What's your name? What are you doing here?"

Conner hesitated only a second. He told the officer James had hired him to repossess the boat, but he didn't say anything about Folger or the scene with the Japanese killers. The cop wrote Conner's name and address on the notepad.

A young girl burst into the shop. She looked panicked. Conner recognized her as the girl who worked the register for James. "What's going on?" She rushed toward the young cop. "Oh, my God! Is Mr. James okay? Has something happened?"

"Crap." The cop moved to intercept the girl. She started crying and shaking, grabbing hold of the cop's arm.

Conner slipped back into James's office. He was careful not to touch anything. The office looked like it had been searched recklessly. One drawer of the filing cabinet stood open. Conner craned his neck, looked without touching. The drawer was marked F–J. An empty space in the front of the drawer. The Folger file. It was missing. James's murder had something to do with Teddy Folger and the boat.

Shit.

He looked over his shoulder. The young cop looked distressed, the girl sobbing on his shoulder.

Conner realized he was being a bit selfish, but he couldn't help thinking he obviously wasn't going to get paid for repossessing the *Jenny*. All that work. He'd been beaten up, even shot at. To come away empty-handed . . .

He flipped open James's humidor, grabbed a fistful of cigars, and shut it again. He stuffed the cigars into his pocket, left the office, walked past the cop and the still-weeping girl.

"Can I go now?"

"Uh . . . sure." The cop waved the notepad at him. "We have your information. A detective might come see you. If we have any more questions."

"Fine," said Conner, who couldn't think of a single question he wanted to answer.

PART TWO

In which Conner Samson
is James Bond.

12

He was known as Toshi X, the Kyoto Destroyer. His job description included cruelty and death, punishment and pain. He was as hard and thin as a blade, long Elvis sideburns, alert eyes that blazed with eager violence. He loved his job, and his job was to make everyone sorry.

And his growing contempt for Billy Moto was becoming harder to conceal.

Toshi had been happy to receive Cousin Ahira's phone call. In Toshi's opinion, it had been a mistake for Ahira to retire from the Yakuza, but now his cousin was showing signs of his former self. Ahira had become soft and weak playing at businessman. Toshi despised weakness. He despised Moto.

"It goes without saying that the incident at the river was bungled badly," Moto said. "If I'd been there, Mr. Kurisaka might have his card now. Your rogue tactics are inappropriate and inefficient." Moto paced the hotel suite as he talked.

Toshi wasn't listening. Instead, he mused how he would go

about killing Moto. He imagined Moto's pencil neck in his tight grip, a short, sharp jerk, the sound of snapping bone. This made Toshi smile.

"Is something funny?" Moto asked.

"Not at all," Toshi said. "Do go on." He reclined easily in the overstuffed chair. His Yakuza sidekick Itchi sat on the sofa across the room. Itchi had ruined his black suit in the river and now wore shorts and a T-shirt purchased at a local gift shop while the suit was at the cleaners. The T-shirt was bright blue and bore the slogan *My friends went to Pensacola, Florida, and all I got was this lousy T-shirt*. For some reason, Toshi thought the garment hilarious.

"Mr. Kurisaka will want a progress report soon, and I'm not optimistic about his reaction," Moto said.

"And who is to blame?" Toshi asked. "It is your tentative, milk-water approach that has failed to yield results. You mince about, ask subtle questions, consult with the insurance woman. For what?"

"We need information."

"We are wasting time," Toshi said.

Moto's face reddened. The man's barely controlled rage amused Toshi. Perhaps he could provoke Moto into a physical confrontation. He welcomed an excuse to spill Moto's blood, damage his smug self-assurance. Toshi was an impatient man and loathed waiting for Moto to finesse the situation. Toshi failed to understand why his cousin found Moto useful. In the old days, Kurisaka would not have tolerated such weakness. Toshi decided to make it his business to show his cousin the light.

Toshi's methods were more direct. More satisfying. Find someone and squeeze them until they talked. But whom to squeeze? Toshi hated to admit it, but Moto was right about one thing. They needed information.

Toshi stood, signaled Itchi to do the same. "We'll leave you to wait by the phone. Who knows? Perhaps the Becker woman will call with useful information after all, but it has been three days. I warn you. I will not sit idle for much longer. Mr. Kurisaka wants the

DiMaggio card. If you can't get it for him your way, then I'll get it mine."

Toshi and Itchi left the hotel suite, Moto steaming and frustrated behind them.

Something was going on.

Joellen Becker had a sixth sense, an instinct. It had failed her often, got her kicked out of the NSA in fact, but it was a pick-at-a-scab feeling that just wouldn't go away.

She'd chased down leads, tried to ferret out where Folger was hiding himself. She'd narrowed the possibilities, but Folger wasn't holed up with his ex-wife. His house was empty and up for sale. She'd broken in through the back door, searched. Nothing and nobody. Several other leads also turned out to be a bust.

Joellen had discovered Folger owned a sailboat, one big enough to live on full-time, but when she'd found the slip at the marina the boat wasn't there. She got ahold of the boat's registration number and performed an Internet search to see if the boat triggered any red flags in the Coast Guard database. Nothing. With the registration she was able to follow the trail to Derrick James. James didn't have a lot of useful information, but he had coughed up a name.

Conner Samson.

The name wasn't much to go on. Samson was a repo man James had hired to take back the boat. A nobody. But that hit-'n'-miss instinct said she needed to find the guy and talk to him. Samson was a loose end floating around out there, and Joellen wanted to tie it up and move on.

She looked at her watch. She was due to call Moto but decided to put it off. She didn't want to admit she'd been temporarily stymied. He'd just have to keep for a while.

Joellen poured herself another white wine, paced circles around her house the way she did when mulling jumbled ideas that refused to gel. Through the living room, into the bedroom, back through to the kitchen. She noticed, not for the first time, how spartan her apartment was. No pictures on the wall, furniture uninteresting and functional. She had never allowed herself to feel anywhere was permanent. Had never been fully satisfied anywhere. No reason to stay where she was; no reason to go somewhere new.

After Father's death and her resignation from the NSA, she had run out of family and had been run out of her career.

She was thirty-six years old, and her own life didn't interest her. The insurance company was a waste of her time and talents. Now she had a goal. Something worthy of her, something that would make life interesting again.

She hoped.

13

Conner awoke, blinked, remembered he was unhappy and hung-over and tried to go back to sleep. Sleep told him to fuck off. He rolled out of bed, groaned. His apartment smelled like throw up and cigars.

He shuffled into the bathroom, saw the puddle of vomit. He'd missed the toilet by a good foot. He'd clean it up later when his head stopped pounding. His toe nudged the empty vodka bottle. Memory crept back slowly. He'd been up all night trying to forget the two thousand dollars he owed Rocky Big.

With no money from the boat repo and rent looming, Conner had placed a thousand-dollar bet on the Red Sox, who blew a three-run lead in the ninth. He'd gone double or nothing on the Mets and lost that bet too. He was flat broke. The refrigerator was empty, and he was out of ideas. He went into the kitchen, looked in his cupboard for coffee.

He was out of coffee.

In the living room, he sank into the couch and pulled the phone into his lap, looked at it a long time.

Tyranny would lend him money. If he asked.

The thought of her made his sour stomach churn, and asking for money would only highlight his loserness.

He dialed the number.

"Hello?"

"It's me," Conner said.

"I tried to call you," Tyranny said. "Yesterday. Or maybe the day before. Don't you have an answering machine?"

Conner looked at the short table at his elbow. A perfect square in the dust marked the absent answering machine. "Sometimes I forget to turn it on."

"What are you doing tomorrow night?"

"You tell me."

She laughed, a tinkling sound like a wind chime. "Dan is throwing a reception for Jasper Dybek. You know who that is, don't you?"

"Short stop for the Dodgers?"

She tsked. "He's only the hottest new contemporary artist there is. He lives in SoHo, but he's touring a few universities. He's on his way to Tulane, but he's stopping here because Dan knows him personally. We're going to show some of his work here at the house. Dan's even hired a caterer."

"Old Professor Dan is one important dude."

"Don't be sarcastic," she said. "This could be very important for me."

"Is that why you married Professor Dan? Because he's good for your career?" Conner grabbed for the words as they left his mouth, tried to reel them back in, but they'd already flown, sprinted the phone line into Tyranny's ear. "Sorry."

She was silent a second. "My marriage isn't any of your business. It's complicated."

"Sure."

"Look, I didn't call to have a fight. I wanted to invite you to the reception. I wanted to see you."

"Yeah, that sounds like big fun. Then all of your art friends can explain the pretty pictures to the dumb jock." He couldn't help himself. The conversation was a runaway train heading for a school bus parked on the tracks. He couldn't make it stop, maybe didn't want to. "A little too snobby for me."

A longer silence this time. "It's black tie, so you'll need a tux. Show up or fuck off. It's all the same to me." She hung up.

Conner slammed the receiver down, jerked the cord out of the jack, and hurled the phone across the room. It slammed against the wall, shattered into five plastic pieces. He balled his fists into his eyes, fought down a wave of nausea. He curled into a ball on the couch, tried to hide from the sunlight and the sound of his heartbeat pounding between his temples.

And he still needed two thousand bucks.

Tyranny Jones looked at the phone, expecting Conner to ring back immediately. He didn't.

Stubborn fucking asshole.

She felt the familiar rush in the blood, the roar in her ears surging. She clenched and unclenched her fists. Violence and sex and rage all boiled together inside her. She had a problem. She knew it. She wasn't normal. Knowing it and making it stop were a million light-years apart.

"You okay?"

She started, looked up into Dan's face suddenly in the doorway. Her husband. "What?"

He searched her face, eyes piercing and blue. "Who was that on the phone?"

"Nobody." She unclenched her fists, realized how she must look, red-faced. Eyes wild. She pulled the plug on her rage, let it drain, offered Dan a weak smile. "It was nobody."

He nodded. "Sure. Okay." He returned the smile, a message: *It's okay if you don't tell me.* Dan's teeth were white and straight. He was older, gray at the temples. Anchorman handsome.

Tyranny would never leave Dan. Couldn't. Their agreement was too good, too necessary for her. He knew about her. Knew she didn't always have control. Special needs. Dan only insisted he never hear about it and that she go to therapy. He wouldn't pry, she wouldn't tell, and they'd pretend to be a regular married couple. Once in a while there was a crack in the façade, a slip in the playacting. Dan wouldn't push it, but Tyranny could tell he knew something, suspected. He'd asked about the phone call.

It was because Conner made her so crazy—no, not crazy. Dr. Goldblatt had warned her against words like that, even in jest. But it was so easy with the other men. She popped them like Valium, got what she needed, and forgot about them. She didn't wear them on her face like she did with Conner, and Dan could see the difference.

Something would have to be done.

Conner showered. Hot water helped a little.

The couch cushions and the Plymouth's glove compartment produced $1.43 in loose change. Conner walked the block to the convenience store and returned with a large coffee in a styrofoam cup. He used it to wash down four aspirin, then spent an hour putting his phone back together with a roll of masking tape.

He called Odeski, begged for work, said he would repossess anything from anybody. The gruff Slav said to quit bothering him.

He picked the phone up three times, intending to call Tyranny with gushing, eager apologies, but it seemed hopeless. Life seemed gray and useless and some kind of bad joke on him. All his second chances had been used up, and he didn't deserve pity or charity or a break from anyone he knew. Rocky Big would send Fat Otis to ask just exactly when he would be getting his two thousand dollars, and that would be the final defeat. Even his friendship with Otis wouldn't save him forever. *This is it, God. If you have a trick up your sleeve, some kind of last-minute mercy. Anything at all. Now's the time.*

A loud knock at the door.

That was fast. Praise Jesus.

Conner opened the door, looked into the face of a stern, handsome woman wearing a beige pantsuit. Her eyes were hidden by dark, sleek sunglasses. She had an air of authority that kept Conner from acting on his gut instinct, which was to slam the door in her face.

"Conner Samson?" She pushed the sunglasses to the end of her nose, regarded him over the lenses. The action made her look predatory, dangerous.

"Who's asking?"

Her mouth twitched, almost smiling. "Joellen Becker. I have some questions about Derrick James and Teddy Folger."

The cop at the crime scene had said somebody might be around to ask more questions. A detective. Great. *You're a funny guy, Jesus.* Conner formed and rejected several replies: *Never heard of those people. I'm sorry, but I don't answer questions without my lawyer. I don't speak English.* Finally, he said, "Okay. Come on in."

She entered the apartment, closed the door behind her, slipped her sunglasses into a shirt pocket. She scanned the room, eyes darting into every corner. She sniffed, wrinkled her nose. "Christ. Open a window, will you?"

She spoke to Conner, but her eyes finished scanning the room in the way cops look at everything. Conner told himself to stay cool. Rule number one: Keep your mouth shut until you know the score.

"I understand you were repossessing a sailboat for James," she said. "Folger's boat."

"Yeah."

"You repossess a lot of boats."

"Just this morning I hot-wired the *QE2*," Conner said.

The corners of Becker's mouth twitched again. Her mouth might have been trying to smile or grimace. "I can't decide if you're funny or tiresome, Samson." She produced a folded piece of paper with a photo paper-clipped to it. She handed them to Samson. "The *Electric Jenny*, right?"

Conner took the picture, looked at it apparently without interest. "Right."

"I need some information, okay?"

"Am I under arrest? Last time I checked, repossessing boats wasn't a crime."

"I'm not the police, Samson."

Conner's brow furrowed. He reappraised the woman. She sure as hell acted like a cop. And the slight bulge under her jacket was probably a pistol. "Let's start over. Who are you, and what's this about?"

"I'm an insurance investigator," she said. "I talked to Derrick James, and he said he'd put you on to the boat repo."

"I couldn't find her," Conner said too quickly. "Sorry. Wish I could help."

"I'm looking for Folger, not necessarily the boat."

"Haven't seen him." Conner *had* seen him. Tied to a chair, eyes swollen, lips bleeding, a couple of Asian guys working him over. The memory made him wince. He couldn't look Becker in the eye, so he pretended to look harder at the picture of the boat. "I checked all the marinas. No sign of her or Teddy Folger." Conner looked at the paper to which the photograph of the boat was clipped. It was the insurance information from Allied Nautical, a fuzzy photocopy, the same exact page Samson had looked at, the same scribbling in Derrick James's handwriting up in the corner.

James was dead, the file missing from his office. And here was a woman who said she'd talked to James. Conner's stomach flip-flopped. He glanced again at the bulge under her jacket, licked his lips nervously. Maybe Joellen Becker had been the last person to see James alive.

"You okay?" she asked. "You look pale."

Conner cleared his throat. "Hungover."

She offered Conner a business card. "I can make it worth your while if you happen to remember something."

Conner stared at the card, didn't take it. "Uh-huh."

She said, "Best to try my cell phone. I always have it with me."

"Uh-huh."

"Any time, day or night." She wiggled the business card like it was a crust of bread she was offering to a petting-zoo goat.

"Sure."

"Are you going to take this fucking card or not?"

"Excuse me just a moment, will you?" Conner said.

He left her standing there, went back to his bedroom, and slid open his closet door. He rummaged past old baseball cleats and his winter coat, found the Webley, the old British service revolver Fat Otis referred to as the antique. He held it tightly, his heart thumping madly. *Easy does it, Samson. If she killed James, then she won't hesitate to kill again. Don't get cute.* He didn't like guns, but he wanted to do this quickly and decisively. He took one more deep breath. *Now go citizen's arrest her sorry ass.*

Conner walked into the living room, the Webley leading the way. Becker saw him, raised an eyebrow.

She said, "Does Indiana Jones know you have his gun?"

"Don't move," Conner said.

"Or what?"

"What do you mean, or what? Or the usual. I'm pointing a big fucking gun at you."

"What's this about, Samson? We were getting along so well."

"You killed James," Conner said. "I saw his body. And the Folger file was missing, and now here you are with a page from that file."

"You're adding two plus two and getting five. Put the gun down."

"Lie on the floor and . . . uh . . . put your hands behind your head."

Becker laughed. "You watch too much *NYPD Blue*."

"You're not supposed to laugh at me. I'm holding a gun."

"What reaction did you want?"

"Fear and compliance," Conner said.

"Fat chance. Your revolver's not even loaded."

"What?" He brought the gun up to his face, looked down into the empty chambers. When was the last time he'd cleaned this thing?

When he was no longer pointing the gun at her, Becker spun, her leg flying out and knocking the gun from his hand. No time for him to react. She kicked again, clocked him on the jaw. His last thought before everything went black was *Does everyone fucking know karate but me?*

14

Conner's eyes opened. He tried to focus, blinked up at the Amazon blur standing over him. Becker. Beyond her was the cracked and stained ceiling. He said, "Had enough?"

"I didn't kill James," she said. "Just out of curiosity, what did you think you were going to do?"

Good question. "Take you to the police?"

"You really want the cops involved?"

He didn't say anything, rubbed his jaw.

"Let's put our cards on the table," suggested Becker.

She helped him up. They sat across from each other at Conner's kitchen table, and Becker explained how James had been alive and well when she'd been there.

"You were probably the last person to see him alive."

"Except for whoever murdered him," Becker said flatly.

"Sure. Right."

"I *didn't* kill him."

Conner threw up his hands. "Fine. I believe you." And he did.

Now that he thought about it, he couldn't figure a reason for Becker to do it. Somebody else had whacked James. Somebody with a motive. It was all guesswork and gut instinct. On the other hand, his gut instincts had put him in the hole with Rocky Big. His gut instincts were shit.

"Why did you go see James if you hadn't found the sailboat?" she asked.

He thought about coming clean but lied instead. "To tell him I was dropping the case. Folger and the boat are long gone. Probably Mexico or Jamaica."

She looked at him hard, didn't speak for long seconds. She put her business card on the table between them, tapped it with an index finger. "I think you know more than you're letting on, Samson. Shit happens. Things got dicey or maybe more complicated than you thought, so now you want to wash your hands of the whole deal. Am I close?"

"It's not like that." *Yes it is!*

She shook her head. "I don't want any explanations. James meant nothing to me. Too bad he's dead, but I have my own concerns. So chill. I'm not going to rat you. I meant what I said. I can make it worth your while."

"Why are you looking for Folger?"

She thought for a second, then said, "He made off with something valuable. The rightful owners want it back."

"What is it?"

She said, "None of your business."

Conner scratched his chin, bit his lip. "How much are we talking?"

She shrugged. All casual now. "You give me something good, a name, an address, something to put me back on Folger's trail, I could go five hundred. Cash."

That wouldn't even get Rocky Big off my back. "I'll call you if I remember anything."

"I'd prefer you remember now."

"And I'd prefer two thousand."

She looked around Conner's dank kitchen, stood, wiped dust off the counter. "Take what you can get, Samson. The cell phone is always on."

She showed herself out.

Samson knew something. Becker was sure of it. It might even be something worth two thousand dollars, but the thought of some two-bit repo man putting the bite on her irritated Becker more than anything. In the old days, she'd gotten a little impatient with some of the rat-fink informants she used on a regular basis. A black eye here, a broken wrist there. There had been complaints, warnings. That special ops stuff didn't rub with routine fieldwork. She had refused her superiors' suggestion to think about anger management therapy. They had trained her to kick ass and now wanted a kinder, gentler intelligence community. She'd been caught in the shift, set adrift between administrations. Her file was a checkerboard of iffy judgment calls and reprimands.

All of this had been used against Becker at her final performance evaluation. She'd been given two choices. Resign from the NSA or staff the company's office in Blue Elk, Alaska.

"I didn't know we had an office in Blue Elk," Becker had said.

"We'll open one," the evaluation board had assured her.

So she'd gone into the private sector. Security consultant, investigations, easy money with no challenge.

Now she was looking for a baseball card. Enough was enough. With the potential payoff she could buy a villa in Spain and forget all this. But would that really satisfy her? She tried to picture herself living a life of leisure, reading a trashy romance novel by the pool, but she couldn't quite see it. Right now, anything was preferable to the drudgery of the insurance office.

She climbed into her black Oldsmobile and drove once around the block. She came back, parked under the low-hanging branches of an oak tree and watched Samson's apartment from a safe distance. *He knows something. I get the vibe. The way he doesn't make eye contact. Let's see what's on Mr. Samson's plate today.*

She lit a Virginia Slim and waited.

After Joellen Becker left his apartment, Conner watched his front door, waiting for her to walk back in.

She didn't.

"Fucking shit."

He should have taken the five hundred. What in hell made him think he could negotiate her up to two thousand? She'd been right. Conner should have taken what he could get.

He grabbed Becker's business card and ran for the phone. No time to be proud. Take what you can get. Damn right. He picked up the phone, and it fell apart. His tape job hadn't held up. He spent twenty minutes trying to put it back together again, but the telephone was finally, irrevocably, deceased.

He put the keys to the Plymouth in his pocket and headed for the front door. He'd drive to the convenience store and use the pay phone.

As soon as Conner was outside, big black hands fell on his shoulders.

15

Fat Otis put a huge arm around Conner's shoulders, crushing him in a half hug, lifting him off the sidewalk. Conner's feet momentarily dangled six inches off the ground.

"Conner, pal." Otis grinned. "Going someplace?"

Conner smiled weakly.

"Man, you know I don't want to do this shit. Why do you put yourself in this position?" Otis asked, his voice plaintive.

"Bad karma?" Conner said.

"You gonna bad karma yourself two broken legs if you keep it up."

Conner thought about squirming out of Otis's grip, making a run for it. But that wasn't really a very good idea. Conner was pretty sure he could count on Otis's friendship just a little while longer. Hopefully long enough to come up with Rocky's money. Besides, it was a bad idea to make Otis run after him. Fat Otis didn't enjoy running. Make him run and you got extra bones broken. No, best to play it cool. Conner was safe. For now.

Otis looked at Conner, read his mind. "Yeah, you off the hook for today. I talked Rocky into giving you some more time, but he wasn't happy about it. So you got to come talk to him. He wants to see you face-to-face."

"How about I just send him a postcard?" Conner said.

Otis shook his head. "Nope."

"A nice letter with a promissory note for the money."

"Get in." Otis tossed Conner into the passenger seat of the yellow Lincoln. "Buckle up."

Rocky Big haunted the dark, cavernous back rooms and hallways of a dirty downtown building on the cheap side of the arena where the Ice Pilots hockey team played. Pensacola was hardly infamous for its rough neighborhoods. The small city didn't have a Bedford-Stuyvesant or a South Bronx, but there were a few places somebody could buy crack or get knifed. Playerz Gentleman's Club fronted Rocky's building. Otis led Conner past some sleepy-eyed women dancing topless in the smoky red light, past the sluggish day crowd to a back door, which opened into a narrow hall that took them past an unused kitchen and ended finally at Rocky Big's Forbidden City, a secret hideout of criminal activity that wasn't really so secret if you were a Pensacola lowlife or a cop on the take.

Conner had heard of Rocky's Forbidden City, but this was the first time he'd seen it. It was like stepping through a door and suddenly you were in Willy Wonka's chocolate factory. But instead of candy, there was stolen merchandise. Instead of Oompa-Loompas, there were sweaty guys who looked too ugly to be longshoremen. Men loaded trucks to one side of him, unloaded other trucks on the other side, pushed carts or racks filled with Nintendo GameCubes or fur coats or cartons of cigarettes or a hundred other things. Anything stolen that went east or west across Interstate 10 came through the Forbidden City.

"I'll take you through Applianceville to Rocky's office," Otis said.

Applianceville was a long, wide hallway lined with washers, dryers, refrigerators, and microwave ovens. Most were brand-new and still in the original boxes.

At the other end of Applianceville, they entered a dark warehouse, stacks of CD players, digital video cameras, laptop computers piled high. The commotion of men loading trucks faded behind them.

They passed a reedy little man sitting on a forklift. He had a thin moustache, hair slicked back and oily. When he heard Conner and Otis approach, he reached for the compact machine gun in the seat next to him but left it when he recognized Otis. He went back to reading the newspaper and smoking a stubby cigar. The smell made Conner's stomach pinch.

They walked past the forklift guard, down another short hall to a door lit by a single bare lightbulb swinging from the ceiling. Otis knocked three times.

A voice on the other side, Southern, slightly high-pitched. "Come in, please."

They went in.

At first, Conner thought there must have been a mistake. The little man behind the desk could not have been the Rocky Big that Conner had heard so much about. Conner had always pictured a big, hairy guy with a scar down his face and a gold tooth. Somebody who could make you cry just by looking at you.

The man behind the desk was neither rocky nor big nor anything else Conner had expected. Rocky had buttery skin and thick pink lips and dark red hair combed back and wavy like some actor from a 1930s movie. He wore a starched white shirt and a plaid vest buttoned halfway. He stood to offer Conner his hand. Short, barely five and a half feet tall.

"Nice to meet you, Conner," Rocky said. "Can I call you Conner? I hope you'll call me Rocky. Otis has told me so much about you. Glad we could finally meet."

He shook Rocky's hand. Conner tried to smile but his face wouldn't do it.

"Please have a seat." Rocky motioned to a chair. "I'm sorry my desk is such a mess." He indicated an adding machine, ledgers, stacks of computer printouts. "There's simply an obscene amount of paperwork involved in an organization like this. You wouldn't believe it."

Rocky sat, smiled. They looked at one another. Otis hovered in the background.

"Well." Rocky cleared his throat. "It seems we have an unpleasant financial matter to discuss."

Conner squirmed. "Rocky, I—it's just that—maybe . . ." Conner couldn't figure any positive spin he could put on the fact he didn't have any money.

A knock at the door.

Rocky said, "Hold that thought, won't you, Conner?" He looked at Otis, raised an eyebrow.

Otis opened the door a crack, had a quick mumbled conversation with someone on the other side. Otis looked over his shoulder at Rocky. "Jeff is here."

"Oh, damn." Rocky suddenly looked stricken. "He's early. Damn damn damn. I really hate this sort of thing."

Otis looked concerned. "Let me handle it, Rocky. You shouldn't have to do this."

Rocky took a deep breath. "No, no. It's okay. I have to do this in person once in a while, or people will begin to wonder." He put a thick phone book in his chair, sat on top of it. He appeared marginally bigger. "Conner, I hope you don't mind. Just some business that needs my attention. Could you have a seat over there, please?"

Conner wasn't sure what was happening, but he was glad the focus had moved away from him. He took the chair on the other side of the office.

Rocky said, "Okay, Otis. Tell him to come in."

Otis mumbled at somebody through the door crack, and a few seconds later he opened it wide, ushered in a squat man with a scruffy beard. He wore a polo shirt, jeans, sneakers, a gold hoop in each ear. Brillo-pad hair.

"Have a seat, Jeff." Rocky's voice was suddenly lower and rough. A slight scowl on his face, which Conner couldn't quite decide was convincing or not.

"Sure, Rocky." Jeff's wide smile looked tight and strained. He sat.

"Jeff, I think we need to discuss the twenty-five thousand dollars you owe me."

Jeff's eyes slid sideways to Conner a moment, then back to Rocky. Conner noticed Otis had moved to stand behind Jeff's chair.

"Like I told your boys, Rocky," Jeff said. "It's just a little delay. My dumb-ass brother-in-law had to make a run to Mexico, right? And he had the dates wrong and now it's just a simple delay with the merchandise."

"I made you a loan," Rocky said. "The particulars are of no interest to me."

"Right, right. I know. I hear you." Jeff bobbed his head. Agreeable. "And I totally respect what you're saying. But I give you my one hundred percent promise that this deal I'm working on is a slam dunk. We needed you to finance us because we were up against a time thing, but as soon as my idiot brother-in-law comes back with the goods, we got a buyer waiting no problem and everybody gets paid." He snapped his fingers. "Just like that."

Rocky sighed. "Otis."

Otis grabbed Jeff's right arm, held it.

Jeff squirmed. "What is this? Hey!"

Otis took Jeff's hand, grabbed the pinky finger, twisted. *Snap.*

The noise made Conner flinch.

Jeff howled.

"Again." Rocky's voice was barely above a whisper. He looked straight into Jeff's face, didn't blink.

Otis grabbed the next finger.

Jeff tried to pull away. "Hey, now wait—I said wait just a—"

Snap.

Jeff screamed. He'd gone pale, a thin sheen of sweat across his forehead. "Rocky, please, I—"

Rocky nodded, and Otis broke another finger. Then another. A strangled, agonizing noise caught in Jeff's throat. He went from pale to red to green in two seconds flat. Conner decided to look at his shoes. He felt cold and sick.

"They're only fingers," Rocky said. "So you can still walk out of here. But next time we do the legs. Then after that, you don't walk out of here at all. Are we clear on this?"

Jeff's mouth hung open. He looked at his wrecked hand, nodded.

"Otis, give the man his hand back. Jeff, see you in three days. Bring money."

Otis helped Jeff stand. He wobbled on trembling legs, cradled his hand against his chest. Otis led him out of the office, shut the door behind them.

Rocky stood, shook his soft hands, shivered. "God, but I hate that. Oh, I think I'm going to be ill." He shoved the phone book off his seat and onto the floor. "I simply detest violence." He sat down again, breathing deeply.

Otis returned with a glass of water. He dropped in two tablets, and the water fizzed. He went to Rocky, put a gentle hand on the little man's shoulder. "Your stomach?" He handed Rocky the glass. "Drink it before it goes flat."

Rocky took the glass, drank it down, made a sour face, and put a hand on his chest. "When I heard the first finger break, I really thought I was going to lose it." He set the glass on his desk. Otis's hand was still on Rocky's shoulder. Rocky covered the big guy's hand with one of his own, offered Otis a grateful look. "You're too good to me."

"You need anything else, Rock?"

Rocky shook his head, smiled. "Let me have a word with your friend Conner, okay?"

"Sure."

Otis flicked a two-finger salute at Conner. "Later, Conner-man." He left.

Rocky gestured Conner back to the seat across from his desk. "I'm sorry you had to see that."

Me too, thought Conner.

"Conner, I've decided we're not going to take any more bets from you. I'm letting all my bookmakers know, so that's really all there is to it."

"What?"

Rocky looked slightly embarrassed. "Now, don't be hard on Otis. It was his idea. He thinks you're going to get yourself in trouble. Otis speaks highly of you, so I'd like to start considering you a friend of the family. It would be extremely awkward if you got in over your head, and we had to break every bone in your body. And I think you know now that having to do that would upset me just as much as it would upset you."

Conner doubted that, but kept silent.

"In fact, Otis says you might be a useful fellow to have around," Rocky said. "If you're having money troubles, perhaps some sort of employment in my organization . . ."

"That's okay, Rocky," Conner said. "I always get by somehow."

"Of course. You know best. All that's left is to settle up the two thousand you owe me."

Conner gulped. "I thought, well, since I'm pals with Otis, and since, you know, you're cutting me off from the bookies . . . I thought you were letting me off the hook."

Rocky sucked air through his teeth. "Mmmmmmmm." He shook his head, looked genuinely pained. "I'm afraid business is business. I just can't do that. I hope you understand it's nothing personal. My goodness, no. I can't let *anyone* off the hook. It wouldn't look right."

A lead weight settled in Conner's stomach. His mouth was dry. Conner wondered if he'd been allowed to watch Otis bust Jeff's fingers in order to make a very specific point.

"I can see this comes at a bad time," Rocky said. "How about this? Take a few days, get your finances in order, then bring me my money. Let's say by the end of the week." He picked up a pencil, flipped open his Rolodex. "I'll even call you with a friendly reminder. What's your number?"

Conner briefly explained his current telephone woes.

Rocky tsked. "When it rains, it pours, doesn't it? Come with me."

Conner followed Rocky out of the office.

They passed the machine-gun man, and Rocky said, "Hello, Pete. Have you met Conner?"

Pete grunted.

Rocky and Conner climbed into a golf cart that was parked on the other side of the forklift. Rocky drove. They whizzed past crates of stolen tennis shoes, blenders, sporting goods, and three red BMWs parked in a row. Rocky took the sharp turns at high speed, and Conner held on tight.

They screeched to a halt in front of a row of plastic garbage cans and climbed out. Rocky went to the can with the sign PREPAID written in green Magic Marker. The can was full of cell phones, all shapes and sizes. Rocky plucked one from the top, examined it, then tossed it back. He found another, turned it on, and nodded.

"This one has a full charge," Rocky said. He scrolled down the cell phone's menu and found the number. He scribbled it into a little book, which disappeared into a vest pocket. He handed the phone to Conner.

"Thanks." Conner turned the phone over in his hands, wondered if he really wanted it. He stuck the phone in his pocket.

"Now we can stay in contact." Rocky rubbed his hands together. "Anything else you need?"

"I could use a tuxedo." Conner had meant it as a joke, but the smile died on his face. He joked when he was nervous, a bad habit that had earned him a few black eyes over the years.

"Come on," Rocky said.

They sat in the golf cart, and Rocky unfolded a map of the warehouse. "Tuxedos on the other side. You look like a perfect forty-two to me."

Conner hung on tight as the cart lurched forward, the warehouse becoming a dark blur of stolen goods. His life had taken a turn for the surreal. He was unable to decide if he was afraid of Rocky or if he'd just made a new pal.

"Shoes," Rocky said. "You'll need shoes too."

16

Joellen Becker knew a hired thug when she saw one, and the big black guy who'd pushed Samson into the Lincoln was definitely a leg-breaker. No wonder Samson needed cash. He probably owed a loan shark. Or maybe he was behind with his dealer. Samson didn't seem like a junkie, but it was hard to tell these days.

She'd put her car into gear and followed them at a safe distance. They'd ended up in front of Playerz. Becker knew about the place, knew who owned it. If Samson was going in there, then there was a good chance he wouldn't come out again. She mentally scratched Conner Samson off her list of leads.

Just for the record, she grabbed her digital camera out of the glove compartment, zoomed in, and snapped a picture of Samson. She flipped open her laptop, downloaded the picture from camera to computer. Her computer and software, like all of her equipment, was top-of-the-line. She brought up the photo, cut it down to a shot of Samson's head and shoulders. She fiddled with the contrast a bit, but really it was a pretty good shot. Then she added some text underneath, an off-the-cuff, thumbnail profile. Now she had a brief record in case she might find Samson useful in the future.

Her cell phone twittered, and she flipped it open. "Becker."

"I want a progress report." It was Billy Moto.

"Not now, Moto. I'm on top of it. Call you later." She flipped the phone closed and tossed it into the passenger seat.

The last thing she needed was the prim half Jap breathing down her neck. She'd gotten nowhere fast finding Folger. It was frustrating. She considered herself a good investigator. This should have been simple. Perhaps it was time to drop in on the ex-wife. Maybe Becker would get lucky. Pissed-off spouses and lovers were often fonts of information. Hate made people talk.

Then she reconsidered the picture she'd just taken. Moto wanted a progress report. Okay. No problem. Anything to get the man off her back. She'd send Moto the photograph and the brief profile. Let him chew on Conner Samson for a while.

Toshi X watched Billy Moto's face go blank. Moto was stoic, hard to read, but Toshi sensed a deep frustration in the man. Toshi believed Moto's frustration stemmed from the man's own weakness and inefficiency. He did not have the will to carry out Ahira Kurisaka's wishes. Unbeknownst to Moto, Toshi had orders. Orders that he was dangerously close to implementing. Kurisaka was not a patient man, and so far Moto had been a disappointment.

Toshi sat on the sofa in Moto's hotel room, wondered if Moto could feel Toshi's hard eyes watching him. Toshi wanted nothing more than to hold the half-breed's still-beating heart in his iron fist. He felt the hatred and rage surging in his veins. Toshi was not ashamed of these impulses. They gave him strength.

Moto closed the cell phone, slipped it slowly into a jacket pocket. "I think the Becker woman has failed us. We must think of something else."

Toshi stood. "You were wrong to place such faith in an outsider."

Moto went to the French doors, which opened onto the room's balcony. He threw the doors open. The sounds of Pensacola traffic flooded the room. "First of all, we are the outsiders here." He stood with his back to Toshi, took in a calming lungful of fresh air.

I'd expect a half-breed to say such a thing. Toshi took a quiet step toward Moto. He could smell the salt water even though the Gulf was several miles away. The switchblade dropped out of his sleeve and into his right hand. He held his breath, took another silent step toward Moto.

"Second," Moto said, still facing away from Toshi. "I'm well aware of your opinions, but the roughshod way you handled Teddy Folger produced no results, as you might recall. Folger's tolerance for pain was lower than you thought. Now if you don't have anything constructive to say, I'd appreciate your remaining silent. I need to think of what to do next."

I'm happy to relieve you of that responsibility. He planned to take Moto from behind, stick the man like a pig. In Toshi's mind, it was what Moto deserved. Toshi thumbed the button on the switchblade, and it flipped open with a small *snick*.

Moto's shoulder's tensed, and Toshi realized immediately that Moto had recognized the noise. It all happened in a fraction of a second, Toshi deciding to leap at Moto while he still had some advantage. Toshi lunged, knife outstretched for a strike under the ribs.

Moto spun fast, blocked the knife thrust, locking wrists with Toshi. Moto kicked hard, caught Toshi in the chest, and knocked him back. Toshi tumbled over a coffee table, landed across the room. He picked himself up, went into a fighter's crouch, the knife moving from side to side in front of him.

Moto had also gone into a crouch, hands at the ready, chin down, eyes up in perfect black-belt form.

"Did you think it would be so easy?" Moto's voice was rough with anger. "Just because I'm not a rabid dog like you does not mean I am without a bite. What do you think Mr. Kurisaka will say when I report your behavior?"

Toshi rubbed his chest. "Idiot. Who else would have ordered your demise?"

Confusion passed over Moto's face, but only briefly. "So that's how it is. Then I must tender my resignation when I take Mr. Kurisaka your head."

Moto hurdled the coffee table and swung a fist at Toshi. Toshi ducked it easily, but realized too late it was a feint. Moto kicked Toshi's left knee. Pain lanced up his leg, and he grunted, went down. Another fist from Moto. It slammed into Toshi's jaw. He tasted blood.

He ducked under another punch, rolled away, and sprang to his feet. He put weight on the bad knee, tested it. It hurt, but it would support him. He'd underestimated Moto. A bad mistake. The two men stood facing each other a few feet apart, breathing heavily.

This time Toshi struck first, slashing wildly with the switch-blade, then jumping into the air, spinning, landing a kick on the side of Moto's head. Moto came right back with a flurry of punches. The two men traded blows and blocks. Toshi tore a deep rent in Moto's jacket with the switchblade, but it didn't touch skin. As Toshi pulled the knife back, Moto caught his wrist, dug a thumb into a pressure point, and twisted.

Toshi yelled, dropped the switchblade.

Moto dove on him, connected a solid jab on the point of Toshi's chin. Toshi blocked another punch but missed the one that landed in his gut. Toshi sucked for air. He jumped back, overturned a chair between himself and Moto. This wasn't going well. He needed a moment to regroup.

Moto pressed the attack, lunged hard and fast. Toshi tried to catch Moto by surprise, reversing his retreat, charging forward. A warrior's scream tore from his throat. He brought both fists down hard toward Moto's head.

Moto grabbed Toshi's arm. A twist. A shift in weight. Toshi was in the air, looking at the ceiling. The room spun past. He landed flat on his back. The air *whuffed* out of him.

Toshi more sensed than saw Moto coming from behind. Toshi kicked out hard and got lucky. The heel of his shoe landed square into Moto's balls. Moto grunted low and guttural, stumbled back several steps onto the balcony, bent in half, hands cupping his testicles.

Toshi gasped for breath, propped himself up on an elbow and reached inside his jacket and pulled out his .380 automatic. He knew now he couldn't take Moto in a fight. Moto was better. He lifted the automatic, fired twice.

The first shot missed. Moto stood, backed against the balcony railing, flinched away from the shot. The second bullet caught Moto on top of his left shoulder. Blood sprayed. The impact pushed Moto back. He fell.

Over the railing.

And down.

Toshi blinked. He heaved himself up, forced air into his lungs, and stumbled out onto the balcony. He leaned over the railing, looked down. It had been a six-story plummet. Palm trees and bushes obscured the view. What was down there? Toshi tried to remember. A patio area, a tiki bar. His instinct was to run downstairs, make sure Moto was finished. But already he heard a woman scream. A crowd would gather. An ambulance. Police. Toshi wanted to avoid all that.

No, he decided. He would not need to check Moto's pulse, look into his dead, unblinking eyes. The fall had killed him. Toshi was sure. He returned his automatic to the shoulder holster, buttoned his jacket. Now to contact Cousin Ahira, inform him the task had been completed.

The phone rang. A series of beeps, and the fax machine across the room hummed to life. Toshi went to see what was coming in. It was from Moto's informant, Becker. A picture of a man. Conner Samson. Name, address, and a short note from Becker. *He might know something.*

Toshi retrieved his switchblade before leaving the room. He lamented not being able to slide it between Moto's ribs. Nothing felt so good as the easy glide of steel into flesh.

17

Tyranny's husband, Professor Dan, had hired parking valets. The teenager in the red jacket looked at Conner's Plymouth like it was a spaceship from Planet Crap. As Conner handed the kid his keys, he thought he caught a whiff of ganja.

"Be careful with the car," Conner said.

The kid grunted, parked the Plymouth between a Land Rover and a Mercedes.

Conner's tuxedo fit perfectly. He'd even shaved, cut his fingernails. He looked good but still felt out of place. These weren't his people. He didn't belong here. He almost didn't knock on the front door but rapped quickly before he changed his mind. He almost turned around, almost sprinted for the Plymouth. The door swung open.

If it had been anyone but Tyranny, he'd have bolted. She looked stunning, loose black evening dress, V-neck plunging low, skin tan and glowing. Her eyes were soft. She sighed at him, an indulgent smile spreading warm on her face.

Conner's longing was a palpable thing. It made his head buzz, traveled the length of his spine and burrowed into his gut. He wanted to gather her into his arms, run his hands all over her, dig his fingers into her soft flesh. He wanted to bawl like a little kid because he couldn't.

He said, "Hi."

"You came." She turned the smile on full blast now, caught his sleeve, and led him into the house. "You look good in a tux." She ran her hand down the lapel. "Like James Bond."

"Which one? Connery or Moore?"

"The new one. Remington Steele."

She led him into the throbbing ebb and flow of the reception. Other tuxedos and evening gowns milling about, sipping champagne and exchanging prefabricated party chitchat. The place squirmed with culture and wealth and influence. One lady wore diamonds as big as peanuts around her neck. Conner expected to see the Monopoly guy wearing a top hat and a monocle. The whole scene gave him the heebie-jeebies.

But then there was Tyranny. She led him across the house, gracefully weaving a path through the mingling mass, nodding to various guests. Finally, they arrived at a small salon where three paintings sat on easels behind a velvet rope.

She stood close to him, whispered in his ear. Her breath was warm silk. "These are the Dybeks. Aren't they magnificent? Last week in New York one of his pieces sold for eighteen thousand dollars at auction. He's up-'n'-coming."

Conner squinted at the paintings. Each was the size of a Denny's place mat with a large, ornate wooden frame. Fuzzy blotches of bright color streaked with darker colors. To Conner it looked like a chimpanzee high on model airplane glue could have painted all three of them in about twenty minutes. What he said to Tyranny was, "Yeah. They're great."

"Jasper Dybek is around here somewhere," Tyranny said. "I'll try to introduce you later."

"I tingle with anticipation."

Tyranny ignored the sarcasm, looked past Conner to a chubby young man who stood gawking at the three paintings. "Randy, are you enjoying the Dybeks?"

Randy saw Tyranny, and his round face lit up with a gap-toothed grin. He waddled over, stood next to her. His tuxedo fit awkwardly, stretched across his belly, the sleeves just slightly too short. A zit the size of a jawbreaker perched on the tip of his nose. "Well, you know, Tyranny. Not really my cup of Earl Grey."

She smiled. "I know, but it was good of you to show up. Randy, this is my friend Conner. Entertain him a moment while I check with the caterer, will you?"

Conner cleared his throat. "Uh . . ." He didn't want to be entertained.

To Conner, Tyranny said, "Randy Frankowski is one of Dan's grad students. Just hang out for a while, okay? Dan's trusted me with arranging everything, and we have almost two hundred guests. It's very important to him that this evening goes well. I'll be right back." She vanished among the partygoers.

Conner looked down at the thing called Randy, groped for conversation. "So you're an artist, huh?"

"Yeah, but not like this." He nodded at the Dybeks. "That's way too abstract."

"If by abstract you mean a waste of everybody's time," Conner said, "then I agree."

Randy started to laugh, then let it trail off.

A white-jacketed waiter glided by with a tray of champagne glasses. Conner snagged a glass in each fist when the waiter came within range. Randy looked at one of the glasses expectantly, but Conner made a point of sipping from each one. *Every man for himself, dude.*

Conner had thought he was doing a good job of ignoring Randy, but the guy stood there staring at him. Anybody else would have drifted away by now, but Conner realized what was happening. Tyranny had asked the guy to entertain Conner while she was gone, and like a trained spaniel, Randy stood there wagging his tail. Conner felt suddenly awkward and rude. He'd let his bad mood take over. He didn't have anything against Randy. Might as well try to be polite.

Conner said, "So what kind of art are you into?"

"Dynamic displays of the human figure in fantastical contexts."

"And what the hell does that mean in English?" He was *trying* to be polite. He really was. He drained both champagne glasses, looked around for the waiter. Maybe he could drink Professor Dan into bankruptcy.

Randy smiled. The guy wasn't easily offended. "It's basically fancy talk for comic-book art. In grad school, you have to translate simple things into fancy talk to make people believe you're worth a damn. You may have noticed I'm not hobnobbing with the other grad students. They don't really consider me a real artist." He made air quotes with his fingers around the word *real*. "My dad says he'll only keep paying my rent if I'm in school and earning passing grades. What I really want to do is start my own comic-book company and graphic novel publisher."

Conner sighed inwardly, resigned himself to hearing the guy's life story. The waiter came through again, and Conner grabbed two more glasses. He gave one to Randy this time. "I used to read *The Hulk* when I was a kid," Conner told him.

"That's okay, I guess, but the indy companies are putting out the really cutting-edge stuff."

Conner realized Randy was going easy on him. It wasn't cool to like *The Hulk*.

"I write *and* draw my own comic. It's really the ultimate medium for the modern renaissance man." He pulled a sheet of paper out of his ill-fitting tuxedo, unfolded it. A blue-skinned woman wielding a flaming sword. She had impossibly large breasts and a suit of gleaming armor that didn't seem to cover or protect her at all. "I draw it with pencil, ink it, then scan it into the computer, where I add the color. When it's slow at Planet X, I work on my own stuff."

"What's Planet X?"

"A comic-book and collectibles shop. I'm assistant manager." He produced a business card. It had the name, address, and phone number of the shop. In the lower corner was Randy's name followed by the words *Superior Being*.

Conner focused on the card. "Do you know a guy named Teddy Folger?"

"Oh, his shop's gone now," Randy said. "Besides, we've always had a better selection. More gaming stuff too, D&D, Gamma World, Shadowrun."

"Sorry to interrupt." Tyranny. She smiled at Randy, and the guy melted. "Randy, Dan is about to make a little speech to welcome our guest of honor. You don't want to miss it."

"Right. See you later, Conner."

"Good to meet you."

Randy left toward the sound of distant ringing. Somebody was tapping a spoon against a water glass. Tyranny took Conner's arm, walked him through the back of the house, out to the pool. "Come on. I want to show you something."

The view of the bay from the pool was perfect, moonlight glinting off water. A half dozen men and women smoked cigarettes, escaping the hubbub of the reception. Soft music wafted. Their eyes met, Tyranny nibbling her lips, looking at Conner like she was trying to decide something.

"It's sort of unreal, isn't it?"

"What do you mean?" Conner asked.

"The moonlight, the music. You in a tux. It's like we've taken a break from reality, like we're in a Cary Grant movie." There was something faraway in her eyes.

Conner agreed. It didn't seem real.

Nobody took notice of Tyranny leading Conner around the other side of the pool and into the little pool house. It was dark inside. Conner reached for the light switch. Tyranny stopped him.

"We only have about ten minutes. They'll start the buffet soon after Dan's speech, and he'll be looking for me." She kissed him long and softly, reluctant to part her lips from his.

She pushed Conner into a sitting position on the rattan sofa, fumbled for his belt. He couldn't believe it, so sudden, what he'd been wanting, needing. She was there with him now in the dark pool house, quiet except for their quick breathing. She pulled up her dress. Black stockings, garters. No panties. She sank on top of him, rocked, riding up and down.

He slipped a strap off her shoulder, lowered her dress, took an erect nipple into his mouth, bit lightly. She moaned, her head back. Tyranny slammed down on him hard now, sucking harsh breaths with each thrust until she was grunting like an animal, gritting teeth, digging into Conner's shoulders with her nails. Conner's sore ribs flared momentarily. He ignored it.

Conner thrust back, wondering how long the Cary Grant fantasy would last before reality came crashing down, not wanting to think about when they would be finished and she'd scurry back into the house to tend to Professor Dan's party. But he couldn't help it. He thought about it. Maybe this was finally it, what Conner had been waiting for. Maybe Tyranny was showing him right now her true feelings, demonstrating that she'd chosen him.

Tyranny's orgasm demanded his attention. He focused totally on the now. She locked herself around him, shuddering as she came. Conner came too. She collapsed against him. Breathing easier, their hearts thumping against one another.

Her hair smelled so nice.

18

Tyranny stood, smoothed her dress down, ran a hand through her hair. She wouldn't look at Conner.

"Do you love Dan?" Conner asked.

Tyranny sighed. "I'm not prepared to talk about this."

Something had changed. She was different. He could hear it in her voice, see it in her posture.

Conner said, "Leave him and be with me."

"Look, it's all very—"

"Complicated. You told me that already."

"I have to go," she said. "I'd appreciate it if you'd wait two minutes before following me back to the house." She looked at her watch. "Shit. Dan wanted to introduce me to Jasper. There's an internship available at MoMA this season, and Jasper might be able to put in a good word."

She saw the look on Conner's face, touched his cheek, and smiled wistfully. "Try to enjoy yourself. Get something to eat. We'll talk about this later." And she was gone.

Conner knew they would not talk about it later. They'd never talk about it. He realized what he'd always secretly known on some level. Things would stay the same. She would not leave her luxurious, beautiful life with Professor Dan.

Conner had been fucked, and that was all.

He pulled up his pants, left the pool house. The smokers had gone inside. Out of spite, Conner picked up a heavy potted plant and heaved it into the deep end of the pool, his ribs protesting only a little. The pot splashed big, plunged to the bottom, and landed with a ceramic *tunk*. He felt a vague, juvenile satisfaction, which faded by the time he was back in the house.

Tyranny reinserted herself into the swirling party, returned pleasantries without thought, avoided being drawn into lengthy small talk. Her head buzzed, couldn't form cold, logical thoughts. She felt sick at her stomach.

So stupid stupid stupid. It had seemed so right, a perfect little romantic moment. Moments, however, never stay moments. They never stay preserved, like a picture-perfect scene in a snow globe. The fantasy leaks out, seeps into reality, spoils everything.

She found her husband.

"I've been looking for you," Professor Dan said. "We're starting the buffet, and I need you to—what is it? Are you okay?"

"Yes."

Her mind raced. She knew Conner so well; poor Conner, he would never forgive this. He surely thought this was the beginning of something beautiful. His expectations were so pure and final. Tyranny was complex, a churning cauldron of thoughts and emotions and conflicting desires, and Conner would simply *never* understand that Tyranny could not be tied down to Conner's idea of love. It was impossible, all simply broken and ruined and impossible.

"You're crying." Dan took her arm, pulled her aside, and looked over his shoulder to see if any of the partygoers had noticed.

"I'm not crying. Don't be ridiculous. I'll be back in a minute."

"I need you down here," Dan said.

"Just a few minutes."

She avoided meeting anyone's eye, went upstairs to her room, closed the door, locked it. She picked up the phone and hit Dr. Goldblatt's home number on speed-dial. The doctor answered.

She told him what happened.

"Do you love this man?"

"I'm not even sure what love is anymore."

"Some say love is merely a set of electrical impulses formed by our brain after receiving specific external stimuli. All of that romantic nonsense was invented by poets."

"I hate you, Dr. Goldblatt."

"My wife often expresses a similar sentiment."

19

The reception had shifted to the long dining hall, where food was being served buffet style. It was too crowded. Conner backed out, intercepted a waiter on his way in with a trayful of champagne, and snagged two more glasses. He gulped them down. Burped. It was still too crowded to get at the buffet. He thought he spotted some roast beef, little red potatoes, good stuff, but there were fifty tuxedos in the way.

A side table offered a spread of tortilla chips with salsa and pigs in a blanket. He plucked a white cloth napkin from the table, filled it with pigs in a blanket and wrapped it up. He put the napkin wad into the side pocket of his tuxedo. It made a nice warm weight against his hip.

The room was too crowded and loud. He didn't see Tyranny anywhere and didn't look too hard.

He retreated to the quiet part of the house. Stray partygoers huddled in twos and threes, private conversations. Conner wanted to be alone. He pushed on deeper into the house, found a room that looked like a small library or maybe a big study. A giant globe on a highly polished wooden stand. Oaken desk. Shelves lined with books. French doors with a view of the bay. This must be Professor Dan's office.

On the corner of the desk a silver tray supported a glass decanter half-full of amber liquid. Four clean highball glasses around the decanter. Conner took the lid off the decanter, set it to the side, filled one of the highball glasses to the top.

"I wouldn't do that." A voice behind him.

Conner started, turned.

A pear-shaped man, short. Thinning blond hair. He wore thick, round glasses that made him look like an owl, a tuxedo with a vest instead of a cummerbund. He stepped into the study, closed the door behind him.

"That's the cheap stuff," he said. He went to the big globe and opened it up. It was hinged at the equator. Inside were more bottles and glasses. "Johnnie Walker Black." He poured himself a tall one, then offered the bottle to Conner.

Conner took a fresh highball glass, held it out, and the guy filled it for him. He quickly drank half, smacked his lips.

The guy asked, "You're not a goddamn art lover, are you?"

"No."

He smiled, took off his glasses, and rubbed his eyes. "Good. I've been to a hundred of these things. They're all the same. If I hear another son of a bitch go on about brushstrokes, I'll stick a gun in my mouth and blow my fucking brains out." He sipped his drink, put his glasses back on.

"Uh-huh." Conner emptied the highball glass, held it out for more.

Pear-shaped Guy filled it again. "Did you ever notice how nobody has to know anything to have an opinion about art? Music too. Simply by virtue of having eyes and ears, anyone at all can spout off about art or music or literature or anything. Half the people out there haven't given art two seconds of thought before tonight. They've never been to art school or studied in Paris or picked up a book about art or subscribed to any art magazines. As soon as they get a few little paintings in front of them, they're more than ready to say why it's good or bad or significant or worthless. Shit."

He drank his drink. Conner drank his too. They filled up again on Professor Dan's expensive booze.

"You're not too talkative. Bad night?" asked Pear-shaped Guy.

"I don't know," Conner said. "It was pretty good for a while. Now I'm not sure."

"Girl trouble?"

"How did you know?"

He shrugged. "That's the only kind of real trouble when you get down to it."

"I'm broke too."

"Small potatoes," said Pear-shape. "I never know where my next dollar's coming from. One day I'm rolling in it, the next I'm stealing Scotch from a giant, pretentious globe."

"Are you a stockbroker or something? I could use a hot tip."

"Not quite, but this advice works for anything. You have to visualize your goal, decide you're not going to be a bottom-feeder anymore. Set specific goals with specific, definable steps. Tackle each step one at a time. Sounds too simple, but it really does work."

"And this will solve my girl trouble?" Conner belched burning Scotch. The fumes came out his nose, made him cough. Thinking about Tyranny didn't mix well with the booze. His belly gurgled.

"Jesus, no. You're not listening. Women are an unsolvable problem. Be nice to them, and maybe they'll deign to put out. That's about all you can do. For everything else: visualize."

"My guts hurt," Conner said.

"Visualize the pain floating away as a bright orange balloon."

Conner ignored him, bent in half, and stumbled out of the room. He felt anxious, hot, and dizzy, realized he'd drunk too much too quick. He tried a door. It was a bathroom. His guts knotted, and he was just able to get his pants down and his butt on the toilet seat when his bowels exploded, a steaming, liquid mess. His face was slick with sweat. It was so hot. His mouth dry.

All that booze on an empty, nervous stomach. He hadn't even eaten the pigs in the blankets.

He cleaned himself up. Flushed.

He reached down to pull up his pants and pitched forward, toppling off the toilet and landing in a tangled heap on the floor. The room spun. He took deep breaths until everything fell back into place. *Visualize standing up.*

He braced himself against the tub, lurched to his feet. *Visualize pulling up your pants.* He did it, zipped himself. He leaned against the sink, looked at himself in the mirror. *Conner Samson, bottom-feeder.* He resolved to do something, take some kind of step forward. Even if it was something wrong. He wasn't going to take it anymore. No more wishy-washy middle ground for Conner Samson.

He splashed water on his face, toweled off, and left the bathroom.

Conner made his way back to the small salon where the Dybeks were on display. A young couple nodded appreciatively at them, discussed the finer points. Conner thought he caught the word "brushstrokes" and giggled.

They scowled at him, eyes tough and offended. She had a nose ring and a butterfly tattoo on her back. He was shaggy-haired. White socks. A couple of Professor Dan's students, Conner figured. They left the salon with their noses in the air.

Conner checked the window, opened it all the way, stuck his head out, and looked both ways and down. Rosebushes underneath. He'd need to be careful of thorns. Nobody was around. It would be an easy jog around the house to where the valet punks had parked the Plymouth. He looked back into the salon. Nobody. He listened ten long seconds but didn't hear anyone coming.

Visualize a major crime.

He ran to the three Dybeks, pushed the velvet rope aside, grabbed each one off its easel, and sprinted back to the window. He reached out with one of the paintings, leaned as far as he could without tumbling out the window. It was still a good five feet to the ground. He didn't want the painting to land hard and crack the frame into pieces. He thought about tossing them into the bushes to ease the landing, but he didn't want the rose thorns to rip the canvas.

Maybe he could climb out the window, then reach back through for the paintings. He bit his lip, tried to judge the distance. It was a little too far down. He wouldn't be able to reach them.

Conner swung one leg over the windowsill. He picked up one of the paintings, put another under his arm. Maybe he could get partway out, still holding the paintings, then position himself to jump down. He squirmed into position. Awkward. Even if he could jump and land without busting his ass, there was no way he could reach back in for the third painting.

"Go ahead and climb out," a voice behind him said. "Then I'll hand them down to you."

Conner yelped, startled. He turned to look into the thickly bespectacled eyes of Pear-shaped Guy. "What?"

"Go on out. Be careful. Don't turn an ankle." He took the painting from beneath Conner's arm.

"Uh . . . okay." Conner swung his other leg over the sill, looked questioningly over his shoulder.

"Go ahead." Pear-shape nodded encouragement.

Conner moved slowly. He lowered himself inch by inch, watching Pear-shape with suspicion, until his feet were on the ground. The window was about a foot over his head. Pear-shape leaned out, handed him the paintings one by one.

"You all set?"

Conner nodded.

"Okay, good luck. Don't take any wooden Injuns." Pear-shape's head vanished back through the window.

"Wait!" Conner had to know.

Pear-shape stuck his head out again. "Yeah?"

"You don't seem to mind I'm stealing these paintings."

"Nope."

Conner asked, "Don't you think Jasper Dybek will be upset?"

The guy laughed. "I *am* Jasper Dybek."

Conner looked at the paintings, back at Dybek. "Don't you need these? I heard you get paid a lot for them."

"An obscene amount," he said. "But I only manage to unload two or three a year. It's not exactly a steady paycheck. If you steal them, I can collect the insurance. Now get moving. In about twenty minutes, I'm going to raise holy hell." He ducked back inside and shut the window.

Conner scooped up the paintings and ran around the house. He told the valet punk on duty to fetch his Plymouth. The kid brought it around within sixty seconds. Conner popped the trunk, loaded the paintings. The valet didn't seem concerned.

"I'm taking these out to be cleaned," Conner said.

"What? Huh?" The kid's eyes were red and glassy, and Conner definitely smelled marijuana on his clothes. The valet didn't know what planet he was on.

"Keep up the good work," Conner said.

The kid grinned stupidly, held out his upturned palm. "How 'bout a tip, dude?"

Conner had zero cash. He patted his pockets, looked apologetic. He found the napkin wad of pigs in a blanket, put it into the kid's hand. *"Bon appétit."*

The kid shrugged, popped one into his mouth.

Conner climbed in behind the wheel, cranked the Plymouth's V-8, and slammed it into gear. He squealed the tires down the driveway, took the turn onto the road too sharply, and exploded a small statue of a naked lady into dust. One of the Plymouth's headlights winked out.

Visualize driving drunk. Visualize not wrapping the Plymouth around a telephone pole.

He drove fast until he was well away from the house. He forced himself to slow down, drive straight. Getting pulled over now would be stupid. More stupid. Now what? He didn't want to go back to his puke-smelling apartment. It symbolized everything weak and worthless in his life. Going back would smack of defeat, and tonight was about taking charge of his life. The new Conner Samson was a go-for-it, damn-the-torpedoes kind of guy.

So. Visualize what the hell to do next, smart guy.

20

Ahira Kurisaka's hot tub had been custom-made to accommodate his massive girth. There was also room for the three blond *gaijin* women. They were white and soft and their large breasts floated amid the bubbles and steam. They lounged, the women surrounding him, idly rubbing his body as they talked and giggled among themselves. They sipped Budweiser beer and listened to KC and the Sunshine Band on CD. Candles flickered and reflected in the room's wall-to-wall mirrors.

Ahira was only distantly aware of the naked women, their blond chatter fading into background noise. He thought about Billy Moto and his hotheaded cousin Toshi and the DiMaggio card. Had Ahira made the right choice about Billy? Had he been unfair? Perhaps he'd made a mistake, placing so much trust in Toshi. The whole situation was unfolding on the other side of the globe, and all Kurisaka could do was wait by the phone for sporadic progress reports.

Ahira felt restless, frustrated. He needed another distraction.

He thumbed the intercom at the side of the hot tub. "Send in the redhead."

A voice through the intercom. "At once, Mr. Kurisaka."

Ahira clapped his hands twice. The blondes ceased their talk, rose from the tub, left the room, grabbing towels on the way out.

The red-haired woman entered from the other door. She dropped her robe, skin so white that Ahira's erection was immediate and painful. Round green eyes. She'd been specifically selected for these characteristics. Round hips, full breasts with pink nipples like oversized pencil erasers. Her copper hair fell straight to the center of her back.

Ahira licked his lips. His voice nearly breathless, he said, "Come to me."

Her smile was somehow simultaneously demure and aggressive. She circled the hot tub, approached him from behind, knelt. She massaged his shoulders. He felt her breasts pushing against him. Ahira leaned his head back into her fleshy goodness, closed his eyes. He had to resist reaching for his own erection. Patience. She would be there soon enough.

Through half-closed eyes, Ahira glimpsed the redhead in the mirror, her hands high in the air. She held something, brought her hands down. His adrenaline surged, and his hands flew up in front of his face just as the piano wire tightened.

It had been meant for his throat, Ahira realized. The wire bit deep into his hands, drew blood. She pulled hard on the wire, grunted. Pain, stinging and wet.

Ahira sat up, gripped the wire, forced it away from his face and over his head. He twisted, grabbed at the woman, caught her ankle. She kicked with the other leg. Her heel smashed against Ahira's mouth. He spit blood, but didn't let go of her ankle. He pulled her toward him. She thrashed, but he kept pulling, grabbed a fistful of her copper hair, and yanked.

She flipped into the hot tub, water washing over the edges, dousing several candles. He slammed a fat hand down on the back of her head, pushed her underwater. She flailed, clawed at his hand and wrist.

Ahira's heart beat a mile a minute. An assassin! Right here in his home, where he thought himself safe and secure. She was supposed to have been searched. Had she been? Or had someone on the inside helped her get past security? Maybe one of the household servants had been bribed to hide the garrote wire among the bath towels. If he wasn't even safe in his own home . . .

She struggled wildly now, panicked. Ahira leaned forward, using his full weight, and pushed her to the bottom.

Of course, a powerful man like Ahira had many enemies, but the attacks had been more frequent as of late. *Why now? Could Hyatta . . . ? Would he . . . ?* Could Hyatta want the DiMaggio card so badly that he would go to such extremes to keep Ahira from obtaining it? The thought made him shiver despite the steam.

There was no time to lose. He pressed the intercom button.

"Yes, Mr. Kurisaka?"

"Ready one of my jets," Ahira said. "I'm going to America."

"Right away, Mr. Kurisaka."

The woman's struggles had ceased. He held her under another minute to be sure, then released her. She floated to the surface, swirled in the hot tub's water jets.

He grabbed a towel, dabbed at his bloody lip, wrapped his hand.

The time had come for him to attend to matters personally, Ahira decided. He would have his DiMaggio card, and he'd wave it triumphantly in Hito Hyatta's face.

21

The sensation was new.

Conner had previously experienced the day-after head-pounding and the obligatory room-spin and dry mouth and all sorts of discomfort associated with ye olde hangover, but he'd never before awoken to a gentle rocking, a slow sway that almost lulled him into a false sense that maybe his hangover would be relatively mild. When he tried to sit up, his eyes throbbed in his skull. Electric alarm bells shrieked in his ears. This was more like it.

Conner looked around and immediately understood the rocking. He was aboard the *Jenny*. Bright morning light washed through the master cabin, gentle waves lapping the hull. Last night's misadventures snapped back into focus.

Conner had decided to make Folger's boat his new hideout for the time being. It was well hidden, stocked with food, and smelled better than his apartment. He hadn't been all that drunk when he'd parked the Plymouth in an out-of-the-way spot and found the inflatable dinghy where he'd left it tied up under some low-growing elephant ears. He'd rolled up the pant legs of his tuxedo and hung his shoes around his neck after tying the laces together. At first, he'd thought the sailboat had been discovered and taken away, but eventually he'd found her, boarded, and made himself at home.

It was the last of Teddy Folger's rum that had taken him to a new level in the hangover department.

Teddy Folger.

Conner thought again about the unfortunate comic-book store owner. What had happened to him after Conner and Jenny had fled with his sailboat? Conner tried to tell himself he wasn't responsible for Folger's troubles. A pang of guilt kept him from fully enjoying a couple of granola breakfast bars he found in the galley. He still felt a little bad when he stripped down to his boxers and took a sun nap on the *Jenny*'s deck.

After a quick shower in the cramped head, Conner searched the boat for some new clothes. Nothing. Not a stitch. He put the tuxedo pants and shirt on again, poked around the boat to see what else he could find. Jenny had been certain her ex-husband was hoarding something valuable.

Conner found a big folder held together with metal rings, like a kid's school binder. He opened it. Plastic pages with pockets. Inside the pockets, a variety of baseball cards. Conner flipped through them. It seemed like a good way to both protect and display the cards. Many of the cards were from the sixties and seventies. Only the Atlanta Braves Hank Aaron card was autographed.

He put the binder aside, kept looking.

Nothing else of much interest on board. Plenty of food. Beer too, but it was warm. In fact, the entire boat was damn hot. The *Jenny* had an air conditioner and a small fridge, but Conner either had to put in someplace and hook up to an outlet or run down the boat's batteries.

Conner found tools, took the little outboard motor apart, and went at it with a tin of WD-40, cleaned the single spark plug. When it cranked and sputtered alive, he whooped with the childish glee of simple accomplishment.

He took another nap.

He awoke, fixed a meal, and drank a warm beer. He watched the sun go down and finally decided he couldn't sit on the *Electric Jenny* eating corn chips and granola bars the rest of his life. The new Conner Samson was off to a slow start. Time to do something. What he needed, he decided not for the first time, was money. Not money like everyone else needs money, for groceries, bills, the daily expenses of living life. No, he needed real money. He needed enough to make being Conner Samson mean something. Conner wasn't dumb enough to think you could buy happiness. But having money and what you did with it was a sign of something else. A signal to the world who you were and what you were about.

He thought about Professor Dan and his big house and Tyranny.

He lowered the inflatable dinghy into the water, checked the ridiculously small gas tank on the putt-putt outboard. Half a tank. He climbed into the dinghy, pants rolled and shoes around his neck again. He'd put on the tuxedo jacket. The outfit somehow didn't feel complete otherwise.

The outboard coughed and spit but finally turned over after a dozen yanks on the cord. He pointed the dinghy upriver and opened up the throttle. The outboard sounded like a Volkswagen on crystal meth. It was slow going. Paddling would almost have been as fast. At least Conner wasn't wearing out his arms.

Joellen Becker had told him Teddy Folger had something that wasn't his. Something hidden and valuable. Conner had no trouble convincing himself he deserved some kind of payment for all the trouble and pain he'd endured.

When he got within a hundred yards of Folger's bungalow, he killed the engine. He paddled the rest of the way and tied up where the *Jenny* had been. He peeked over the concrete retaining wall, scanned the house and yard. All quiet.

Back aboard the sailboat, Conner had figured he'd come have a look-see, but returning to the scene of a crime wasn't the most genius thing he'd ever done. As a matter of fact, the last time he'd been here, a little Japanese guy had kicked the shit out of him. But whatever the "valuable something" was, it sure wasn't aboard the *Jenny*. Maybe Folger had it hidden in the bungalow.

He heaved himself over the wall and put on his socks and shoes. Conner approached the bungalow quietly and slowly, but he didn't bother with the war-movie crouch. The house was dark. He cupped his hands and looked through a window, as he had before. A small, dim light, maybe from the bathroom or a closet, but otherwise the house seemed deserted. He looked through windows on the sides and in the front. This time the kitchen was clear. Whatever had happened here before, it was all over now.

The front door was locked. Around back, one of the sliding glass doors slid open quietly. He went in, closed the door behind him. At first, he thought the house smelled only stale, stuffy, but somewhere there was a stink. A bad one.

He moved through the small house, into the kitchen. Bloodstains on the tile floor and an overturned chair corresponded with what Conner had seen through the window on his last visit.

Conner went into the bedroom, where the smell was worse. Much worse.

The smell came from a dead body. Teddy Folger spread eagle on the double bed, naked, bloated and gray, skin slack. He had a bloody plastic bag over his head. Conner grimaced, pinched his nose between thumb and forefinger. Folger didn't look real. He looked like a bloody movie prop, something out of a kid's haunted house for Halloween. The way his body lay, limbs loose at odd angles, almost made it look like he didn't have bones. A limp sack of jelly. A bag full of raspberry jam for a head.

"Not a pretty sight, is he?"

Conner jumped at the sound of the voice. "Jesus fucking Christ." He leapt back, heart thumping up in his throat. His eyes focused on the person sitting in a dark corner. She leaned back in the overstuffed easy chair, legs and arms crossed. It was that woman. The one who'd kicked the gun out of his hands in his apartment. "Becker?"

"Yup."

"You scared the hell out of me."

"What's with the tux?"

Conner ignored the question, rubbed his chest, willed his heart rate back to normal. "What are you doing here?"

"I told you I was looking for Folger." Becker lifted her chin at the corpse on the bed. "I think that's him."

"It is."

"How do you know?"

Because I saw some ninja dudes punch him raw. "It's Folger's house. I just figured."

"Right."

Conner didn't think she was buying it. He didn't blame her.

"I think we'd better talk," Becker said.

"We are talking. Aren't you enjoying it?"

"Cut the shit," she said. "Maybe we can help each other."

"I'm still trying to repossess the sailboat," Conner lied. "I told you I'd given up before because I thought you were competition."

"You're a bad liar. Try again."

Conner put on his innocent face, the one he used when big, scary guys caught him repossessing their cars. "Honest."

"If you're still looking for the boat, then why did you go see James?"

Oh, yeah. All those lies he'd told her last time. He'd forgotten. Conner backed toward the bedroom door a step. Maybe he could just run for it. He didn't want to talk to Becker. His story wasn't holding up, and her cop eyes kept drilling into him. Even in the dark, he could see her hard stare gleaming suspicion.

"Chill out, Samson," she said. "I'm not going to do anything to you."

"I'm chilled. No worries here." He kept edging toward the door.

"You mentioned two thousand dollars." She paused long enough to light a cigarette, the lighter flame bathing her face momentarily in hellish orange. "I suppose that can be arranged."

Conner froze. "I'm listening."

22

Becker puffed her cigarette, knew she now had Samson's attention. Almost everyone understood threats and money. The threats might become necessary later. Hopefully not.

"Let's talk in the other room," she suggested. "It stinks in here."

Samson nodded, backed into the living room, keeping an eye on her. He was so wary. Again she sized him up. She could see the indecision and caution in his posture. He was acutely aware of his own ineptitude, a man smart enough to know he was in over his head. She made him nervous. Then again, Joellen Becker made a lot of people nervous. They'd taught her that at the Agency, how to make a man squirm with a cold stare. How to intimidate with a glance.

She followed him out, sat on the sofa, stubbed out her cigarette in a candy dish full of Hershey's Kisses. Conner stood there, waited for her to get on with it.

"I'm going to level with you," she said.

"Okay."

"It's a pretty good story. You might want to get comfortable."

"I'm good." Conner remained standing.

"You know what Teddy Folger did for a living, right?"

Conner said, "I know he owned a plaza and ran a comic-book store. It burned."

"I work for the insurance company that paid the claim after the fire," Becker said. "Folger reported that something very valuable had burned in the fire. It didn't burn. He collected the money but still has this thing hidden."

"That's why you said it was something that doesn't belong to him," Conner said. "Okay. So what was it?"

"A one-of-a-kind, autographed baseball card."

"This is about a baseball card? Are you shitting me?"

"I don't have time to shit anybody, Samson."

Conner asked, "So what happens now?"

"I've searched Folger's house and this bungalow. No dice. If he was planning to skip the country, I'm thinking he has the card aboard the *Electric Jenny*. Show me where the boat is, and you'll get paid."

"Cash?"

"Of course," Becker said. "As soon as I deliver the card to my employer, he'll give me the money, and I'll give it to you."

"When?"

"A few days."

She watched Samson turn the offer over in his head. He knew where the boat was, she was sure of it. What he was doing here in Folger's bungalow wasn't much of a mystery either. She'd told him Folger had something worth money.

"What card is it?" he asked.

"I told you, a baseball card."

"I mean, who's on it? The player."

"Joe DiMaggio."

Samson bit his lower lip, shook his head. "What's it worth?"

She thought about telling him the truth, but only for a split second. He'd needle her for more money if he knew its real value. Samson wouldn't settle for the two thousand. But he knew the card must be worth something. Why else go to all this trouble? "It's auto-graphed, and that makes it worth a lot. Twenty thousand."

"For a baseball card? Now I *know* you're shitting me."

She drew the automatic from her shoulder holster, pointed it at Conner's leg. "If you say that again, I'll shoot you in the kneecap."

Conner gulped. "Right. Sorry."

"Listen, I don't know why a kid's baseball card should be worth that kind of money, and I don't care." She put the gun down on the coffee table, shook another Virginia Slim out of the pack, and lit it. "These hard-core collectors are crazy. They can get obsessed. But if some rich nerd wants to fork out for a slice of cardboard, it's fine with me. You want a 10 percent finder's fee or not? Two thousand bucks."

Conner rubbed the back of his neck. He looked nervous and un-happy. "If I know where the boat is—and I'm not saying I do—but if I do, I'll go fifty-fifty with you."

Becker blew out a long stream of smoke, shook her head, and rubbed her temples like she was weary. Let Samson think he was playing hardball, wearing her down. Finally, she nodded. "Okay, Samson, you win. Fifty-fifty. But only if we find the card. Otherwise, no deal. You go your way, and I'll go mine."

"I still have your phone number," he said. "Let me poke around. I'll call you."

"When?"

"Soon."

"How soon?"

"Very soon," Conner said.

"Don't fuck with me on this, Samson. I'll make you hurt."

"I'll bet you say that to all the boys."

Becker said, "If I don't get a call from you tomorrow, I'll stomp you so hard, you'll think that kick in the chops I gave you yesterday was foreplay."

Conner said good-bye and left by the front door.

She sat, waited, finished her cigarette, and listened for Conner to start his car and drive away. She kept listening, but never heard anything. Had he walked? It didn't matter. Becker wouldn't be able to stall Billy Moto much longer. She needed Conner Samson to come up with something. Even if she paid him ten thousand dollars, she'd still be way ahead in the end. Ten thousand was chump change.

Or maybe she'd save ten grand and put a bullet into Conner Samson's brain.

23

Conner waited until he was out of Folger's canal, cranked the putt-putt motor, and returned to the *Jenny*.

With eager, shaking hands he flipped open the binder, looked for the DiMaggio card. *Ten thousand dollars. Ten thousand dollars. Ten thousand dollars.* A mantra of desperate hope. Fleetingly, he entertained the thought of going around Becker, collecting the whole twenty thousand for himself, but he wouldn't know how to go about it, and frankly Becker scared him stiff. No, Conner didn't have the stomach for a double cross. He'd take his ten G's and run.

He flipped every page, slowly reading the name of the ballplayer at the top or bottom of each card. Mickey Mantle, Joe Morgan, Catfish Hunter, Steve Garvey, Stan Musial, and on and on.

No DiMaggio.

He started over at the beginning, went through the binder again. Then he took out each card, turned it over in case one of the plastic pockets held an extra card or in case two cards were stuck

together. He bent and twisted the binder itself in case there were secret pockets.

Then he hurled the binder across the cabin. "Goddammit!"

Conner sat, put his face in his hands. *I should have known it
wouldn't be that easy.* He'd already mentally spent the ten thousand.
He knew a man in Fort Walton Beach who'd make him false registration papers for the *Jenny.* He'd slap a new name on her, stock her,
head to Mexico. Find a dark-eyed *señorita* to make him forget about
Tyranny.

It would have been nice.

He stripped off his tuxedo, put out the lights, opened the port-
holes in the master sleeping cabin, and flopped into bed. He lay
awake a few minutes thinking about the baseball card. He wanted to
find it, wanted the money. Even with the gentle breeze off the water
it was hot as hell, but sleep came quickly enough, the waves rocking
the boat.

Conner dreamed. He was playing left field for the Yankees, but
somehow everything seemed weird, the color faded, bleached, like
he was in a home movie. The other guys on the team were all famous.
Willie Mays came up and started talking to him. The wind kicked
up, and Willie folded in half, fluttered. He was two-dimensional. All
the other guys on the team were baseball cards. The wind gusted,
lifted them up and out of the stadium.

The wind scooped up Conner too, lifted him without effort, as
if he were without weight, like there was nothing to Conner at all.

He awoke early the next morning, threw on the tuxedo again,
and motored the dinghy to his illegally parked Plymouth along the
river. He had the binder of baseball cards with him. A couple of little ideas rolled around in his head, trying to become bigger. He
jumped into the Plymouth and drove to his apartment.

After a shower and a shave, Conner traded his tux for a pair of
jeans and a Flounder's Bar & Grill T-shirt. Nike sneakers. A Ping
baseball cap. He felt almost human again.

Then he packed.

Conner was disappointed to find all the clothes he wanted to keep fit into one large tote bag. A baseball glove, the remaining Macanudo cigars, various personal items, and the Webley revolver filled another small backpack. While searching the dark depths of the closet, he found a box of .45 bullets and the metal rings that would allow them to fit into the ancient gun.

He stood in the middle of the apartment, spun a slow, full circle, taking in everything, the shabby furniture, dull walls, light fixtures filled with dead mosquitoes. How alarmingly easy to abandon this old life, leave everything in dust and ruin and the lingering stink of vomit. It was so easy, Conner wondered why he hadn't done it before.

He picked the tuxedo off the floor, went through the pockets. He found Randy Frankowski's Planet X business card, put it in his pocket, and dropped the tux back onto the floor. He went into the kitchen and fetched Joellen Becker's business card from the kitchen table.

Then he turned on the cell phone Rocky Big had given him, dialed the number. "Hello, Rocky? I'm coming to see you. I'm ready to settle up."

PART THREE

In which Conner Samson
is Captain James T. Kirk.

24

Pete met Conner at the door to Playerz, escorted him past what looked to Conner like the same regulars watching the same dancers do the same things, like robots in an X-rated Epcot exhibition. Pete didn't say much, but his little rat eyes were always moving.

Conner carried the Jasper Dybek paintings under his arms.

Pete took Conner to Rocky's office door and left him. Conner knocked with the toe of his shoe. His arms were full of abstraction.

"Come in."

Conner juggled the paintings until he could get a hand on the knob, turned it, went inside. "Hello, Rocky."

Rocky squinted at Conner, looked at the paintings, raised a curious eyebrow. "Well, what's this then?"

"An offer."

Rocky motioned Conner to the empty seat across from him. Conner sat, leaned the paintings against Rocky's desk. He was a little nervous about this, didn't quite know if Rocky would go for it.

Today, Rocky wore a dark gray suit, obscenely bright floral tie.

He spread his hands, indicated Conner should look at the item on his desk. "I'm trying to figure this thing out."

Conner looked.

A plastic fish on a wooden plaque. Rocky snapped his fingers near the fish's head. The fish sprang to life, body twisting, mouth opening and closing to the mechanical sounds of "Don't Worry, Be Happy." It sang a few lines, then went still again.

"What exactly do people do with these?" Rocky asked.

"You've never seen those?" Conner said. "It's a singing bass, a very annoying novelty that was a trend about a million years ago."

Rocky sighed. "And we have an entire truckload." Rocky tossed it over his shoulder, and it landed in a pile of junk behind him. "So, let's hear your offer."

Conner put the paintings on his desk. "These are worth a lot more than two thousand."

"What are they?"

"Paintings."

"I can see that," Rocky said. "Specifics."

"By a guy named Jasper Dybek. He's getting famous. His last painting went for nearly twenty thousand dollars."

Rocky looked embarrassed. "I don't usually take items in barter."

"There's like sixty grand worth of art here."

· Rocky considered, picked up the phone. "Julie? Get me Burt Rosenthal at Sotheby's. Yes, I'll wait." He put his hand over the phone. "Only because Otis vouches for you. I really am becoming a ridiculous softy. Sometimes I think— Hello, Burt? Yes, it's Rocky. How's your boy? He still at New Haven? That's grand, really. Super. Listen, I'm calling about the usual. You know what I mean. Uh-huh. I know it takes time. No problem. Three abstracts by an artist named—" Rocky looked at Conner, raised an eyebrow.

"Jasper Dybek."

"—Jasper Dybek," Rocky said into the phone. "Yes, it does look like some sloppy work. I've never been a fan of abstract myself. Can we move them? Uh-huh. Right. No, that's good for now. Call me later with the details. Thanks, Burt." He hung up.

Rocky sighed. "Okay, I'll take them."

Conner clapped his hands. "Thanks, Rocky. You won't regret it. What's my cut?"

"Your cut of what?"

"That's sixty thousand dollars worth of art!" Conner's voice had leapt up an octave.

"We're square." Rocky's voice was flat, a warning tone.

"But—"

"Conner, these are original paintings, not DVD players. You can't put them through a legit auction. That means we have to find a private collector or somebody in Europe or somewhere to buy them. Burt will take a cut, and the fellow down the line will take a cut, and maybe they won't sell for a year or two or maybe never. I'll probably lose money on the whole deal. Do you understand?"

Conner nodded. "Yeah. Sorry, Rocky."

"Don't pout," Rocky said.

At least Conner's slate was clean, and right now that was no small thing.

Conner Samson walked out of Playerz, climbed behind the wheel of the Plymouth Fury, and put plan B into motion.

Planet X was a small shop in a plaza on the navy base side of town, wedged in between a pizza joint and a computer store. Conner walked in with the binder full of baseball cards.

The owner of Planet X had gone all the way. Models of space-ships and dragons hung from the ceiling on fishing line. Life-size cardboard cutouts of Batman, Green Lantern, Spider-Man, and the Punisher. Movie posters on the walls, *Star Wars*, *Blade Runner*, and others. Conner moved around a big display of Dungeons & Dragons accessories to look at a display inside a glass dome. It was a model of a castle under siege, lead figurines with swords and spears assaulting the defenders along the castle walls. The figurines had been painted with excruciating detail. Even dabs of red blood on the tips of the spears.

Somebody had a lot of time on his hands.

Conner bypassed several shelves of sci-fi and fantasy novels, Star Trek toys, and found what he was looking for. A long glass case filled with baseball cards. They ranged in price from $1.50 to $125.00. Conner put the binder on the counter, flipped through it, and wondered what he could get for them.

"Conner?"

Conner turned. "Hi, Randy."

Randy Frankowski looked just as awkward in denim shorts and a Wookie Anti-Defamation League T-shirt as he did in a tuxedo, but the kid seemed happy and comfortable, in his element with the Star Trek collectibles and comic books and sci-fi stuff all around.

"Did you hear about the Dybeks?" Randy said. "Somebody stole them. Can you believe it? Right in the middle of the reception. Professor Dan was livid."

"Wow. Do they know who did it?"

Randy shook his head. "Not that I've heard. The cops crawled all over the place looking for clues or whatever, but last I heard they were stumped."

Good.

"I really didn't expect you to come in here," Randy said. "You didn't seem like a comic-book sort of guy. Unless you want to start reading *The Incredible Hulk* again. We have the latest issue."

"Do you guys buy baseball cards?" Conner asked.

Randy pointed to a poster on the wall. It depicted a triple-breasted, green woman riding a unicorn and wielding a flaming whip. "That's one of mine over there. I drew it and went to this place and had a hundred posters run off. We sell them here in the store, and I've sold like eight or nine already. That's pretty cool, huh?"

"Focus, Randy. I asked about baseball cards."

Randy looked at the binder, nodded. "Ah. You want to unload the collection, huh?"

"I could use some cash."

"The boss set up two standard methods," Randy said. "First, we can sell them on consignment. We'll put them on display with whatever price you want, and when they sell, Planet X gets 15 percent. You get more money that way, but it's a slow sort of system." He pointed at a card in the case. "That Wade Boggs has been in the case a year. I could have sold it ten times, but the owner won't come down on the price."

"I don't have time for that."

"The other way, Planet X buys the cards from you outright, but only at half the Price Guide value."

"That's good." Conner tapped the binder. "Let's do it."

"Are you sure?" Randy asked. "You lose a lot of the value that way."

"Start adding them up."

Randy shrugged, went around the other side of the counter, and pulled out the Price Guide. Randy went through the binder, finding the prices in the guide, writing the numbers in a long column on a legal pad.

Selling Folger's old cards wouldn't be enough to get out of town, but it might carry him awhile. Conner thought he might have to sell the Plymouth Fury. It was in good shape, mostly original parts. One of the custom shops could probably turn it into a classic show car. But Conner knew he wouldn't get good money. As with the cards, he would want to unload the Plymouth in a hurry.

What he really needed was the ten grand from the DiMaggio card, but he didn't know where it was. Maybe Randy knew something that could point Conner in the right direction. After seeing the prices on the cards here at Planet X, it was difficult to believe a card could be worth so much, even to a rabid collector. A few hundred bucks was a lot, sure. Twenty thousand was a whole different ballpark.

"How much more valuable is a card if it's autographed?"

Randy looked up from the Price Guide. "Depends on the card, I guess."

"As much as twenty thousand dollars?"

Randy wasn't shocked by the number. "Sure. Still depends on who the player is, though."

"How about Joe DiMaggio?" Conner said.

"Oh, you're talking about Teddy Folger's card, huh? Yeah, that's an expensive one for sure."

"You know about it?"

"Everyone knows about it. Everyone in the business anyway. I heard it burned up with Folger's shop. Too bad. Jerry was bummed out for a week when he heard."

"Who's Jerry?"

"He's the card guy here at Planet X. I'm more of a comics guy, but Jerry knows cards like it was his religion. He could tell you every detail about the DiMaggio card, what it's worth, all that."

"When does he come in?"

"He's at the Other Worlds Sci-Fi, Comics & Collectibles Convention in Montgomery and won't be back until next week."

Hell.

Randy said, "I tallied up all the cards. Looks like $810. Half of that is $405. That okay?"

"Yeah," Conner said. "Is there anyone else I can ask about the DiMaggio card? I'm curious."

"You could ask Teddy Folger about it, I guess."

I could ask. I wouldn't get any answers.

Randy went to the register and came back with $405, handed it to Conner. "I'm going up to the convention tomorrow with a load of comics. I'm trying to sell a set of Frank Miller *Daredevils* in mint condition. I'm talking totally original, not one of the Marvel reprints."

When Randy said this, Conner heard, *blah blah blah blah blah.* "Uh-huh."

"If you still want to talk to Jerry, you can ride up with me."

Conner would rather hit himself in the face with a hammer, but he wanted to know about the DiMaggio card, its value, any small scrap of information that might help. This Jerry might know what sort of person would pay so much for a card, maybe even provide a list of buyers should Conner actually get his hands on the card. "When?"

"In the morning about nine A.M. We'll have fun. I usually pack a cooler full of sodas and sandwiches for the trip."

"How much does this cost?"

Randy said, "If you pay ahead of time, it's cheaper. At the door, it's going to be twenty dollars to get in, I think."

Twenty bucks. Possibly worth the investment.

Randy interpreted the hesitation on Conner's face as reluctance. He snapped his fingers. "I know how to get you in for free."

"Yeah?"

"Leave it to me."

"Okay." Why not?

"One more thing. I should really warn you about Jerry. Some people think he's a bit strange. He's really an okay guy, but he's kind of a nerd," Randy said.

25

Murder.

It was the thought uppermost in Conner Samson's mind, that he would murder Randy Frankowski if he didn't shut the hell up. Conner kept these thoughts to himself as they sped up Interstate 65 toward Montgomery in Randy's 1998 Geo sardine can, Randy pinballing from lane to lane, Conner gripping the armrest. The kid really didn't seem to notice that he drove like shit, didn't signal when he changed lanes, sped up or slowed down for no discernible reason, and veered onto the shoulder whenever he leaned down to slide a new CD into the stereo.

And all the way, the nonstop chatter. Mostly about comics, but the topics ranged all along the big nerd spectrum. For the last twenty minutes, Randy had railed against the new Star Trek series *Enterprise*, claiming it had not been what the show's producers had advertised and was merely a watered-down version of *Next Generation* and *Voyager* and wasn't really new or innovative at all.

"I could give a shit," Conner mumbled.

"What?" Randy shouted over the music. They Might Be Giants blasted full throttle out of the stereo's tinny, crackling speakers.

Conner raised his voice. "I said let's pull over. I have to take a leak."

"No problem."

They took the next exit, pulled into a Shell station right next to a McDonald's. Randy went next door to load up on McStuff. Conner relieved himself in the service station's restroom. He purchased a Pepsi and a *Fortune* magazine.

He stood next to Randy's Geo, waited for the kid to return from Mickey-D's.

Conner spotted a shiny black Land Rover parked across the lot. It was new, tinted windows, gleaming rims. He felt suddenly angry that there were people in the world with lots of money, nice cars, big houses while he was riding in a chubby kid's Geo on the way to a sci-fi convention. It wasn't that Conner had any particularly strong political convictions about the redistribution of wealth. If he could be one of the rich people that others hated, then that would be just hunky-dory with Conner. Someday.

Randy returned with a bag of food and a chocolate milk shake. "We're only about forty-five minutes from Montgomery. You want to go ahead and get changed now?"

"Changed for what?"

"Oh, I forgot to show you," Randy said. "I told you I could get us in for free, remember? Today's costume day. Wear a costume, and you don't have to pay the entrance fee."

"Please don't say what I think you're going to say," Conner said.

Randy set his food on the Geo's roof and popped the hatchback. He pulled out a tote bag, unzipped it. Within were two sets of clothes: a blue shirt and a pea-green shirt, two pairs of pants. The legs on the pants were short, ending just below the knees. Boots.

"These are modeled on the exact Federation uniforms from the original series," Randy said. He beamed. "The green shirt is for you. It fastens around the front. I thought you'd be Captain Kirk. I'll be Spock in the blue shirt."

"And you really think I'm going to wear that?"

"It'll fit. The material's real stretchy."

"I hate to disappoint you," Conner said. "But there's no way in hell I'm putting that on."

"You'll have to pay to get in then."

"I'll think of something."

"Hey, whatever, man." Randy grabbed the blue shirt and the pants. "I'm going to change."

He went into the Shell station, came back a few minutes later. The shirt was at least a size too small. He wore sneakers instead of the boots.

Please not the ears. Please not the ears. Please not the ears.

Randy took the plastic pointy tips out of his pocket, fastened them to his ears. He was now a complete Vulcan.

"How do I look?" Randy asked.

"Great."

They got back into the Geo and onto the interstate, headed toward Montgomery. Conner noted only casually that the Land Rover had fallen in behind them.

The Montgomery Airport Holiday Inn buzzed with geeky activity. Randy screeched the Geo into the hotel parking lot, nearly splattering the shortest, skinniest Batman Conner had ever seen. Randy slammed on the brakes three inches from Batman's leg. Batman screamed, flourished his cape, and bounded away.

Conner pitied the men and women of Gotham.

As they parked, a posse of Klingons spilled out of a minivan. They barked at each other in a made-up, alien language. Conner could only shake his head. What was with these people? Conner realized, even as he gawked at a frizzy-haired Wonder Woman with a wiener dog on a leash, that his view of these people was far from enlightened. He didn't really consider himself intolerant. He could never have been part of his high school or college baseball teams if he didn't get along well with his black and Hispanic teammates. Maybe it was his jock training. These were the kids people made fun of in high school. Back then, it seemed the natural order of things, and now, into adulthood, something of the cruel adolescent still clung to Conner. He didn't want to stick their heads in a toilet, or throw eggs at them, as many of his old jock chums had. But he wanted to scream *Get a life!*

Yeah. Right. As if Conner's life was so enviable.

They crossed the parking lot, and Conner noticed the black Land Rover pull into the lot and park several spaces away. Escambia County license plates. Conner didn't believe in coincidences. He watched, waited to get a look at the driver.

"Come on, come on." Randy's voice was begging and eager. "I want to check in, then cruise the dealer room before the afternoon panels start."

Conner followed Randy into the hotel lobby, still glancing over his shoulder at the Land Rover. Nobody got out. Conner imagined bad people stalking him. He'd recently embraced paranoia.

He stood with Randy in a long line and watched him register for the convention. When the woman behind the counter asked if Conner would like to register also, he shook his head. Randy started in about wearing the costume. Conner explained that he was going to push Randy's face in if he brought it up again. Randy said Conner couldn't get into the dealer room unless he registered and wore a name badge.

Conner pulled Randy aside. "Look, I don't need to sign up for all the whatnot and hoo-ha. Just go get Jerry and bring him out here, so I can ask him a few questions about the DiMaggio card."

"I don't think Jerry would go for that," Randy said. "He won't want to leave his table."

"Everyone needs a coffee break. Just ask him."

Randy shrugged. "I'll ask, but don't hold your breath."

Randy left, and Conner decided if he couldn't sneak in, he'd go ahead and pay the twenty bucks and get on with it. Conner looked out the window at the Land Rover. It was still there. Somebody might have gotten out when he was arguing with Randy, or maybe—

The Rover's driver-side door swung open, and a tall, thin man climbed out, expensive blue suit, gleaming wing tips, well-coiffed hair with gray at the temples. It was Professor Dan.

Shit and fuck and hell and damn and sonofafuckingbitch . . .

Conner leapt behind a potted palm, watched Professor Dan between fronds. *What the hell is he doing here?* The realization struck Conner like a cartoon anvil being dropped on his head. Professor Dan knew Conner had taken the Dybeks. Wait, why wouldn't the professor call the police? Did he want to confront Conner *mano a mano*, some kind of macho showdown? It didn't seem like Dan's style.

Randy returned, tapped Conner on the shoulder. "Jerry won't come out right now. I told you. He's not what you'd call the most social person."

Conner ignored Randy, watched Dan. The professor looked lost, seemed befuddled by a couple of teenagers wearing crude homemade armor and wooden swords wrapped in aluminum foil. He started walking toward the hotel.

"Anyway," Randy continued, "Jerry says he'll talk to you later if—"

"Shut up," Conner said. "We've got to hide."

Conner ran into the hotel lounge, Randy trailing behind him. Dan entered three seconds later, stood in the lounge doorway, and scanned the room until his eyes landed on Conner. He walked over, chin up, stride confident.

"Samson," Professor Dan said. "You and I need to talk."

"So talk."

Professor Dan looked Randy up and down like he was inspecting a turd. "Alone. Over at the bar."

Conner and Professor Dan leaned at the bar. The bartender took their orders, a draft beer for Conner and a Beefeater and lime for Dan. The professor didn't say anything, sipped his drink. Conner was nervous, didn't want to talk first. He gulped beer, waited, kept his eyes glued to the professor's face, but Dan was unreadable. If he accused him of stealing the Dybeks, Conner would deny it. He would just flat out look Dan in the eye and claim to have no idea what he was talking about.

"I want you to stop seeing Tyranny," Professor Dan said.

"I'm not . . ." Conner couldn't even finish the lie. He felt suddenly leaden, his gut heavy. He couldn't look at Professor Dan. He felt guilty and small and embarrassed. He felt caught.

In fact, Conner had often imagined a confrontation with Dan, fantasized about telling him off, telling him he wasn't good enough for Tyranny, that he was a pompous, arrogant has-been. Then he'd sweep Tyranny into his arms and drive away in his new Ford Mustang. Convertible.

Instead, all Conner could do was wait for what Dan said next.

"I want to be clear on this," Dan said. "You're going to stop seeing her. End of discussion. I felt it was something I had to say in person." He downed his drink, turned to leave.

Somewhere from the bottom of Conner's throat, he said, "No."

It had come out in a croak, had almost been lost amid the bar din. Conner almost didn't have the breath to utter it, his feeble defiance. Dan, in fact, hadn't even heard him, was still walking away, when Conner cleared his throat and said a little louder, "No."

Dan stopped, looked back at Conner. "What?"

"I said no. It's not up to you. It's up to Tyranny."

Dan laughed, came back to the bar, and motioned for the bartender to refill his drink. "How do you think this will work? I mean really. You think Tyranny is like a dog? We'll both call her and see who she comes to? You think she'll make the right choice?"

"I think she'd choose me," Conner said. "She loves me, not you."

"Love. Huh. She likes you. I'll admit that," Professor Dan said. "That's why I wanted to talk to you face-to-face. She was very agitated after the reception the other night. She claimed not to be feeling well, but I know she was upset about you. She might even like you better than the others."

"Others?"

A slight smile. Smug. "You don't know, do you? How delightful. You can't tie down a woman like Tyranny. She isn't built that way. She has problems. Needs. I'm an adult, so I take it in stride like an adult."

"You're a liar." Conner felt hot up through his face. Sweat.

"As long as she keeps her extracurricular activities out of my face, I'm pretty tolerant, but you're different, Samson. You upset her, and that upsets me. It makes me have to think about it, and that's when it starts to bother me. So you're out, Samson. You can't handle yourself like a grown-up, so I'm telling you to walk away."

"She loves me." Even to Conner it sounded weak. Others? Professor Dan was trying to rattle him.

"Jesus, you're dumb." Dan gulped his drink. "I'm twice the man you are, Samson. I have money, influence, standing in the community. But that's not why Tyranny and I work. I understand her and give her the room she needs. You don't get it. You're a diversion to her. That's all."

"Shut up." The anger roared in his ears.

"You're a textbook loser, Samson," Dan said. "Do you think it's true love just because she humped you?"

"Don't talk about her like—"

"Knock off the chivalry bullshit. You've had your ride. Now it's time to move on."

Conner's fist came around fast, smacked hard into Dan's jaw. Dan spit blood, stepped backward, legs wobbly, then sat down hard on the floor.

He stood slowly, wiped blood on his sleeve. "Feel better? Think that solves anything? Just like your type to—"

Conner hit him again. Dan's head snapped back, but he didn't go down.

"Son of a bitch." Dan charged, leapt on Conner, wrapping his arms around Conner's waist. They fell back in a tangled mass, knocked over a table, scattering mugs of beer. Costumed nerds screamed and fled the lounge.

Conner and Professor Dan rolled on the floor, punching and gouging without effect. Conner bit Dan's arm. He screamed, kicked Conner away. They both scrambled to their feet, facing each other and breathing heavily.

Dan grabbed a chair, threw it at Conner.

Conner caught it, threw it back at Dan, who ducked and yelped. Then Conner rushed the professor. Dan grabbed a drink from the bar, splashed it into Conner's eyes. Conner yelled, tried to punch with one hand while wiping his eyes with the other.

Bodies piled on top of him. Shouting. His hands were pinned behind his back and his face slammed down on the floor of the lounge, rubbed raw against the cheap carpet. It hurt.

All Conner could think of was Tyranny. How many others had there been? The mental images of her with other men burned Conner's brain. He tortured himself with this thought over and over again the way men will do when they're trying to reach that numb place where nothing matters anymore.

26

Conner slumped at one of the lounge tables, holding a bar towel full of ice against his forehead. A slight knot from when his face had kissed the floor.

The bartender, security guard, and busboy who'd gang-piled him had been persuaded not to call the police by a fistful of Professor Dan's money. It wasn't out of kindness. Dan didn't want to be taken downtown for disturbing the peace and destruction of property. He'd given Conner one last warning to stay away from Tyranny before he left.

Tyranny.

Conner couldn't sort through all the jumbled feelings in his gut. All he could do was sit there and hang his head and feel like a world-class sucker.

Adding insult to injury was the Captain Kirk costume.

Conner's shirt and jeans had been soaked with beer during his fight with Dan, a big rip in the shirt too. He'd reluctantly agreed to change into the dry Kirk costume. What did it matter now?

Randy entered the lounge, sat at the table with Conner. Randy lifted his hand, spread his fingers in Vulcan salute. "Live long and prosper, Captain."

"It's too late," Conner said. "And don't call me Captain."

"Just trying to cheer you up."

"In case you haven't noticed," Conner said, "I'm having a shitty day. So I'm not really in the mood."

Randy looked away, drummed his fingers on the table. Finally, he said, "Let me tell you your problem, Conner."

"I can't wait."

"Your problem is that you fail to comprehend some universal truths. Truths that are so true they're cliché but true nonetheless."

"Is this going to take long?"

"If you want a ride back to Pensacola, shut up and listen."

Conner shut up.

"Here are a few examples," Randy said. "What goes around comes around. The pot calling the kettle black. Takes one to know one."

"You forgot Be Kind Rewind."

Randy went on like Conner hadn't said anything. "I see how you look at me, how you look at all these people around here. We're big dorks, right? Geeks. Let me tell you something. I wake up every day just fine with who I am. I don't have to apologize to the cool people. What you don't seem to realize is that you're getting the same treatment. Professor Dan thinks you're nobody. He thinks less of you than you think of me. You're just shit he's trying to scrape off his shoe. If you want to live in a world where everybody has to look down on somebody else to feel good, then that's your world. That's where you live. Count me out."

Conner didn't say anything, closed his eyes, held the ice tighter against his head.

"Here's another thing," Randy said. "I fell in love with Tyranny too."

Conner's eyes popped open.

"She's one of those people with a magic light around her. And she doesn't treat me like a comic-book geek. You're lucky to even know her. But you're not grateful. You think you've been slighted. You think you've been robbed. You're one of the lucky ones, and you don't even know it because you're so good at being a sarcastic, miserable bastard."

Randy stood. "By the way, I arranged for Jerry to come out and talk to you on his dinner break. Oh, and *you're welcome*."

Conner watched Randy leave. At first, he was angry at the kid. What did he know about anything? What did Comic Book Boy know about Conner Samson? But Randy's Universal Truths echoed between Conner's ears for the rest of the day.

In the hotel restaurant, Jerry ordered a cheeseburger (hold the lettuce, pickle, onion, or anything resembling a vegetable), a double order of fries, and a Dr Pepper. Conner sat across from him, sipped a cup of black coffee.

Jerry was tall, skeletal thin, hunched over, blond hair thinning and brushy. Nose like a beak. He mistakenly believed he was growing a beard, but to Conner it looked like patchy blond fungus under his lip and along his jaw. Jerry ate like a condemned man, smacking lips. Little noises of desperate enjoyment. Occasionally, Jerry even chewed once or twice before swallowing.

Conner let him eat, waited until Jerry was ready to talk.

Jerry belched, shoved fries into his cheek like he was a chipmunk storing up for winter. "You wanted to know about Teddy Folger's Joe DiMaggio card."

"Please."

"You're lucky I'm talking to you," Jerry said. "I'm an expert. I know everything there is about baseball collectibles. I have special knowledge. Don't people with special knowledge get a consulting fee or something?"

"I'm paying for your cheeseburger."

Jerry shrugged. "Well, you're a pal of Randy's, so I'll help you out. What do you want to know?"

"All I know is that it's an autographed card," Conner said.

"*Was*. It got destroyed in a fire, so if you were thinking about buying it, you're out of luck."

"I'm just curious why it's worth twenty thousand dollars."

Jerry scoffed, looked at Conner like he'd taken stupid to a new level. "More than that! Try a hundred thousand smackers. At least that's the insurance amount."

Conner blinked, realized his mouth was hanging open. "It's a fucking baseball card! I put them in the spokes of my bike when I was a kid."

"Well, that's your dumb luck, isn't it?" Jerry gulped Dr Pepper, burped again. "If you'd archived them properly, they might be worth something now. Like I said, a hundred thousand is just the in- sured amount. Any collectible is really only worth what somebody is willing to pay."

"But . . ." Conner shook his head. He was still in shock. "So if I went back in time, bought twenty cards, found Mr. DiMaggio, and made him sign them all, they'd each be worth a hundred thousand dollars?"

Jerry barked laughter, bits of half-chewed french fry flying halfway across the table. "Jesus, no offense, but that's a dumb thing to say. You don't know how this works at all, do you?"

"Maybe you'll explain it to me." *Asshole*.

"Rarity is always a consideration with something like this. If there's a million of something, then they won't be worth so much. One of a kind, worth more. It's just common sense."

Conner actually did feel a little dumb not realizing this. It was obvious.

"It's not just the DiMaggio autograph. Lots of those around," Jerry said. "It's the other signatures that make it worth so much."

"What other signatures?"

Jerry rolled his eyes. If he was about to call Conner dumb again, he mercifully changed his mind. "You really are at square one with this card, huh? Marilyn Monroe and Billy Wilder also signed the card. It's a famous damn card. You didn't know? It's like one of the

Holy Grails of collectibles. Sports collectors and film buffs would both kill for it. It's like if you found an ancient autographed picture of Moses, and Charlton Heston and Cecil B. DeMille had signed it too."

Conner was beginning to understand. It still seemed an outrageous amount of money, but he was getting the idea now that collectors took this kind of thing very seriously. He remembered that DiMaggio and Monroe had been married. Right before she was married to the playwright. Or was that after?

Conner asked Jerry who would buy such a card, how would somebody find them. Jerry told him collectors came from all walks of life. There were trade magazines and Web sites that put collectors in contact with each other. And conventions. Lots of conventions.

"By the way, I brought you this book." Jerry picked his backpack off the floor, found a thick hardcover book, and slid it across the table to Conner. "If you're interested in Monroe and DiMaggio, this is the best one. It's half pop culture analysis and half biography."

Conner took the book, read the cover. *The King and Queen of America* by Adam Oppenheimer, Ph.D. "Thanks."

"It's thirty bucks." Jerry held out his hand.

Conner almost threw the book back in the jerk's face but decided he was curious. He kept the book, gave the money to Jerry.

"I don't see why you're this curious," Jerry said. "It's pointless now. The card burned up with Folger's shop. Damn shame."

"Did you ever see the card?" Conner asked.

"Sure, lots of times. He had it hanging behind the counter in his shop. I'd see it anytime I went over to trade some cards. It was about so big." Jerry spread his arms up then down to indicate poster size. "It was all framed up along with Monroe's letter. Shit, I almost forgot about the letter. He had a personal, handwritten letter from Monroe too. It was all set up just beautiful. Before he put it in the frame, he used to take it out of the safe to show me."

"Safe?"

"Yeah, Folger had a safe built into the floor, hidden behind a se-cret panel under the register. I think he thought it was cool or some-thing. But I guess he was too proud of the card to lock it away and liked to have it on display instead."

Conner only half listened. He thought about Joellen Becker. She either didn't know the card's actual worth, or she was taking him for a ride. And Conner Samson was getting a little sick of being pushed around and lied to.

Jerry had demolished his burger and fries. He looked around the table in case he'd missed something. "Say, how about some dessert here?"

Conner stood, dropped a twenty on the table. He didn't know if that would cover dessert or not. "Thanks, Jerry. You were helpful. I have to get going." He walked away.

Jerry called after him. "I can get you a signed DiMaggio in mint condition for a good price. It won't have the other signatures, but it's a good card."

Conner didn't even look back.

As they'd arranged, Conner met Randy at the Geo. Randy had a pair of shopping bags with him and looked pretty pleased with his purchases. They got in the car, headed south.

Conner stared out the window, plans coming together in his mind. It didn't take him long to decide what he was going to do. It was clear, so very clear and obvious. He wondered if this was what people meant when they talked about inspiration or the muse. As soon as he returned to Pensacola, he'd get started.

His new copy of *The King and Queen of America* wasn't an easy read. He flipped to a spot in the middle, had to read it twice to get anything out of it. The author talked about Jacques Lacan and some kind of fake persona Marilyn Monroe put out for the public and how deep inside there was the "real" Marilyn that maybe got lost somehow. Conner wondered which persona DiMaggio loved, if he'd ever caught a glimpse of the girl who'd been Norma Jean. He closed the book, put it away.

He decided he needed to say something to Randy. "You were right." He cleared his throat. "All that stuff you said about my attitude and everything. You were right. I was out of line, and I'm sorry."

Randy didn't say anything for long seconds. Finally, a sly smile spread slowly from ear to pointy ear. "You can't help it. You illogical Earthlings are all governed by your human emotions."

27

A dull shred of daylight remained when Randy dropped Conner at his Plymouth. The whole ride back, Conner thought about the Joe DiMaggio card, where it might be. It hadn't been aboard the *Jenny*, in the binder with the rest of Folger's collection.

There were a few things Conner wanted to see for himself.

He drove to Folger's torched strip mall on Davis Highway. The place was a muddy, scorched mess, halfhearted, yellow police tape draped around the scene. It looked a shambles, but not particularly hazardous. He parked on the side in the shadows, stepped over the police tape.

There was still something of a roof left in places, held up by ash-black beams. Conner couldn't immediately tell which store was which, but he found a half-burned, life-size cardboard stand-up of Spider-Man and figured he'd found the comic-book shop.

Conner poked through the rubble, but there wasn't much left to see. Burned and melted shelves and display cases. He estimated where the cash register might have been and started kicking through the ash. It was dirty work, and Conner felt suddenly like he was wasting his time. But he quickly found the outline of a panel in the floor. It was caked with grime and ash, and he had to work it back and forth to slide the panel back.

He had the vague notion that he'd check the safe tonight, simply see if he could find the thing, and if it was undamaged, he would come back the next day with some heavy equipment and drill it out.

Conner felt simultaneously excited and silly. Secret safes were the nonsense of Nancy Drew treasure hunts.

He finally worked the panel all the way back. The safe underneath was unscorched, and presumably whatever might be inside was still undamaged. Conner had mulled the possibilities, thought it possible Folger had left the DiMaggio card in the hidden safe with plans to come back and pick it up later. Conner didn't know much about safes but figured a good one should survive a fire. He examined its surface, a combination lock and a handle. He reached out, turned the handle.

It was open.

The elation of his good luck quickly segued into discouragement with the realization nothing of value would be within. Otherwise, Folger would have locked it. He might as well have a look. Conner didn't currently have any better ideas.

He reached in, came out with a copy of *X-Men*. A yellow Post-it note stuck to the plastic covering said *#172 First Byrne*. Conner had no idea if this was significant. He put his hand back in the safe. The sum total contents consisted of four Star Wars action figures (Han Solo, Luke Skywalker, Darth Vader, and something called a Jawa) all in the original packaging, a Rubik's Cube (unsolved), a videotape labeled *Space: 1999 Bloopers*, and a red lace brassiere.

No DiMaggio card.

"Damn." But he wasn't really surprised.

It had been difficult enough to find a thirty-six-foot sailboat. Something as small as a baseball card could be hidden in any of a million places. He reconsidered Jenny Folger. Conner had to admit, without her he'd never have found the sailboat. After all, she'd been married to the guy, knew his habits. If he told her about the card, got her thinking, she might be able to come up with something useful. He toyed with the idea of calling her, but decided the long, quiet drive across the Bay Bridge might help him think.

He pointed the Plymouth toward Mobile.

Conner arrived at Jenny's complex. He didn't immediately go up to her apartment, sat in the car a moment, leaning on the steering wheel. There had been something mildly disappointing and fatigued about their parting. He'd honestly not expected nor wished to see her again and assumed she felt the same way.

Conner would try to keep it all business. Jenny Folger would understand that, appreciate it. There was a mercenary quality about her, nothing cruel, but something born of necessity and survival. He'd appeal to her righteous sense of greed and revenge, and maybe she'd know something useful about Teddy's prize baseball card just as she'd known about the sailboat.

He took a deep breath, went to her door.

When he knocked, the door creaked open, darkness within.

Hell.

"Jenny?" He pushed the door open the rest of the way, took a tentative step inside. "It's Conner."

No answer.

It happened sometimes. People leave in a hurry, late for work or a date, and they forget to lock the door. Leave it wide open sometimes. Even as Conner thought this, he knew on a gut level that this wasn't one of those times, that he wouldn't find anything but bad news in Jenny Folger's apartment.

He found her in the bathroom.

She lay faceup, blond hair down over her face. Her right arm and leg hung over the side of the tub. She wore matching green bra and panties. She was so obviously dead. Conner looked at her from the doorway, unwilling to move closer. He didn't want to see what had happened, couldn't stomach a slit throat or a bullet hole or a caved-in skull, whatever had done her in.

With the life gone out of her, she suddenly seemed older, skin rubbery and fake-looking like the other bodies he'd seen recently. Too many bodies.

Who's next? Me?

Conner recalled their sudden sex in the cheap riverfront motel. She'd been so heated and animated and desperate. It seemed impossible that this was all that was left of her.

He left the apartment. Closed the door.

28

Toshi stood at the bow of the small, rented speedboat. Itchi piloted. The boat motored slowly along the shore, the night deep and dark, stars fuzzy behind low clouds. Toshi fished around with a handheld spotlight.

After ten minutes of violent coaxing, the Folger woman had offered precise directions to where Conner Samson had hidden the sailboat. She'd eagerly spilled the information, hoping it would purchase her life. No sale.

To Toshi, one patch of steaming swamp looked much like another, so he and Itchi had been searching for nearly two hours.

A glint of white among the cypress.

Toshi swung the spotlight back like a pistol, aimed down a narrow inlet that at first seemed too small to accommodate a large sailboat. "Back up. Turn us around."

They swung the speedboat into the inlet, and the *Electric Jenny's* stern hove into view. Toshi ordered Itchi to cut the engine. They drifted in silence toward the *Jenny*, bumped the hull gently. They leapt aboard with lethal grace, intending to move through the boat quickly, subduing Samson or whoever else might be aboard.

Nobody was home.

Toshi ordered the boat searched. When Itchi couldn't find the DiMaggio card, Toshi flipped open his switchblade, tore into the cushions and the bedding. No sign of the card.

Toshi had not really expected to find it. His feeling was that Samson had the card. Rather than search further, Toshi would much rather find Samson and make him tell where it was.

"Itchi."

"*Hai.*"

"Stay here," ordered Toshi. "Lie in wait for Samson in case he should return. You know what to do."

"It shall be done," Itchi said.

"Do not let him throw you off the boat this time," Toshi said.

Itchi reddened but kept silent.

"Remember to restrain yourself," Toshi said. "Samson will die soon enough, but we must make him talk first."

Joellen Becker had made half a bottle of Jack Daniel's disappear a little at a time with a shot glass shaped like a shotgun shell. The evening had started with her chewing through Folger's insurance file. She read and reread every line, looking for some hint. Anything. Did he have another property, an office someplace? A safety-deposit box? Folger had no friends, no living relatives. And Folger himself wasn't talking.

It was useless. Hell, maybe the card *had* burned with the shop. More likely, Joellen admitted to herself, she'd simply come up empty. She had not found the card, nor had she any leads where it might be. She hadn't found Folger in time to ask him any useful questions. Then she'd called Samson twenty-five times. No answer. He was a bust too. Useless. All useless.

She twirled her father's Old West–style six-shooters. She always brought them out when drinking, not often but once in a great while. The general had been a George Patton worshipper. The pistols were so corny, gleaming nickel, ivory handles, but Becker had to admire the craftsmanship. This is what washed-up spooks did, she imagined. Drink into oblivion, play with guns and wonder where everything went wrong.

She remembered that day she resigned from the NSA. It had been a bad day.

She stood at the foot of his bed, watched him while he slept, a cigarette dangling unlit from her lips. She would wait until he awoke. There was no hurry and nowhere to go.

Her father, the retired three-star army general, looked sallow and shrunken, dark circles around his hollow eyes, face pinched. The cancer had eaten its way through most of the major organs, spreading suddenly and rapidly and without mercy. In six short months, Joellen had watched him deflate, this man who'd once been like some ferocious god.

The television above her head blared a cable channel Western. She reached up, flipped it off.

The old man's eyes flickered open. "I was watching that." He produced the remote from beneath the bedcovers, turned the film back on. "It's John Wayne. The Searchers."

"At least turn it down."

He thumbed the remote again, cut the volume to almost nothing.

He shifted in bed, only slightly, but it looked like his bones would shatter, like they couldn't possibly support the weight of his slack skin. He grunted, moved his legs.

Joellen did not offer to help.

He finally found a comfortable position, sighed, exhausted, and closed his eyes. For a moment, Joellen thought he'd fallen back to sleep. But he opened his eyes again, and said, "I hear you got fired."

"I just came from the meeting," she said, plainly irritated. "How did you find out?"

"I still know people in this town," he said. "A few who still respect me enough to keep me in the loop."

"You already know, then." She shrugged. "There it is." She took the lighter out of her purse, almost lit her cigarette but remembered she was in a hospital. She put away the lighter, didn't know what to do with her hands.

"What will you do now?"

"Go someplace," she said. "Get my head together. Figure things out."

"I know someone at Langley," the general said. "And there's always consulting. I have a few names."

"I don't need any of your names, Father."

He frowned. "Don't you?"

"No."

A long pause, then he said, "I suppose you don't. Or, if you did, you wouldn't say."

"No."

"Fair enough." His eyes shifted to the small table under the window. "Your inheritance is over there." He closed his eyes again.

She went to the table, opened the highly polished wooden box. Two pistols inside, spotless, nickel six-shooters. In their hometown library, there was a picture of her father in Korea wearing the pistols. To the best of Joellen's knowledge, the revolvers had never been fired in combat. Her father was simply a ridiculous show-off.

"The brilliance of John Wayne in The Searchers,*" her father said, eyes still closed, "is that he clings to his quest even when it's obvious his quest is doomed. What else is there for him to do? He has come home in defeat, a Confederate who's refused to surrender his sword. He has no cause. What else can he do but invent a new one for himself?"*

"What are you telling me, Father?"

He said, "I'm just telling you about a good film. His quest becomes his life." He opened his eyes, looked at his daughter. "Goals are nothing. That you pursue them is everything."

Somehow, Joellen doubted that was what John Ford had in mind.

"I'm leaving the house and the money to Eliot." Joellen's brother.

"It's yours," Joellen said. "Do as you wish." You rotten old bastard.

A thin, weak smile spread on his face. "I know what you're thinking."

"I'm thinking that you've complained for years about Eliot wasting his

life as a painter and wasting your money studying in Paris and Rome where he was doing a lot more screwing and drinking than painting. So naturally you want to reward him with a big inheritance."

"You don't understand," he said. "Eliot doesn't stand a chance. The world would eat him alive. It's the only way."

"I know." She put her hand on the rail of the hospital bed, touched his thin arm with a finger.

"I'm going to die now," he said.

"I know."

"Don't leave, please." He put a frail hand over hers. "I might fall asleep again, but don't go. I don't know why, but I hate the thought that I'd die and nobody would be here. The doctor gives me fifty-fifty on lasting the night. I'm full of narcotics."

"I won't go anywhere."

"I'll see your mother soon," the general said.

"I like the pistols, Father. I'll keep them. If I move somewhere with a fireplace, I'll put them on the mantel."

"Do you remember that dog we had in Virginia? What was it? When you were a teenager. Some kind of terrier."

"It was a Jack Russell terrier," Joellen told him.

"Yes, I remember. That was a damn fine dog."

And five minutes later he was gone.

Joellen understood she was drunk, pushed the bottle away, and it tipped over, spilled the remainder of its contents across the table. She left the mess. To hell with it.

She pushed herself away from the table, stood on rubbery legs. She made it as far as the couch and fell asleep with her clothes on.

Conner drove back to Pensacola.

Jerry had said the thing was insured for a hundred thousand. Conner remembered something else Jerry had said.

Any collectible is really only worth what somebody is willing to pay.

There must be somebody else out there, a serious collector who didn't mind throwing a lot of money around. If Conner could find another buyer, he wouldn't have to deal with Becker. He was so close to doing something right. There was a stack of money right there in front of his face. All he had to do was reach out and grab it. If only he knew how.

Rocky Big. Rocky would know what to do. Rocky had known whom to call about the Dybek paintings.

But he couldn't go to Rocky empty-handed. Conner needed to get his hands on the card. He had to show Rocky he could deliver the goods.

He started the Plymouth, pointed it toward the *Electric Jenny*.

He'd need to search the sailboat one more time. Conner was certain the card was someplace simple, right under his nose.

Conner drove thirty seconds, stopped, turned around. What he really needed was to talk to Rocky first. No sense getting all involved with this scheme if Rocky knew a dozen reasons it was a bad idea. Maybe Conner wouldn't be able to sell the card even if he found it somehow.

Conner changed his mind yet again, headed for the beach. It had been too long since he'd visited his favorite stool at Salty's Saloon. And what he really needed was a drink.

Conner walked into the empty bar and said, "Sid, I want an Absolut martini straight up."

Sid tore his eyes from the television behind the bar. A baseball game. When he saw Conner, he raised an eyebrow. "You know I can't float you with the expensive stuff. How about a beer?"

Conner slapped a twenty-dollar bill on the bar. "My friend Andrew Jackson is buying."

Sid put his hands together, bowed his head, and mumbled a prayer.

"What are you doing, Sid?"

"You've got cash," Sid said. "That's one of the signs of the apocalypse, ain't it? I want to get right with God."

"It's too late for you. Fix the drink."

"Uh-huh." He threw ice and vodka into a shaker, splashed in some token vermouth. He shook it all up, poured it into a delicate glass with a long stem. Two olives. He shoved it in front of Conner, and said, "What's that crazy outfit you're wearing?"

"Kirk," Conner said. "I'm a captain, so show a little respect."

"Whatever. There was a woman in here looking for you."

Conner's hand froze halfway to the martini. "The hell you say."

"Scout's honor."

"I thought you discouraged women from coming in here."

Conner's hand found the glass, hoisted it to his lips. His mouth made a third of it disappear. His stomach received the gift, turned up the heat. All of his body parts working together in harmony. Togetherness made the world go round.

"Sure I discourage them," Sid said. "This ain't no hoochie pickup bar. It's a guys' bar. Sports on the tube and cheap beer."

"Uh-huh. What did she look like?" Conner worried it was Becker. She didn't seem like the kind of woman who would tolerate being jerked around. Conner didn't want another kick in the teeth.

Sid described the woman. Tyranny.

Conner's heart and stomach did a strange flop-and-flutter thing, the result of curiosity, worry, excitement, and desperate hope all mixed together. He threw down the rest of the martini, told Sid to build him another. "Not so much vermouth this time."

Sid brought the drink. Conner drank.

"Hey, turn up the TV," Conner said.

Sid glanced at the screen. "It's a commercial."

Conner leaned over the bar, grabbed the remote, and turned up the volume. It was a commercial telling people they could own their own business. *Be your own boss.* Internet access terminals about the size of ATM machines. Put them in hotel lobbies and malls. Conner liked the simple idea of making the rounds once a week, picking up the money, letting the machines do all the work. But the more he thought about it, the more he saw the problems. People would vandalize the machines. He'd need insurance. Maintenance. They'd turn out to be more work than a regular job.

Conner thought about Tyranny again. "What did she want?"

"She wanted to see you."

"I know *that*," Conner said. "What about? Did she say?"

"She didn't say. Not exactly. I don't think she's happy with you."

"What makes you say that?"

"You know that wooden cricket bat hanging next to the door?" Sid asked.

"Yeah."

"Well, she just took it off the wall, and she's coming at you fast."

Conner spun on the stool, saw Tyranny's blazing eyes a split second before the bat came down hard, cracked Conner on the forehead with a sharp *thok*. Conner's eyes crossed, his head swam. He fell back in Sam Peckinpah slow motion, scattered three other stools, and landed flat on his back among the cigarette butts. He tried to sit up, but it took a second, bells ringing in his ears.

He blinked the dancing colors from his eyes, climbed to his knees, reached for the bar, and pulled himself up. He looked side to side, thinking maybe another whack was coming.

"She left," Sid said.

Dammit.

Conner found his legs, stumbled for the door. He ran out to Salty's parking lot, jumped in front of Tyranny's BMW. It was a calculated risk. She wouldn't run over him. Probably not.

She screeched the brakes, bumped Conner's leg, but he held his ground.

She rolled down the window, stuck her head out. "Dan has a black eye, you shit."

"I can explain."

"Explain in hell." She revved the engine.

Conner yelped, leapt on the hood. "Tyranny, please! Let's talk."

She sat there a moment glaring at him. He looked back, projected puppy-dog sadness through the windshield. She stuck her head out again, still mad but not hysterical. "Get in."

He slid off the hood, froze a moment watching her. Maybe it was a trick. Maybe she'd plow over him when his guard was down. No, she was cool. He got in the passenger side, and she peeled out of the lot. Conner death-gripped the door handles, fumbled for the seat belt.

She drove fast, pushing her luck with yellow stoplights. They didn't talk.

Conner didn't know how to start, didn't know how they related to each other anymore. He thought, now suddenly in the speeding BMW, the streetlights and restaurant neon smearing the windshield, that she was a foreign thing to him, that there'd always been more to her, dark complex secrets he couldn't know or wouldn't understand if he did. The simple fantasy that they'd love each other and be together and cue the sunset seemed ridiculous now.

She'd been playing chess the entire time he'd been playing checkers.

"You'd better slow down," he said. "Cops."

She slowed down. Glowered and fumed.

"I've spent a long time trying to get my life to make sense," she said at last. "I can't be how you want me to be. Dan lets me be myself, and that might include something ugly or perverted or something you can't understand, but that's how it is. That's how it's going to stay. It's how I stay sane. I never asked you to do anything or change or be anything but what you are. I need the same from you or we'll never see each other again. And, man, I mean fucking *never*, because I can't have Dan come home with a black eye every night. You get me? I don't need this bullshit."

"How did I rate such special attention from Dan?" Conner asked. "Or does he chase down all the other guys you fuck and threaten them too?"

Conner hoped that she'd deny it. If she denied it, he'd believe her. He was desperate to believe in her, to reinvest his faith in the portrait of her he'd painted in his head. And he also realized, had to admit, that what he mostly wanted was for her to hurt, to feel guilt, feel the same pinch in her gut that he felt whenever he thought about her with somebody else.

But she wasn't hurt or shocked. She didn't deny anything. "Do you know why I'm always so reluctant to see you? It's because I do love you. I love you more than the rest, maybe more than I love Dan even."

Conner almost said something, but he was learning. *Shut up, man. Let her talk. Maybe this is going your way.*

"I know you, Conner," she said. "And I know me. You'd never be happy unless you possessed me totally. I just don't have the capacity for what you need. I'd end up making you miserable. I'd make myself miserable. We're doomed as a couple, baby. We don't fit. Dan tried to warn you off because I like you. I've always had deep feelings for you. That's why you're dangerous. The others don't mean anything. They just help me push funny little buttons in my brain. Dan knows you're different."

"Buttons?"

"This is pointless."

Conner said, "Take this." He snatched a scrap of paper from the car's ashtray, an ATM receipt. He scribbled a phone number on the back. "I have a cell phone now. Call me, please. When you're not so pissed. Let's figure this—"

"I'm not going to call you."

Conner couldn't think of a damn thing to say. He folded the scrap of paper, slipped it into the ashtray where she could see it. She'd come to her senses. She'd call. Wouldn't she? He shrank in the passenger seat, feeling small and lost and that maybe the universe was running him over. All Conner Samson could do was sit there in Tyranny's Beemer and get taken for a ride.

30

Tyranny dropped Conner back at his Plymouth, then sped away into the night. Conner stood, watched her taillights shrink to nothing. He wasn't a crier. He'd never been outwardly emotional, but he wished he could just curl into a ball in Salty's parking lot and blubber and blubber, great, snotty wracking sobs until he'd cried himself right out of existence.

He went into Salty's and made himself drunk.

Sid warned him not to drive. The bartender would call him a cab. When Sid turned his back, Conner headed for the parking lot, climbed behind the Plymouth's wheel, and took off. He headed for his secret parking spot along the river, turning onto the dirt access road, the swamp trees a green blur in his headlights, making for the copse of elephant ears where he kept the dinghy hidden.

I'm not too drunk. I'm driving fine.

Then the rapid-fire slap of foliage on his windshield. The bump. His axles slammed the ground as he bottomed out, bounced in his seat, and bashed his head against the roof. The Plymouth dove forward, angled down sharply. The mud-brown splash against the windshield.

Conner sat, took his keys out of the ignition. He looked around. The front of the Plymouth was in the river, the trunk and back wheels still on the bank. He opened the door, and the river spilled in around his ankles. He climbed out, shut the door again. He hiked up the bank, back down the short trail carved by his rogue Plymouth.

He saw what had happened. The road curved, but he hadn't.

He hiked back down to the Plymouth, judged he could open the back door without too much more water getting in. He retrieved the backpack of meager belongings he'd salvaged from his apartment. At the top of the bank, Conner found a clear spot, took inventory. He pulled out the Webley revolver.

Anger surged drunkenly in his veins. He stood abruptly, jerked the trigger at the Plymouth. "Piece of shit!"

Click. Click. Click.

Unloaded. He sighed, sat down again, and loaded the revolver with the metal rings that held the bullets in tight. The next time he was angry he'd want to hear some noise.

He swung the backpack over his shoulder, held the pistol loosely as he walked five minutes to the dinghy. He shoved off, jerked the cord on the putt-putt motor. He headed upriver toward the *Electric Jenny*.

Bad luck still had a few surprises for him. A half mile from the *Jenny*'s hiding place, the putt-putt motor shuddered and conked out. Conner jerked the cord twenty times before realizing he was out of gas. He was almost mad enough to blast the engine to smithereens with the Webley but restrained himself.

He reluctantly took up the oar and paddled, cursed, and kept paddling. He was sweaty and nauseous from the exertion. His bruised ribs still ached in a vague way. All he wanted was to slip into the master cabin and fall long and hard into dreamless sleep.

The narrow inlet came into view, the boat's white stern barely visible in the nearly complete black of night. Conner dipped the oar into the water, stroked long and smooth, drifted toward the *Jenny*, gliding in quietly. And then, just above the stern, he saw it. The floating, bright cherry pinpoint of a glowing cigarette.

Adrenaline pumped, and Conner stood up in the dinghy, not thinking what he was doing. The little boat rocked, threatened to dump him out. Beyond all luck, Conner didn't tip over. He aimed the Webley at the *Jenny*, blazed away without really aiming.

Blam blam blam blam.

Ricochets. The tambourine tinkle of shattered glass, the sound of a porthole dying. The shots were deafening. They still echoed along the river as Conner settled back into the dinghy, paddled furiously for the *Jenny*. He pulled alongside the boat, grabbed the rope ladder, and hoisted himself up, the Webley stuck in his pants. He drew it when his feet hit the deck, swung it full circle looking for the intruder.

Nobody.

He went belowdecks, rushing around, the revolver leading the way. Only after he confirmed nobody was hiding anywhere did he really look around and see what had happened. The interior was trashed. Whoever had been here had been merciless in their search for . . . what?

The DiMaggio card.

Conner wondered if they'd found it. Did they really have to trash his boat? He realized he now thought of it as *his* boat.

He went back out on deck, held his breath, listened. What if it hadn't been a cigarette? Maybe it had only been a firefly. Conner was pretty drunk. Even now, with the rush of danger subsiding, his vision was a bit blurry, the revolver heavy in his hand. Maybe it was just—

A big splash off to the right.

He swung the Webley, squeezed off the last two shots into the black swamp. "Cocksucker!"

He tossed the gun into the cockpit, circled the deck, casting off lines. How many were out there? Did they have a boat? Would they come after him? He leapt into the cockpit, cranked the *Jenny*'s inboard. It chugged to life on the first try. He threw it into reverse, tree limbs screeching on fiberglass as he backed out.

When Conner had the boat in the middle of the channel, he gave it full throttle, headed downriver. He piloted the boat into implacable blackness. He reached for the running lights, but suddenly had the startling thought he was dragging the anchor. Had he pulled it up? His brain was addled. He started forward to check.

The boat shuddered violently. The sound of the world breaking. Conner flew forward. In midair, he realized the boat had collided with something in the dark. He landed, skidded headfirst across the deck. His skull smacked against something. The white noise. The long tunnel into cottony silence.

31

"Mister! Hey, mister." The voice was young, female. "Are you dead? You need some help?"

Conner opened one eye. Early morning, but the sun was already searing and rippling orange on the water.

He lifted his head, which throbbed angry above his left eye, touched the wound, sticky with blood. He lay on the deck at an odd angle. *He* wasn't at an odd angle. It was the deck.

He'd hit a sandbar in the middle of the river. The prow pointed up at an angle, the stern dipping nearly below the waterline. The engine was still running, blades spinning, churning in the water and propelling him nowhere fast.

"Mister?"

He focused on the voice. A teenage girl in a blue bikini. A speedboat. Five teenagers in all, boys and girls on the river for a good time. Blue Bikini Girl kept looking at him, waiting for a sign.

Conner waved. "It's okay. Not dead."

They waved. The dude behind the wheel throttled forward and the speedboat shot down the river like a bullet.

Last night's memories congealed, lined up for inspection as Conner half slid down the deck into the cockpit. He remembered Tyranny and his car in the drink and shooting the Webley at what might have been an intruder. He hadn't been sure. Then he remembered the trashed cabin. Somebody had searched the boat. There had definitely been an intruder. Whoever had been there had probably not found the DiMaggio card, or else why had they stuck around waiting for Conner?

The Japanese? Maybe they wanted to question him the same way they'd questioned Folger. Tied to a chair.

Conner killed the engine. He checked the gas gauge. Only a few gallons of fuel left. He checked his watch and tried to estimate how long the *Jenny* had chugged uselessly against the sandbar, but his head throbbed, his mind cluttered with other worries.

He went below and forward to check the bilge, see if there'd been a hull breach. No leaks. No problems.

The main cabin was a mess, dishes and bottles scattered, items jarred loose on impact. Even the ugly seagull painting had been knocked off the wall. The glass in the frame had shattered. Conner would need to wear shoes until he could sweep up.

He picked up the seagull painting. The wooden frame had cracked too, and it almost came apart in his hands. He sighed, let it drop. *Fucking mess is going to take forever to clean up.*

Again, Conner had fallen into thinking of the *Jenny* as his boat. Somebody had violated his property, invaded *his* space. He kicked the seagull painting where it leaned against the bulkhead. The frame splintered the rest of the way, broke apart. The painting pulled away, folded over, and slid out of the broken frame.

Behind it a stunning blonde with a gleaming smile held her white dress down as the hem blew up around her. Red letters above her head: THE SEVEN YEAR ITCH.

Conner frowned, focused on the film poster. It took him a

minute to understand what he was looking at, the letter and the DiMaggio card encased in hard, transparent plastic.

Through the fog of his disbelief and pounding head, Conner almost thought he saw Marilyn wink at him. *Took you long enough, big boy.*

32

Itchi shivered in the morning light, welcomed the sun, which quickly baked him humid, his wet clothes heavy. Finally, the night was over. He'd been afraid to venture in the dark, the too-near sounds of furtive movement among the shrubs and cypress trees terrifying. He'd heard that Florida swamps teemed with alligators and venomous snakes and the occasional sodomizing redneck.

The thought he should call Toshi on his cell phone and ask for rescue tempted Itchi more than once. But he was much more afraid of Toshi than he was of alligators. Toshi tolerated failure poorly. Itchi had been careless, had let Samson sneak up on him. When Samson started shooting, Itchi's reflexes had taken over. He'd leapt into the water, and when he'd tried to climb back aboard, Samson had opened fire again.

Itchi had bungled, been caught by surprise, had let Samson escape and cowered in the dark swamp wallowing in fear and indecision. No, Toshi wouldn't be pleased. Toshi, it seemed, was nearly always displeased about something. Itchi was supposed to have broken into Derrick James's office and slipped out again without anyone knowing, but had been forced to kill James when the man had walked in suddenly. Toshi had called Itchi a careless oaf.

As a young man Itchi had been told he would be feared and re-spected as a Yakuza. At the moment, he felt only wet and hungry.

He stood, stretched his legs, and looked about. No path, no ob-vious way through the swamp and back to civilization. He made his way down to the river's edge, looked across. If there'd been a house or something, Itchi would swim the river and make his way back to the hotel. He scanned the far bank. Nothing.

The ancient gods, however, were occasionally merciful. That's what Itchi's grandmother had often told him and what he thought now when he saw the little inflatable dinghy hung up on a low branch and bobbing with the current.

He gleefully waded into the river up to his thighs, grabbed the side of the dinghy and heaved himself into it. He pulled the cord several times before ascertaining the little outboard was out of gas. Sometimes the ancient gods were not all they were cracked up to be. He dumped the outboard into the water, grabbed the paddle, and headed downriver.

The river seemed to stretch on forever, at least in comparison to last night's quick journey in the speedboat. He stroked, fell into a rhythm. When he rounded the bend and saw the *Jenny* stranded on a sandbar, his heart leapt. Perhaps all was not lost. He could still board the sailboat, find Samson. Toshi need not know the unfortu-nate details of Itchi's misadventure.

He paddled faster.

The water was high at the *Jenny*'s stern. Itchi tied up and scram-bled easily over the transom. He went through the boat quickly. No sign of Samson. Had he marooned the *Jenny* intentionally for some reason? More likely Samson had fled wildly in the dark and ended up here by accident.

Itchi jumped back in the dinghy, continued downriver. His arms grew sore. Itchi was in excellent physical condition, but paddling used a whole new set of muscles.

Ten minutes later he saw activity on the left bank. It was far ahead, and he could only make out vague shapes. Another minute and three men came into focus. A tow truck. A car with its front end in the river. One of the men seemed to be gesticulating frantically over the fate of the automobile.

Samson.

Itchi recognized him from the photograph.

He redoubled his paddling, headed for the riverbank.

"Watch it!" screamed Conner. "That's a vintage automobile."

The tow truck had backed up too fast, bumped the Plymouth. The driver was a sticklike man with an overbite and springy red hair on his chin. He wore a dirty undershirt and a cap with a Rebel flag patch.

He stuck his head out the window of the tow truck. "I know what I'm doing. Take it easy." He pulled the truck up and backed in again several times before he was satisfied. He got out of the truck, carrying two fistfuls of heavy chains.

Fat Otis stood behind Conner, looked on with amusement. "I don't think the engine will start now."

"Can't they flush it out or something?"

Otis shrugged. "Do I look like a mechanic?"

"I can tow it to the garage," the driver said. "Have one of the boys take a look at it."

Conner agreed and said he'd call about it later.

"Come on," Otis said. "I'll give you a ride. What you got in the garbage bag? Dry clothes?"

"Something I want to show Rocky."

Conner hadn't wanted to fold the poster, so he'd slipped it under the bunk in the main sleeping cabin. The DiMaggio card was already in hard plastic. He'd folded the letter along the creases—careful not to add new ones—and put it in a Ziploc bag. Rocky would know whom to call to fence the thing. Conner wanted to cut Joellen Becker out of the deal if possible. She made him nervous and was one hundred percent totally unlikable.

After sealing the card and the letter into a garbage bag and calling Otis on the cell phone, Conner had discovered the inflatable dinghy was nowhere to be found. It was only after swimming halfway to shore that Conner realized he should have put some dry clothes into the bag also. At least he wasn't wearing the Kirk costume anymore.

"Uh-huh. Well, I got to put a towel down or something," Otis said. "I don't want you dripping on my seats."

They got into the yellow Lincoln, started driving.

A long silence stretched.

"Otis, can I ask you a question about Rocky?"

"You can ask."

"Why do they call him Rocky Big? I mean, he seems more like a Lionel or a Dennis."

Otis half smiled. "Well, you seen him, right? I mean, he ain't exactly anybody that anybody else would be scared of, is he? So he made up that name, helps keep the reputation alive."

"Ah." Conner nodded. But that wasn't really what he'd wanted to know. Conner had been wondering about something ever since the ugly scene with Jeff at Rocky's Forbidden City.

Finally, Conner asked, "Would you have broken my fingers if Rocky said to?"

Otis sighed, considered before answering. "Rocky and I go way back. He helped me when nobody else would, when I had no family, no friends, nothing. He gave me a chance when all my other chances was used up. What else a black man my size gonna do? Be a bouncer in some half-assed nightclub. Rocky thought I was worth more than that. He trusted me. I owe Rocky everything. I'm not sure you know what that means, to owe somebody everything, but take my word for it, it's important. It means something." Otis shrugged; the half smile had drained from his face. "So yeah, I'd have busted you up. I wouldn't have enjoyed it. But I'd do it if Rocky said."

Conner let it hang there. They didn't say anything else for the rest of the ride.

•   •   •

From his shrubby hiding place, Itchi watched Samson and the big black guy leave in the old automobile. He waited a moment, watched the tow truck driver attach the chains to the Plymouth. Itchi looked around, determined he and the driver were alone and isolated.

He stood and walked fast straight for him. The driver looked up at the last minute, mild surprise across his face.

"Hey, what are you doing—"

Itchi chopped open-handed across the man's throat. The driver's eyes bugged. He choked, gasped for air, clutched at his throat. Itchi grabbed the driver's head and chin, jerked sharply. The driver's neck snapped, eyes rolling back in his head.

Itchi caught the limp body, went through the pockets, and found the truck keys before letting it drop. He unchained the Plymouth and planted a solid kick on the bumper.

The axles creaked. The car rolled forward. It slowly slipped back into the river, rolled and rolled until it went under. A single air bubble floated to the top and popped.

Itchi jumped into the tow truck and cranked the engine. He found his way to the road, engine roaring as he poured on the speed. In a few minutes the yellow Lincoln was in sight.

Itchi took out his cell phone and dialed Toshi. "Boss? Yeah, it's me. I'm on Samson's tail right now. No problems at all. It's all going like clockwork."

33

Otis dropped Conner off at Playerz.

"You're not coming in?" Conner asked.

"Shit," Otis said. "My ride smells like swamp water. I'm heading to the car wash." He drove away.

They knew Conner at Playerz by now and waved him through. Conner passed Pete on the forklift. He was reading a *Mad* magazine, the wicked little submachine gun still in his lap. Pete barely glanced at Conner, nodded him on back to Rocky's office. The word seemed to have gone out: Conner Samson was okay.

Conner knocked once, went inside. "Rocky, I got a proposition for you."

"You're all wet," Rocky said.

"Yeah. Long story."

Rocky picked up his phone, pushed a button. "Julie, can we get a couple of towels in here? Thanks, dear."

Conner opened the garbage bag, took out the DiMaggio card

and the letter from Marilyn Monroe, set them on Rocky's desk like he was presenting him with the Holy Grail and an Academy Award.

Rocky donned a pair of half glasses, squinted at the letter, then the card. The glasses added twenty years to his face. "Now, this is interesting?" Rocky turned the card over in his hands. "What is it?"

"A baseball card and a letter from Marilyn Monroe."

"Is that something good?"

Conner explained. He told Rocky about the autographs, the insured value, the possibility of a collector out there willing to pay big money. It felt like a sales pitch, and that was okay to Conner. Conner Samson possessed this thing that so many other people were looking for. It felt good to be lead dog for a change.

Rocky picked up the phone, asked the person on the other end to get him his "associate in Chicago."

Rocky put his hand over the phone, handed Conner a folded piece of paper. "We just ripped off a shipment from the Gap. Go find some dry clothes." Rocky turned his attention back to the phone. "Sal? Yes, good to speak with you too. Listen, I have a specialty item, some baseball memorabilia and a Hollywood thing. Is that one phone call or two?"

Conner left the office, closed the door behind him. He breathed a sigh of relief, didn't realize until now how tense he'd been. Rocky would know what to do, whom to call. Conner felt strangely comfortable leaving it all in the hands of the odd crime boss.

He ran into Julie on the way down the hall. She was thin and pale, pencils stuck in her wad of dishwater hair. She handed Conner two clean towels. He thanked her, and she went back to work.

The map led Conner through the warehouse maze, like a Super Wal-Mart, a mall, and a flea market all rolled into one. Except everything was hot. Otis had told him people had the wrong idea about criminal supergeniuses. People thought they were like James Bond villains, lasers from outer space and nuclear bomb extortion. Nope. The real criminal masterminds were born administrators, super-bureaucrats. Rocky Big had to handle state and local officials, cook the books, duck the tax man, hide cash flow, organize travel schedules, trucks coming and going at all hours of the day and night. It was a logistical, pencil-pushing nightmare and Rocky Big was the best. The ebb and flow of stolen goods in and out of Rocky's warehouse was a magnificent, criminal ballet.

Conner lingered longingly over a collection of plasma flat-screen televisions. Hook one of those babies up to a surround-sound system. Maybe if things worked out . . . Conner shook himself loose from the fantasy, found the boxes of Gap clothing. He dug around until he found his size, a pair of khaki pants and a forest-green V-neck T-shirt. Conner was wet, smelled brackish. He didn't want to put the clean clothes on his dirty body. He walked back to Rocky's office.

Pete had evolved to a copy of *Sports Illustrated*.

"Rocky still on the phone?" Conner asked.

"Yup."

"Anyplace a guy can clean up around here?"

Pete told him there was an employee locker room on the second floor. Conner found a spiral staircase, climbed it, passed a Coke machine, and found the men's locker room. Half the urinals had been ripped off the wall. The tile was an industrial green. He tried three shower stalls, found one that dribbled water that was almost warm. He rinsed off. No soap.

Even in summer there was just something about dripping naked on bare tile that made Conner shiver. He flashed on his baseball days in the locker room. Morons snapping towels. Idiots. He sort of missed it.

Rocky walked in. "I didn't even realize the plumbing still worked up here."

Conner quickly wrapped a towel around himself. "I needed to clean up." For some reason, Conner wasn't crazy about Rocky being too close to his naked body.

"You've done quite well!" Rocky said.

Conner raised an eyebrow, started edging toward his new Gap outfit draped over a stall door.

"There's a million-dollar offer for the DiMaggio card," Rocky said.

Conner's mouth fell open. "What? But that's—it's only worth—" *Any collectible is really only worth what somebody is willing to pay for it.*

"Some tycoon has a collection. Looks like you're gonna be in the chips, as they say."

Conner forgot all about being naked. He was stunned.

"It's a lot of money." Rocky looked serious. "Try not to piss it away."

34

Itchi sat in the tow truck outside of Playerz, watched for twenty minutes to make sure Samson wasn't going anywhere, then called Toshi to report. Toshi ordered him back to their new headquarters, a suite at the Intercontinental just six blocks away.

Itchi drove there in three minutes. He abandoned the tow truck on the street, left the keys in the ignition. The doorman frowned at Itchi's disheveled appearance but wisely said nothing. The elevator took Itchi to the top floor.

When he walked into the suite, he opened his mouth to tell Toshi everything was under control. What he saw made his eyes pop. He shut his mouth again, swallowed hard.

Ahira Kurisaka sat in an overstuffed chair like it was a throne, a dozen hard-faced men around him. Kurisaka looked distinctly cross. Kurisaka's presence could only mean the big man was displeased or impatient or both. That he'd come half a world to see why he did not yet have his baseball card did not bode well for Itchi. Itchi sent a brief prayer skyward, prepared himself to be squashed.

Toshi cleared his throat. If he was as nervous as Itchi, it didn't show on his face. Another awkward second of silence slipped past before Itchi realized they expected him to say something.

"Conner Samson is at a local strip club called Playerz. He's still there as far as I know." They knew this already, Itchi thought, but he couldn't just stand there and not say anything.

Ahira Kurisaka said, "And the DiMaggio card. Did he have it with him?"

Itchi had no idea, but *I don't know* weren't words you said to Ahira Kurisaka. Itchi remembered the plastic bag Samson had carried. It was possible the card was in the bag. Itchi could almost convince himself the card had to be in the bag. Sure. Why else would Samson clutch it so tightly? In any event, it would please Kurisaka to tell him so.

"I believe so," Itchi said.

"Then why did you not take it from him?" Kurisaka asked.

That was one hell of a good question, thought Itchi. He decided to take a kernel of truth and dress it up with a few strategic lies. The big black man with Samson had appeared formidable. He was big enough to be two men. Or even several men.

"Samson had his gang with him," Itchi said. "I thought it best to follow and report back."

"You did well," Kurisaka said.

Whew.

Toshi snapped his cell phone shut. "I just spoke to our people. They ran down the information on the strip club. It's a front for the local syndicate." Toshi laid it out, Rocky Big, the warehouse, everything.

Kurisaka nodded, stared ahead at an invisible point in the distance, deep in thought.

Toshi leaned forward, spoke quietly into Kurisaka's ear, but it was just loud enough for Itchi to hear. "In our blood we are Yakuza, are we not, Cousin? And Yakuza take what they want."

Itchi watched Kurisaka's face harden. The giant billionaire steepled his fat hands under his nose, narrowed his dark eyes. He stood slowly, like a massive planet dislodged from its orbit. Kurisaka lifted his hand, stretched it out, some lunatic god pronouncing judgment.

Itchi tensed, braced himself for the edict.

"Gentlemen," Kurisaka said, "we go to war."

PART FOUR

n which Conner Samson
is Bruce Willis.

35

Conner had dried and changed into his Gap clothes. He felt clean and human again.

Rocky drove them back to the office in the golf cart and explained how fencing the DiMaggio card would go. Rocky was half-apologetic. The deal had to go through a few layers of handlers and finders. Everyone wanted his or her cut, including Rocky himself. When all was said and done, Conner might clear $350,000. Give or take a few thousand.

"At least it's all tax-free," Rocky said.

"Yeah." Conner felt light-headed. It was more money than he'd expected to see his whole life.

And then Conner's elation shifted to dread. At first, he couldn't understand the sudden anxious knot in his stomach. Why shouldn't he be glad? But he wasn't glad; he was afraid. And it was a familiar fear, something that had gnawed him more than once, and in a moment of jarring clarity, he understood. He'd always used his bad luck as an excuse. If he lost a bet, it was just bad luck that the team's star player was on the injury list. If Conner botched a repo job, it was just plain old bad luck the car had run out of gas. If Conner lost his baseball scholarship, it was just more bad luck that he hadn't kept his grades up, didn't happen to study the right chapter an hour before his final exams, happened to get into a class where the professor took an irrational dislike to him. And if the Bay Bears didn't want him, or he was always broke, or Tyranny didn't love him, it was all because of bad luck, bad breaks, the dice just never came up in his favor.

But luck had nothing to do with it. He knew that now, had really always known it deep down. Conner had made his own messes, and it had been easier to pretend it was bad luck than to take responsibility for himself. Things had been so easy for so long. High school had been no problem. He'd lucked into a college scholarship. He was a popular athlete and women wanted him, and he'd been invited to parties and life seemed a thing that had been invented for Conner Samson's amusement. At some point, things had stopped being handed to him. Life became hard. And instead of facing up to the challenge, Conner had pouted like a spoiled kid and invented the myth of bad luck.

Conner had convinced himself that Tyranny could not leave Professor Dan and his money. Could Conner blame her? She'd become accustomed to a comfortable lifestyle. What if Conner had money? What if he could keep her as secure and as comfortable and as happy as Professor Dan could? Conner had clung to that excuse, the belief that only Dan's money made Tyranny choose him over Conner. Now that Conner had money, what if she still preferred Professor Dan? If Tyranny rejected Conner now, it was because Conner wasn't good enough. And that was the fear. The possibility that if he peeled away all the excuses, Conner Samson simply wasn't good enough, not worthy of love, no good to anyone for anything. Useless.

At the Dybek reception, Conner had drunkenly resolved to make himself new. Not to be a bottom-feeder anymore. But he had no idea how to be anything other than what he was.

"You look like somebody crapped in your breakfast cereal," Rocky said.

"It's been a long day."

"This'll cheer you up." Rocky pulled a cedar box out of a bottom desk drawer, slid it across to Conner, and opened the lid. Cigars. "Otis asked me to save a box for you."

Conner lifted an eyebrow, grabbed one, sniffed it. "Nice. What kind?"

"Hell if I know," Rocky said. "You've seen the place. We have all kinds of stuff around here. I thought maybe you'd know since you enjoyed—" Rocky jerked his head up, cocked an ear toward the door. "Did you hear that?"

"Hear what?" Conner lit the cigar with a lighter shaped like a cowboy boot. He puffed, inhaled deeply, and held it a second before tilting his head back and blowing smoke at the ceiling. It surprised him that something as simple as a good smoke could brighten his mood, albeit only slightly. "Not bad. Maybe they're Cuban or—"

"Be quiet, please." Rocky jerked open another desk drawer. His hand dipped in and came out again with a nickel-plated .45 automatic. His hands shook. "God, I hate this thing." He fumbled in the magazine, cocked the pistol. Rocky didn't look at Conner. He stared at the door, still listening. "Are you sure you didn't hear—"

Conner sat up. Worried now. "What is it?"

"I just thought . . . Maybe I'm imagining things."

And then Conner heard it too. The distant *pop pop pop* faint and muffled. A short pause. Conner almost spoke again, but Rocky waved him quiet. Immediately another rapid-fire series of pops. Rocky reached for the phone, but it rang first.

He answered. "What's going on? What? Damn! Yes, do it. Do it now!" Rocky slammed the phone down. "Jesus!" He opened his desk drawer again, came out with another, smaller automatic, slid it across the desk to Conner. "Take this, Conner."

Conner looked at the gun without picking it up. "What?"

Pops again. Gunfire.

"Somebody's here. I don't understand. Nothing like this has

ever— Christ, they're getting closer," Rocky said. "Pick up that pistol. Check the clip."

"Who's getting closer?"

"I said check your fucking weapon," Rocky yelled. "I don't know who they are. They just busted in and started shooting up the place. We got five dead men out there and—"

The phone rang. Rocky grabbed it. "Talk."

Conner saw Rocky go pale.

"Well, stop them. What do I pay you for?" Rocky slammed the phone down again. "They're through the strip club."

Conner detected a tremor in Rocky's voice, and that scared Conner more than anything else. He grabbed the pistol. Checked the load. His palms were sweaty on the grips. "What is this?" He meant the gun.

"A .380. Point and squeeze."

Gunshots exploded alarmingly close. Conner's mouth went dry. The phone rang again.

Rocky grabbed it. "What the hell's going on out there? Jesus, it sounds like they're right on top of us." Another flurry of shots. "In the warehouse? Get them out of there. Get everyone." His voice rose as he spoke, squeaky and panicked. "Don't let them get back here. You understand what— Hello? Hello?"

He threw the phone down. "Goddammit!"

Conner stood, headed for the office door. "I think it's time to go, Rocky."

"Don't go out there!"

"I'm getting out of here."

"I'm telling you my men will handle it." Rocky didn't sound like he believed it. "Stay put. Don't go to pieces."

Screams on the other side of the door. Back-and-forth shouting. More gunshots. Conner jumped back from the door. If he'd ever had a chance to run for it, it was too late now. If the racket was any indication, all hell was breaking loose just outside of Rocky's office. The jagged rattle of a submachine gun.

Conner felt the urge to pee.

Rocky stuck his pistol in his waistband, grabbed the edge of his desk. "Grab the other end. Help me move it against the door."

Conner grabbed the other side of the desk and froze. The world on the other side of Rocky's office door had suddenly gone quiet. They looked at the door, at each other, back at the door again.

Rocky picked up the phone, listened, put it down again. "Dead."

Footsteps. Coming toward the office.

Rocky pulled the automatic from his waistband, swallowed hard. "I wish Otis were here," he whispered.

Conner thumbed off the safety, lifted his pistol toward the door. His knees were water, his spine cold jelly. The doorknob rattled and Conner felt his sphincter twitch. "Shoot through the door!"

"Can't." Rocky crouched behind his desk. "I had it made special. Bulletproof."

The door swung open, and Conner nearly started jerking the trigger, but Rocky told him to hold fire. Pete stumbled into the room, slammed the door shut again behind him. He held the sub-machine gun, the barrel hot and smoking.

Pete tilted on his feet. He didn't look good. "I think . . . I think maybe . . ." He teetered sideways, hit the wall and slid into a sitting position. He dropped the machine gun, both hands going to his gut, the bloodstain widening, making his shirt stick to his belly. "Oh . . . no."

Rocky ran to him. "Hang on, Pete. Oh, Christ. Conner, lock the door."

Conner bolted for the lock, hand outstretched. Whoever was on the other side of the door, Conner wanted them to stay there. A little bit of his brain realized he was locking himself in as well as the attackers out. Trapped. He'd have to worry about that later.

His fingers had just touched the knob when the door flew open. The heavy door smashed Conner's head. Bells went off in his ears. He reeled, fell back, legs rubbery. Next thing he knew, he was on the floor.

Gunshots.

He opened his eyes, blinked away the colored lights. He glimpsed

Rocky for a split second, firing his automatic. Bodies fell. Then bullets tore into Rocky. His body twitched, red blossoms across his chest. He hunched over, fell to the floor. His face turned to Conner, eyes rolled back, blood on his lips.

Conner tried to make his arms and legs work. The buzzing in his ears. He fought to keep his eyes open. The men swarmed the room, stepped over Conner and Pete and Rocky.

Japanese men.

One took the DiMaggio card from Rocky's desk. He showed the others. They smiled, nodded, talked gibberish. Conner tried to reach for the pistol Rocky had given him, tried to lift his head. He felt so heavy.

One of the Japanese saw him struggling. He was lean, wicked, mouth curling in contempt. Sideburns. He said something to his pals, and they all laughed.

He pointed his pistol at Conner's head. Conner tensed.

Click.

The Japanese guy shrugged at his gun, ejected the empty clip, shook his head as he looked down at Conner with waning interest. The heel of his shoe came down hard on Conner's temple.

Darkness.

36

In the dream, Conner moved like molasses.

He hovered near third base waiting for the pitch. At which time he'd take off running for home in the hopes the batter laid down a good bunt. Conner had to start running before he knew if the bunt was down. That was the tough part. It required guts. Faith.

The pitch. And Conner ran. His feet caught in the mud. He strained to put one foot in front of the other. Tyranny was at home plate waving him in. When Conner looked again, she was waving him off. He tried to run, barely able to move, not able to tell if he was welcomed at home or not.

He fell, facefirst in the mud. He tried to see, to blink the mud out of his eyes. Where was the ball? Had the bunt been laid down? He tried to get up, couldn't make his body obey.

The weight of eternity held him facedown in the mud, and from a long way away, a voice called, Conner's name echoing down a dark tunnel.

•   •   •

"Conner!" Big hands shaking him awake. "Conner-man, get your ass up. Come on! We've got to get out of here."

Conner's eyes popped open, tried to focus. He saw Otis shove aside Rocky's desk like it was made of foam rubber. Otis knelt at a cabinet behind the desk, opened the bottom drawer, and withdrew a big leather doctor's bag.

Conner faded briefly, eyes crossing. He felt his body being lifted, arms and legs dangling. His head cleared. How many times had he been knocked cold in the last few days? He looked around. He was being carried. Fat Otis toted him under a huge arm. Bleeding bodies lay around the office. Rocky looked so small.

A wave of dread and grief washed over Conner. He forced it down into his gut, cut himself off from it. "Put me down."

"We don't have time for you to pull yourself together," Otis said.

"I can walk."

Otis put him down. Conner wobbled on his feet a moment, steadied himself. He remembered the Japanese guy holding the DiMaggio card and darted for Rocky's desk.

Otis yelled, "Dammit, come on!"

"One second." Conner rifled the papers on Rocky's desk until he found what he was looking for. The Japanese had taken the card but left the Monroe letter in the plastic bag. Conner snatched it just as Otis grabbed his arm and pulled him out of the office. Conner stuffed the letter in his pocket.

The warehouse was a mess. More bodies. A few Japanese but mostly Rocky's guys. The strip club was worse. The bar was on fire. They coughed their way through and out the open door into the street. They passed a group of determined firemen going the other way. The street flickered in the red lights of the emergency vehicles. More sirens in the distance.

Now Conner understood Otis's hurry. The place crawled with cops (there were already one squad car and a brace of uniforms directing traffic away from the fire), and neither Conner nor Otis was inclined to stick around and answer awkward questions. There was still plenty of confusion, but soon they'd get organized.

Otis had parked his Lincoln just beyond the fire trucks. They drove in a random direction. Conner slumped in the passenger seat, every one of his nerves frazzled. Pensacola suddenly looked like a town he'd never seen before, full of strangers and enemies. Nothing was understandable, Playerz and Rocky swept away in a blazing storm. On a whim. For a baseball card. Conner's life had revealed itself as a surreal, cosmic joke. Somewhere, the gods held their sides laughing. Look at the silly mortals.

Conner figured he must have only been out of it a few minutes. It had seemed like days. "What happened?"

"Shit," Otis spit. "I was hoping you could tell me." Otis relayed his side of it. After the car wash, Otis had run some errands, taken care of Rocky's business. When he returned, he'd found Playerz a smoldering, bloody wreck. He'd run back to find Rocky, only to find his boss shot full of lead. Conner had survived by dumb luck.

Conner felt anger radiating off Otis. He'd been loyal to Rocky. Every muscle in the big man's body was a coiled spring. Jaw set. The vein in his neck throbbing time like a bass drum.

"Tell me what you know about this," Otis said. "So I know who to kill."

Conner spilled the story. It didn't occur to him for a second to hold anything back. The *Electric Jenny*, the Japanese, the DiMaggio card. The whole shooting match. Otis asked the obvious questions. Conner answered. Otis said he didn't think Rocky had pissed off any Japanese dudes, not that he knew of.

"I don't think it's a vendetta," Conner said. "It's the baseball card. They killed another guy for it too." He told Otis about Folger and the bungalow.

"This is fucking bullshit." Otis slammed the palm of his hand against the steering wheel. "Nobody kills a bunch of people and burns down a fucking strip club for no fucking baseball card."

Any collectible is only worth what somebody is willing to pay, thought

Conner. But the price wasn't just money now. It included blood. "Those Asian guys must know there's a reward for it."

Otis's eyes flamed wild with rage. "We got to find these mother-fuckers and do something."

Conner didn't say anything.

"No, no, no, no." Otis shook his head. "Don't you shut down on me. I'm not in the mood for your Conner Samson sit-on-the-side-lines bullshit. You're in this right up to your ass."

"What are you talking about?"

"Your damn attitude. Like you ain't involved. You know what your problem is?"

"Jesus." America's new pastime. Tell Conner Samson his problem.

"You ain't a team player."

"Fuck you."

"It's true. That's why you got kicked off the college baseball team."

"I didn't get kicked off the team," Conner said. "I flunked out."

Otis went on like he didn't hear. "Rocky was my team. And somebody just fucked with my team big-time. And if you think I'm going to sit around with my thumb up my ass, then you're screwed in the head. Now you better tell me on whom I can vent my mighty wrath. Otherwise, the only motherfucker around here to vent on is *you*."

"I have one idea," Conner said. "Somebody who might know something."

"Then call them," Otis said. "What you waiting on? Dial the fucking phone."

37

She couldn't escape the hangover.

She tried lying on the couch, then sitting up, lying in bed. She sprawled on the floor, tried standing in the shower under cold water. She dried off, returned to the couch. Nothing helped. Joellen Becker's head thundered, her stomach queasy. There was no way she could arrange herself that would abate the misery.

Her life hovering in front of her like a rapidly deflating balloon didn't help matters. She refused to return to her dismal desk at the insurance agency. The thought of it made her stomach heave. She'd need to track down some of the old contacts, start looking for a gig. If she stayed in the States, there wouldn't be much, corporate stuff or insurance work again. Better prospects out of the country. She'd had an offer from an old NSA chum in El Salvador, but it could be tough for women down there. Worse in the Middle East.

What would her daddy general think if he could see Joellen Becker now?

The phone rang, like sonic beams shot through her ears to melt her brain. She didn't want to answer. Why bother? But she squirmed off the couch, held her head, picked up the phone before the machine clicked on. "Yeah?"

"This is Conner Samson."

She thought about that a second. "So what?"

"I'm at the Waffle House across from the mall," Samson said. "Why don't you come down here and explain why a gang of killer Japs are so crazy to get their hands on this Joe DiMaggio card."

"Do you have the card with you?"

Samson said, "Be here in half an hour." He hung up.

Did Samson know? If so, how much? For some reason he still needed her. So he didn't have the whole story. He had the pieces of the puzzle but couldn't make them fit together. Conner Samson still needed Joellen Becker.

She made it to the Waffle House in twenty-two minutes.

Becker sat next to Samson in the plastic booth. The black bald behemoth took up almost the entire seat on the other side. When she'd arrived, she'd been shocked to see how bruised and battered Samson looked. He'd been through the wringer.

She sat back, let him tell his story. She knew a few Zen techniques that were supposed to help suppress her headache, but they never worked. She tried them anyway. Then she lit a cigarette.

Conner told her about the Japanese goon squad, how they busted in, shot up the local syndicate, and made off with DiMaggio.

Becker blew a long stream of smoke. "Wait a minute."

Samson froze in midsentence.

Becker asked, "Do you mean to tell me you don't have the card?"

"That's right," Samson said.

"The Japs have it."

"Exactly."

She shook her head. "Thanks for wasting my fucking time, guys. At least the coffee was fresh." She started to slide out of the booth.

"Whoa, hold on. Hear me out." Samson grabbed her forearm.

She looked down at her arm. "You want to lose that hand, sport?"

He let go, held up his hands, palms out. Placating. "No offense. Just give me five minutes."

"You've got until I get to the bottom of this coffee cup," she said. "Talk."

"Okay, well, I'm not exactly sure, okay? But you've got a buyer on the line for a million bucks, right?"

She didn't say anything.

"I know all about it, okay? Well, not *all* about it. I don't know who the buyer is but he's willing to pay a cool million. I figure these Japanese got wind of the reward and now they're trying to collect."

Conner didn't know. The Japanese *were* the buyers. She let that sink in, mulled it, and said, "So what are you going to do, sport? Storm the castle? Take the card back from the Japs? Doesn't look like you did too well against them last time."

Even with the hangover, Joellen marveled at her ability to think through several things simultaneously. The old training never went away. On the surface, she took in Conner's story, sifted what he knew, what he didn't know, and what he *thought* he knew. Another part of her brain gauged how to use this information to her advantage.

"Look, you've been a step ahead of me the whole time," Samson said. "Every time I turn around, you're there. I figure I bring you the information, you know what to do with it. We were talking about a finder's fee before, and I thought maybe—"

She shook her head. "All deals are off."

"Oh, come on, you can't—"

She turned to the big black guy. "What's with Chatty Cathy here?"

"Oh, yeah," Samson said. "This is Otis. I was getting to him. He sort of has a side interest in all this."

Otis leaned forward. "I implied I'd stomp his little ass if he didn't help me find out who fucked up Playerz. I've sort of got a revenge thing going."

"Uh-huh." Becker mashed out her cigarette, lit another. Her wheels were turning.

"If you know the identity of these Asian dudes, I'd appreciate your help," Otis said. "Just point me in the right direction and stand back."

"And why should I help you?" Becker asked. "And please keep in mind I don't stomp as easy as Samson. Take my word for it."

Otis plopped the leather doctor's bag on the table, opened it, and fished out two wads of cash, hundred-dollar bills. "That's ten big. Like I said, show me where to unleash, then step away from ground zero."

Perfect. With these two suckers on board, her plan might just work. Yes, she was starting to like the odds. There were still details to work out, but . . .

In the meantime, she couldn't seem too eager. Becker pushed the money back at Otis. "Look, I don't think—"

Otis went back into the bag, threw two more wads of money on the pile.

She cast about the restaurant. People were looking. "Put it away, you idiot."

Samson cleared his throat. He wanted back in the conversation. "I'm just saying, you can probably track these guys down. A big Japanese mob can't be that easy to hide in a town this size. You can find them and get the card back."

"How do I do that, Samson? Call in an air strike?"

"I don't care about no fucking card." Otis raised his voice. "Just find out where they're at, then tell me. You can at least do that."

The waitress stopped by their table. "A little loud here." She topped off their coffees and left.

Becker lowered her voice. "Okay, I *might* have a few ideas. But not here. Let's discuss it back at my place." She looked at Otis. "Bring your bag of money."

•　•　•

Back at her apartment.

She showed them in, told them to have a seat, went into the kitchen.

She swallowed two Advil and made herself drink three full glasses of water. Put on a pot of coffee. It had been a long time since she'd had so much to drink. The headache was bad, and she suspected she'd feel worse before she felt better. There were some drugs she could take to ease the effects, but there'd be a price to pay later. She'd known some of her fellow agents to become dependent on such drugs, and it could get ugly.

She grabbed a clean dishrag, soaked it in cold water under the faucet, and dabbed her eyes, behind her ears. The headache grew worse by the minute, but she put on her game face, took the .25 caliber Beretta out of the kitchen junk drawer. It was so small and light, she could jam it into her waistband near her navel, produce it quickly.

Only a precaution. Samson was harmless, but there was an angry fire in the big man's eyes. Better safe than sorry.

Her head: *thump thump thump*.

Becker remembered the first time she'd met Samson, the state he'd been in, hungover to his yellow eyeballs, his apartment reeking of sick. She remembered thinking that might be a typical morning for Samson. How did people do it, live like this, boozing as a lifestyle? *Never again.*

Never mind. A lapse. Becker was more in control of her life. Or she was trying to be.

Even as she did all this—the Advil, the water, the .25 caliber pistol, contemplating Samson's self-destructive lifestyle—the part of her brain that was always working sorted the final details of her scheme. She had a good shot at the bounty on Kurisaka's head, and the two chumps sitting in her living room would provide the perfect diversion.

It didn't mean anything to Becker if Conner Samson and his giant pal got themselves shot full of holes.

38

Ahira Kurisaka sat alone in his hotel suite. He gazed lovingly at the baseball card on the desk in front of him. It was his. He alone possessed it, this one-of-a-kind thing. *One-of-a-kind.* Kurisaka paused to consider what that meant. No amount of money, no level of power, nothing could re-create this thing. There was a certain magic in that.

And Hito Hyatta would be positively green with envy.

Kurisaka was sorely tempted to take the card out of the protective plastic casing. He wanted to feel the naked cardboard in his hands, sniff it to see if he could detect traces of the bubble gum. He could not wait to take the card back to Tokyo, so he could casually place it on the table during one of his lunches with Hyatta. He looked at his wristwatch, did the math. Perhaps a phone call . . .

He couldn't wait. He was nearly giddy, reached for the phone, and dialed Hito Hyatta's number. Kurisaka's eager smile was so wide, it hurt his face.

He had to get past a secretary and another assistant before Hyatta answered the phone. "Hello? Is that you, Ahira?"

"Good to speak with you, Hito. I hope I'm not catching you at a bad time."

"I always make time for you, Ahira."

"I just had to call and share news of my latest acquisition." Kurisaka relished the anticipation, this moment, the second before telling Hyatta about the DiMaggio card. Hyatta's brain would be spinning, wondering what amazing thing Kurisaka now had in his possession. Kurisaka let the moment stretch another second, then said, "You might recall we were both looking to add baseball cards to our collection."

"Oh, yes. You have been successful?"

"Completely," Kurisaka said. "I'm actually calling from Pensacola, Florida, in the United States. I have this wonderful Joe DiMaggio card. It's autographed by the player, naturally, but it's also been signed by—"

"Marilyn Monroe and Billy Wilder," Hyatta said. "Yes, I'm aware of that one. A cute card. My agents made me aware that one was available sometime ago, but it just wasn't my style. All that Hollywood and sports stuff mixed together. More of a fun novelty than a serious collectible, I thought."

"Oh. I see." A lead weight landed in the pit of Kurisaka's belly. "When you said you were interested in a Florida card . . . I thought maybe . . ."

"You thought perhaps we'd be competing for the same card." Hyatta chuckled. "Then we would have to fight it out, eh? Maybe have a good old-fashioned bidding war. Not to worry, the card I was interested in was in Orlando. Someone turned up a nearly mint-condition 1911 Honus Wagner."

"Ah." Kurisaka felt sick.

"The owner asked an even million in American dollars," Hyatta said. "But I took great pleasure in grinding him down to seven hundred thousand. A bargain, really."

"I see." So painful. Why wouldn't Hyatta stop talking?

"To me," Hyatta continued, "the Wagner card is more purely a baseball collectible. And I've always considered myself a purist."

"Uh-huh." *Insufferable ass.*

"But for you, well, I think the DiMaggio card is more in keeping with the tone of your collection. Your collection has always been—what's the word I'm looking for—*whimsical.* Yes, that's it. A sort of fun, whimsical collection."

There wasn't a trace of irony in Hyatta's voice. He honestly didn't realize that his every word was a dagger in Kurisaka's heart.

Hyatta said, "There's actually a very interesting story about Honus Wagner. Apparently he—"

"I'm sorry, Hito, but I have a call on the other line. Congratulations on the Honus Wagner. Good-bye." He hung up.

Kurisaka looked at the DiMaggio card, but every drop of his enthusiasm had evaporated. He picked it up, examined it one last time, sighed, placed it in the custom-made attaché case. He wasn't sure, but he thought it possible he might cry.

A knock at the door.

"Come in."

Toshi entered, offered his cousin a nod of respect. "I'm afraid we won't be able to move up our departure. The airport is behind schedule and unable to service the craft until midmorning."

"It doesn't matter." Kurisaka stood, his shoulders slumped. "I'm going to bed."

"Is something the matter, Cousin?"

"It's nothing. I'm tired. Just very tired." He went into his bedroom, closed the door behind him.

Toshi wondered at his cousin's sudden mood shift but finally shrugged and left the suite.

39

It took Joellen Becker three phone calls and forty-two minutes on
her laptop to find the information she wanted. Becker still had good
contacts, local law enforcement, federal. It had been easy to find
out how many Japanese passports had recently come through US
Customs in Pensacola. She found out Kurisaka was on the top floor
of the Intercontinental, that he had more than a dozen men with
him, and that his private jet was scheduled to leave for Tokyo.

Kurisaka. The man himself. Becker's intuition had served her
well. She thought the billionaire might be in America, all of those
Japanese hired guns Samson had mentioned. It wasn't just Kurisaka's
errand boy Moto anymore. She had hoped to obtain the DiMaggio
card so she could use it to lure the billionaire to America. Becker
didn't have the card, but here was Kurisaka right in her own backyard. Kurisaka had a small army with him, but he wasn't home in his
big Tokyo fortress. This might be as vulnerable as he'd ever get.

A few taps at the computer, and she'd accessed the airport's maintenance roster. She'd moved Kurisaka's jet to the bottom of the list. That should hold him up until morning.

If she'd still been with the NSA, she could have had Kurisaka's phone bugged within ten minutes. Now it might take a full day, and there just wasn't time.

"Well?" Otis. The big man had stood behind her the whole time. Too eager. His brooding anger made Becker slightly nervous. There was rage in him ready to be tapped, bubbling just under the surface.

She spun her chair around, faced Otis. Samson had spread himself on the sofa. "I think I know a way," she said. "I think we can get the card back, but we'll need to act fast." She explained what she'd done to delay Kurisaka's departure.

"I told you I don't care about no baseball card." Otis shook his doctor's bag. "I said I'd pay you."

"I know." She held up a hand. "You want payback. I think it's a waste of time, but that's none of my business. But hear me out. You don't have enough cash in that bag, not compared to the reward for the card. I think my plan will satisfy your needs. Both our needs." She explained briefly what she had in mind.

Otis nodded. "That'll work." His jaw was set. He looked determined.

She stubbed out her cigarette, lifted her chin at Samson. "Got an opinion on this, sport?"

Samson laughed. It sounded forced. "My opinion is that I don't want anything to do with this."

"Hey, you called me, remember?"

Samson stabbed a finger at Otis. "*He* insisted. And I thought I could salvage a finder's fee out of all this."

"I'm surprised at you," Becker said. "To endure everything you've been through, then to be so willing to come up empty-handed. I thought even you had more backbone than that."

"Look, what do you want from me? I had the damn card in my hands, and I lost it. I blew my chance, okay?"

"You make your own chances in this business, Samson," Becker said. "Or is a little bad luck all it takes to bust your balls?"

"A little bad—what did you say?"

"Nothing worth a damn comes easy," she said.

Samson opened his mouth. He was ready to spit something sarcastic. But he closed his mouth again, shook his head. He flopped back down on the sofa, crossed his arms, and wouldn't look at her or Otis.

Becker knew what he must be thinking. She could read him like a book. All Samson wanted to do was keep living his little life. But there was part of him that wanted to achieve something, and it was at war with the other part that kept saying not to stick his neck out. She studied him sitting there on the couch but couldn't tell if he was pouting or brooding or deep in thought.

She opened her desk drawer, looking for another pack of cigarettes.

Instead, she saw her father's six-shooters. She stared at them for long seconds. *Goals are nothing. That you pursue them is everything.* She'd risked her life before, many times in her special ops days. Could she honestly say that the reasons she'd risked her life those times were any better or worse than now?

Becker decided to let Conner stew a minute. She got up from her desk, went into her bedroom, motioned Otis should follow. She opened a closet. "Help me with these." They pulled out three metal trunks, heavy, locked tight with thick combination locks. They dragged the trunks into the living room. Becker spun the locks, threw back the lids.

Two contained various weaponry, ammunition. The third held Kevlar vests and electronic equipment. Becker had never had the opportunity to use any of this equipment, all items she thought of as severance pay when the Feds forced her resignation. *Our tax dollars at work.*

"Shit," Otis said. "Your Sharper Image catalog has better stuff than mine."

Conner Samson stood, sighed dramatically, his jaw set, eyes alert and determined. He looked down at the assorted equipment and weaponry. "Okay, tell me the plan again. And be very clear about how easy and safe my part is."

•   •   •

Ninety minutes later, Conner sat in the Lincoln next to Otis. He still wasn't sure how he'd been talked into it. Becker had told them what to do. They'd parked at the rear entrance of the hotel, this Kurisaka and his band of chop-saki killers on the top floor. He felt like a second-rate SWAT team guy, half-assed secret agent wanna-be. He felt stupid and clumsy and afraid.

Joellen Becker had draped him in Kevlar. Nylon straps. Buckles. An electronic headset with a single earpiece and a microphone strapped to his throat. Three guns. Three opportunities to shoot off his own foot. Some kind of automatic on the ankle, a small cali-ber. The little gun felt awkward down there when he walked, so he decided to leave it off and not tell Becker. The other two were nine-millimeter Glocks, one under each arm in lightweight canvas shoul-der holsters. A Batman-style utility belt. Conner was scared to death he'd bump into something and blow himself in half.

If my part of the fucking plan is so safe, then why the hell am I wear-ing a ton of guns?

Better safe than sorry, Becker had told him.

Otis wore the same outfit with two notable differences. One: He also carried a giant, fully automatic twelve-gauge shotgun with an enormous barrel magazine. Conner had not even realized there was such a gun.

The other difference was almost comical. A single Kevlar vest didn't even come close to covering Otis's massive chest. In an awk-ward but serviceable arrangement, Becker had strapped two vests together. The new rig left only a few gaps, dangerous spaces where a lucky shot might find its way through. *Better than nothing*, thought Conner.

"Five minutes." Becker's voice echoed electronic in Conner's earpiece.

Conner felt a sudden urge to call it off. Why was he doing this? Conner wasn't sure he even understood himself, didn't know how to take his jumble of feelings and turn them into words anyone could understand. It had something to do with Tyranny. But it had a lot more to do with himself, like seeing this thing to the finish would somehow snap into focus who he was as a human being. A failed ballplayer, a flunked-out student, a rejected lover. There was nowhere to go but forward, wide-eyed into the open jaws of doom.

But now, he wasn't sure. Fear.

"Otis, maybe this is a bad idea."

"Go then," the big man said. "I'm staying. I know what I'm about."

"You got that leather bag of money. You could take off." *Take me with you.*

"It's Rocky's money," Otis said. "I'd say he'd want to buy revenge with it."

Becker's voice again. "It's go time. Samson, get into position."

Conner touched the microphone at his throat. "Right."

He looked at Otis one more time. Otis said nothing, only nodded.

Conner slipped a windbreaker over his gun rig. It was over ninety degrees even in the middle of the night, but he couldn't chance someone seeing him and calling in the cops.

He left the Lincoln behind, walked fast around the back of the hotel, and found the service entrance Becker told him would be there. His heart pounded in his ears, mouth dry. He didn't touch the knob. Too soon. It would be locked, maybe even have an alarm.

Becker had told him state-of-the-art, modern hotels had state-of-the-art, modern blind spots and weaknesses. She was parked somewhere with her laptop and her cellular modem, tapping into the hotel's computer network. Voodoo magic. Again Conner realized how little he understood about so much.

A long *buzzzzz* followed by a *click*. Becker's voice in his ear. "Go, Samson."

Conner turned the knob and rushed inside. No alarm. He scanned the area. Kitchens to the right. A service elevator to the left. He climbed in, thumbed the throat microphone. "I'm in the service elevator."

"Okay," Becker said in his ear. "Is there a keypad or a lock? You'll either need a key or a code to ride to the top floor."

"A keypad," Conner said.

"Good. If you'd have needed a key, you'd be screwed. We can bypass the code. I'll tell the computer system there's an emergency evacuation. That'll unlock all the restricted elevators. But I'll disable the alarm. Give me a second."

"How'd you learn to do all this?" Conner asked.

"I'd tell you, but then I'd have to kill you. Now clam up. I'm working."

Conner clammed up. Waited.

Then the elevator moved. Up.

Becker's voice. "I'm going to cue Otis. When he starts his commotion it should pull any guards away from the service elevator and give you a clear path."

"What if I don't have a clear path?"

"Then we'll see what you're made of, Samson. You've just got to have faith Otis will do his job."

Yeah, Conner knew this play. The suicide squeeze.

Otis sat stone still in the Lincoln, eyes closed. He'd been working on his breathing, in through the nose, out through the mouth. He was going to walk face-first into danger, and he'd need his mind straight if he wanted to come out alive. But he had to do this thing. He'd feel Rocky's ghost haunt him forever if he didn't.

Otis had graduated high school with average grades, hadn't paid much attention to most of the stuff he'd read in English class, Hemingway stories and *The Red Badge of Courage*. He'd forgotten most of it. One thing stuck with him crystal clear. *Hamlet*. The ghost of Hamlet's father had made a big impression on a seventeen-year-old Otis. The ghost defined certain responsibilities. You don't forget your family. You don't turn a blind eye when somebody does them wrong. He'd been surprised how applicable these lessons had been later in life.

His high school English teacher had asked the question: Was

the ghost real or a manifestation of Hamlet's guilt? What did it matter? Otis thought. Hamlet was fucked up either way.

Rocky Big had been family, and Otis didn't want to risk any ghosts.

A hiss of static in his ear. Otis opened his eyes.

"You're up, Otis," Becker said in his earpiece. "Good hunting."

Joellen Becker typed rapidly on the laptop in her dark car. She'd parked near the garage entrance, where she planned to enter the hotel as soon as she'd set a few things in motion. Otis was on his way, so she only had a few minutes.

The hotel's system codes had been ridiculously easy to obtain even on short notice, an appropriate bribe with an underpaid hotel employee. She tapped a few keys and shut down all the hotel's outside telephone lines and the rest of the alarm systems. It wouldn't take long for somebody to realize they could still call the police on a cell phone. If she'd still been with her old special ops unit, she would have been able to jam those calls with high-tech equipment.

She'd already taken a handful of special pills twenty minutes before. A vitamin blend, alcohol neutralizer, hangover remedy. Now she rolled up her sleeve, found a fat vein, and inserted the hypodermic needle, pushed the plunger, felt the narcotic boost, the special mix she'd used only once before on a covert mission when she'd had to go without sleep for thirty-six hours. She felt the surge. Like she could fly or take on the world.

She set one more program in motion before shutting down her laptop. For months Becker had been tapping into computerized security systems, hotels, apartment complexes, homes, and businesses. Anything that had a silent alarm connected to the Pensacola Police. There had been no reason for her to do so except to keep her hacking skills sharp. But secretly she'd been hoping the computer file would come in handy. She started the timer. In exactly five minutes, every alarm would ring at once. It would delay the authorities just long enough for Becker to make her getaway after she'd accomplished her mission.

Joellen Becker strapped on her pistols, zipped her leather jacket over her Kevlar vest, left the car behind, took five steps toward the hotel, and stopped. She felt overwhelmed by a sentimental urge and tried to fight it. She didn't fight too hard or for too long and finally lost, went back to the car, shrugged out of the shoulder rig and popped the trunk. She dropped her automatics inside and took out the leather holsters with her father's six-shooters, strapped them around her waist.

They hung low, felt so stupidly good that she giggled.

Otis walked into the hotel lobby, a blanket thrown over the automatic shotgun. He stepped up to the front desk. The guy behind it was prim and efficient. "Can I help you, sir?"

"I'm going up to visit some friends."

"It's after hours," the clerk said. "I'll need to call up first. What's the guest's name?"

"Jack Shit."

"Sir?"

"Sorry about this." Otis's big fist came out of nowhere, smacked the clerk between the eyes. The clerk folded, collapsed behind the desk.

Otis found the elevator. He went up, his gut sinking, jaw set. He dropped the blanket, gripped the full-auto shotgun with white knuckles. Becker had called the shotgun an impractical prototype, a silly weapon not good for much.

Except for what Otis was about to do.

The floors slipped by. Soon he'd be at the top. Otis felt nervous. It was a feeling he'd almost forgotten, didn't quite know what to do with. He usually made *other* people nervous. He swallowed, throat rough. Sweat in his armpits, on his neck and upper lip. He heard his own breathing, felt his own heartbeat, saw the elevator doors open.

He stepped out of the elevator, shotgun out front like the hood ornament of death, and pulled the trigger.

Toshi paced the halls one last time before going to bed. He wanted to make sure everything was secure. It was unlikely any of Cousin Ahira's enemies would make an attempt on his life here in Pensacola, but Toshi was a professional and left nothing to chance.

He found Itchi at his post near the service elevator. "A quiet night?"

"All is well," Itchi said.

Toshi nodded. "We leave for Tokyo in the morning."

Itchi said, "It will be good to go home."

"Yes. The hard part is over. Mr. Kurisaka has his prize. Nothing to do now but pass one more quiet evening."

Gunfire erupted down the hall. Screams.

Toshi cursed, ran for the commotion as he drew his automatic from its holster. He glanced over his shoulder, saw Itchi following close behind. He slammed on the brakes, and Itchi ran into him, almost knocking him over.

"What are you doing?" barked Toshi.

"The shots—"

"Back to your post! We'll call if we need you."

Itchi bowed. "*Hai!*"

Toshi ran again at full speed, thumbing the safety off the automatic. He was eager and ready to do harm.

40

The deafening <u>kuchugga-chug-chug-chug-chug</u> of Otis's shotgun shook the hotel, a buckshot blizzard, shredding wallpaper and plaster, shattering light fixtures. The weapon sang, a Wagnerian shotgun opera, the sound track to hell.

The two guards, sharp-eyed Japanese in bright Armani suits, had gone for their guns upon seeing the elevator doors open. Otis sprayed them with buckshot, blood flying and landing on the walls in Rorschach splats. Doors opened, men flooding the halls without regard for their own lives like all good minions. Four men, no, six.

Otis emptied the barrel magazine, the weapon ejecting the shells, which collected in a smoking pile at his feet. He shredded skull and bone, the hallway transforming into a crucible of blood, until finally he was still pointing the shotgun but nothing was coming out. He'd spent the ammo, and four more men spilled out of rooms, firing automatics.

The bullets felt like hard-thrown stones against Otis's Kevlar vests. A chunk of lead caught him in the fleshy part of the thigh, a burning knot of flesh and blood and pain. Otis grunted, dropped the shotgun.

He took a half dozen more shots in the Kevlar, another bullet whizzing too close past his ear. He drew the twin Glocks, opened fire. They sounded like pissed-off firecrackers compared to the shotgun. Otis fired six shots, missed everything, realized he wasn't using the scattergun anymore and actually had to aim.

Another bullet grazed his shoulder. It stung.

Otis aimed, squeezed the trigger three times, killed one of the men, and swung the pistols in a deliberate arc, dropped two more. The last man saw he was alone, turned and ran. Otis filled his back with lead.

The hallway was suddenly silent except for the faint moan of the wounded. Smoke hung in the air, the smell of sweat and death.

Otis slapped two new magazines into the Glocks, stepped over the bodies crisscrossing the hall. His every step sank into the pile carpeting, squished with blood.

Itchi watched Toshi disappear around the corner and exhaled relief. He knew he was supposed to be brave, but running toward gunfire was very low on his list of things to do.

The shots down the hall were louder now, a rapid series of little bombs, a small war. The roar of gunfire was so loud, it was no surprise Itchi didn't hear the *ding* of the elevator behind him, the doors sliding open. Did not, in fact, realize anything was amiss until he felt the cold barrel of the gun pressed to the back of his head.

Damn.

"Drop your guns," said the man behind him.

Itchi had only one. He dropped it.

"Kick it down the hall."

Itchi kicked his gun. It slid out of reach.

"Now step away and turn around."

Itchi did it, looked at the man. Samson. The man looked haggard, determined, and nervous all at the same time. He licked his lips, shook the gun at Itchi.

"I don't want to kill anybody."

Itchi nodded. By fortunate coincidence, he didn't want to get killed.

"Get on the elevator," Samson said. "Get the hell out of here."

He edged past Samson, hopped aboard the elevator. The doors began to close. He saw Samson turn and head away down the hall. His thoughts raced in the two seconds it took the elevator door to shut. Guilt and honor and duty, the feelings Itchi had thought safely suppressed. Itchi's only job was to protect Kurisaka, and he'd botched it. Inattention. Stupidity. The bungling *gaijin* had come upon him from behind. Itchi had put up no resistance. He was a coward.

Itchi slapped the DOOR OPEN button, drew the short dagger on his belt with the other hand. The doors slid open, Samson still visible only a little farther down the hall, the gunfire racket still erupting beyond. Itchi sprinted down the hall, his feet barely touching the ground, dagger up and ready to strike.

When Itchi was six feet from Samson's back, he leapt. Just as Samson turned, brought his pistol around. Samson's face was a mask of terror and surprise.

Itchi wondered how he looked to Samson.

41

If not for the narcotic boost, Joellen Becker would have been winded by the third floor. Instead, she sprinted two steps at a time, up through the hotel's stairway, her hard boots echoing off the cement walls.

Her plan was simple. The behemoth Otis, using Satan's own shotgun, would simply cut a path through Kurisaka's men. Most likely, Otis would be killed in the process. No matter. Otis's rampage might draw any guards away from the service elevator, giving Samson a clear path. Or perhaps not. Samson's survival was of little concern to Becker. He could even keep the DiMaggio card should he actually win through. To Joellen Becker, the most important thing was that the two men cause as much of a diversion and draw as much fire as possible.

She didn't consider she'd duped them, not completely. Otis had his chance at revenge. Samson could chase a baseball card for which there was no longer a buyer. It was what they wanted. *Go for it, guys. Have fun.*

Joellen Becker had bigger plans. While searching the mercenary

Web sites and checking with her old NSA contacts, the name Ahira Kurisaka had sent up a red flag. She'd dug a little deeper and found there was a big fat price on his head. Five hundred million yen. (That's 4.8 million American!) Kurisaka had enemies, and they were willing to pay big to make him go bye-bye forever. She'd withheld that tidbit of information from Samson.

She was two floors from the top when she heard a mob of footfalls rumbling down the stairs toward her. Fuck. Somehow, they knew she was coming. It didn't matter how. She'd have to fight her way up. She'd hoped to avoid as much combat as possible, ideally popping a quick slug into the back of Kurisaka's head and beating feet down the stairs again before anyone tried to kill her.

But when Becker saw the three Japanese men running toward her, she realized what was happening. These men were not coming for her. They were running away. Panicked. *Otis must've given them hell.*

When the three saw her, it took a moment for them to recognize a threat. They lifted their pistols, one even managed to get off a shot, the bullet kicking up tiny chunks of cement a foot over Becker's head.

Becker drew the six-shooters, the nickel flashing in the stairwell's fluorescent light. She squeezed each trigger three times, the cylinders turning in B-movie slow motion as she charged up the last flight of stairs.

Two of the men took the bullets in the chest, fell forward, lifeless bodies rolling down the stairs. Becker leapt over them, pressed forward, firing twice more at the final man. He took a slug in each leg, went down hard.

Becker reached the landing, stood over the man with the ruined legs, pointed one of the six-shooters at his forehead. The man trembled, turned pale. Either from the loss of blood or from the flat, emotionless expression on Becker's face. Probably both.

"How many more men up there?" Becker asked.

The man shook his head.

"Where's Kurisaka?"

He shook his head again. "No . . . speak." He groped for words. "No . . . English."

"I almost specialized in Asian languages," Becker told him. "I took French and Italian instead. Unlucky for you."

She pulled the trigger.

42

Conner Samson screamed, flinched away from the guy jumping
him. Conner threw up his arm—sheer reflex—and the guy sliced
him from wrist to elbow. The wound burned, blood-sticky and hot.
His own blood. Fear and adrenaline. Conner pushed the Glock at
his attacker, jerked the trigger five times fast.

Impossibly, from only three feet away, every shot missed.

The guy bowled into Conner and they both went over. Conner
landed hard on his back, the wind knocked out of him. He gulped
for air. The guy was on top of him, dagger raised. The Glock was
right in the guy's gut. Even Conner couldn't miss. He pulled the
trigger twice.

His attacker convulsed, eyes going wide. He froze a moment,
then very slowly tilted sideways. Conner pushed him off, scooted
away. He looked into the dead man's eyes. *I did that. He was alive.
Then I fired the gun, and now he's dead.* Conner felt dizzy, shook it off.
He looked at his gun. Blood on the barrel. He wiped it on the dead
man's pants and returned it to its holster.

Conner picked himself up, ran down the hall, looking at the room numbers until he found Kurisaka's suite. The DiMaggio card, in theory, lay within. Had Otis's diversion worked? *Here we go.*

He took the specially shaped charge from his utility belt, a black disk the size of a silver dollar, a small switch right in the middle. He peeled off the paper, adhesive underneath, and slapped the charge onto the door right next to the knob like Becker had shown him. He flipped the switch, backed away five feet. His instinct was to run all the way back up the hall, but he needed to be ready to rush inside.

The charge went off after five seconds, a loud *bang*, which made Conner jump even though he'd been expecting it. He ran into the suite, bracing himself for a possible hail of gunfire or a knife in the gut. But as Becker had predicted, none of Kurisaka's henchmen waited within.

He reached for the light switch, flipped it off. Closed the door behind him. He already had another, smaller disk in his hand, tossed it into the darkened room. He turned his head, shut his eyes tight, but still saw and felt the hot flash through his eyelids. He looked back, put on the special night-vision goggles.

The world turned green. Conner turned to see a quivering green blob lumbering toward him. It took him a second to realize it was a man, a giant fat man who filled his vision. The blob's eyes were specter black. Conner stepped aside, and the blob rumbled past him, fell over a chair, and cursed in Japanese.

He knows I'm here, but he can't see me. Conner knew Kurisaka would be here, but he hadn't expected a charging elephant.

Conner drew his Glocks, searched the room quickly. He wanted to find the DiMaggio card fast and get the fuck out of there. He saw a metal attaché case on the table, set down the Glocks, and flipped it open. The DiMaggio card sat in its hard plastic shell in the center of the padded case. *Bingo.* He closed the case, grabbed it by the handle.

White-hot light stabbed Conner's eyes. He flinched, clawed the night-vision goggles off his face. Someone must've switched the room light back on, overloaded the goggles. Conner blinked, spots in front of his eyes. He flailed, bumped into furniture. He blinked again, his eyes clearing just in time to see the giant fist coming at his face.

The big man hit him right between the eyes. Conner flipped backwards over the table, landed in a tangle on the other side. It felt like he'd been hit by a pickup truck. Somehow he hung on to the case. Shouting in Japanese. Bells ringing in his ears.

Conner stood, half-falling, half–backing away from the monster moving around the table to get at him again. He saw a door, ran for it, went through, and shut it behind him. A bathroom. He flipped the lock. Pounding on the door, almost shaking the thing out of its frame. If that guy put his full weight into it, the door wouldn't last long. He checked his shoulder holsters. Empty. He'd set the pistols on the table when he'd checked the attaché case. He looked down at the case in his hand. All things considered, he'd rather have had the pistols. He thought about the little automatic he was supposed to strap to his ankle.

Goddamsonofabitchmotherfuckingshit—

The door shook with impact. That guy wanted through. Now.

Think, dumb-ass.

He checked his utility belt, various items of dubious value. Two more of the shaped charges he'd used to blow the door lock. A miniature first-aid kit he'd use on himself later if he survived. A little camera. Forty feet of tough nylon line with a miniature grappling hook. A granola energy bar. *Who designed these fucking things? What did they think the wearer would encounter? No time. Focus on the problem.*

Conner thumbed the microphone at his throat. "Becker. Dammit, Becker, where are you? I need some help here, and I mean right fucking now!"

The pounding on the bathroom door increased, the hinges groaning. The door wouldn't last another minute.

43

Toshi knew violence. It was his bread and butter. But the carnage in the hotel corridor astonished him. Kurisaka's men lay in steaming piles, blood soaking the floor and walls. Half his mind processed the slaughter in a split second. The other half of Toshi's brain appraised the gargantuan black man rapidly advancing with a set of out-stretched pistols. He was as huge as Kurisaka, round belly, big features. But not as soft or clumsy. He came at Toshi like an athlete, fast and sure of himself, and opened fire.

To a trained killer like Toshi, the entire clash unfolded in slow motion. Toshi charged too, ducked as he ran, raised his automatic, scanned his target, even as the big man's first three shots passed close over his head. Toshi recognized the man's Kevlar instantly, altered his aim from chest to head, squeezed the trigger.

It took only a single shot. The big man's left eye exploded with a wet splat, blood thick, squirting like a ketchup packet squeezed too hard. The bullet exploded from the back of his skull, bone and flesh and goo flying, a horror-movie, special-effects nightmare.

Toshi watched him, fascinated. The giant didn't fall immediately. He stood up ramrod straight, head twitching, mouth opening and closing. He took four halting steps back, lurching stiffly like a windup robot. Parts of his body refused to believe in death. There was a long, slow exhale.

Then he toppled over backward, hit with a floor-shaking impact, arms and legs sprawled wide. Toshi picked his way over and around the bodies of Kurisaka's men. They had not been Yakuza, but they were tough men, good fighters. And this big black man had been a mighty warrior also. It had been a good death. Toshi stood over him, studied the ruined face. Who was he? What had been his part in this? One of the assassins, perhaps, who wished to claim the bounty on Kurisaka.

In the end, he was just another of the many dead.

Joellen Becker emerged from the stairwell and smelled it immediately, the stink of blood and gunpowder and bowels loosened in the final death throes. She looked both directions up and down the hall. At the far end, a man in black stood over Fat Otis's prone form. Otis had done his job well. She'd handle the lone survivor before moving on to execute Kurisaka.

Samson's voice in her earpiece: "Becker. Dammit, Becker—where are you? I need some help here, and I mean right fucking now!"

Becker ripped out the earpiece, tossed it away. *You're on your own, sport.*

She drew the six-shooters again, stalked the hall toward her target, deliberate steps. *Go in quick. All business.* She thumbed back the hammers, the cylinders clicking and turning. Arms up and straight. She took a dozen steps toward him, fixing him in her sights, before squeezing the triggers.

He'd already turned his head, spotted her. He was catlike, leapt to the side. The six-shooters thundered, slugs flying past him. She saw the shoulder material of his jacket rip, dust and thread flying, and she wondered if she'd even drawn blood. She fired the six-shooters until they spun on empty. *Click click click.*

He returned fire from his crouch, off-balance but on target. Three shots slammed into the Kevlar beneath Becker's leather jacket, almost knocked the wind out of her. She dove on the carpet, more shots passing over her.

She looked up, saw him ejecting the spent clip. If he reloaded, she didn't have a chance.

Becker launched herself up from the carpet and into a full sprint in one smooth motion. She pumped her legs and arms as the clip fell, bounced off the carpet. Becker was within four feet of him as he pulled out another clip. She planted herself. He slapped the new clip home.

She spun, a roundhouse kick.

He lifted the pistol, squeezed the trigger.

Becker's boot connected with the gun, the shot going off into the ceiling, plaster and dust. The gun flew away. She aimed another punch for the man's nose. *Put him down quick. Get on to Kurisaka.*

He caught her fist, twisted her arm. She grunted, jerked away, a flurry of fists to his gut and head. He blocked, counterpunched. She blocked the one aimed for her chin, but took a hard hit in the kidney. Becker winced, stepped back to regroup, but he wouldn't let her. He pressed the attack. A kick followed by another punch. She sidestepped the kick by a fraction of an inch, ducked the punch.

This bastard is good.

She dropped to the floor, attempted a leg sweep. She knew he'd dodge it. She popped up again, jabbed three times fast with her tight little fist. She connected on the bridge of his nose all three times, his head snapping back, eyes round and surprised.

He staggered back out of her reach, wiped his nose and looked at the blood. A thin smile. "Not bad for a woman." Thick accent but clear enough.

They dove for each other, collided in a frenzy of punches, kicks, and blocks. He ducked, twisted. She lost track of him. Then the sudden blur of a fist, the impact spinning her head around.

Becker's turn to stagger back. She spit a tooth. It landed on the carpet between them. Blood on her lips and chin.

He charged her, and she punched. He caught her punch under his arm, held on tight, and wrenched. She heard more than felt the *snap*. He let go, and Becker scooted away from him, her right arm dangling useless and limp at her side. Now the pain. Even through the special drugs, she felt it throb the length of her arm. *Oh, God. Oh, no.* She willed the pain down to something manageable, fought off a wave of nausea.

Becker punched with her other arm, but her opponent batted it aside. He spun and kicked the broken arm. She screamed, the pain an electric assault on her system. Dark spots hovered in front of her eyes. She backed away quickly, trying to remember how far the stairwell was behind her. Maybe she could run, get away. Becker knew she was kidding herself.

Another blow to the side of her head, and she went to one knee. A kick and she was facedown on the carpet. She tried to push herself up, felt the man grab a fistful of her hair and jerk her head back, heard the *snick* of his switchblade and didn't have to guess what it was. An odd moment of clarity.

Even as it was happening, she could not quite believe it.

Becker felt the cold steel on her throat, then a white-hot instant of pain, then nothing at all.

44

<u>Bitch!</u>

Conner tried again: "Becker, dammit, I'm in a world of shit here. Where the hell are you?" No answer, and he didn't have time to wonder why. Another jarring impact against the bathroom door, the top hinge almost pounded apart. The giant on the other side was coming through, and the door would soon be so many splinters. Now or never. Conner had to do something.

Even something incredibly stupid.

He tied the grappling-hook end of the nylon line around the pedestal sink. He clipped the other end to his utility belt, made sure it was tight and secure.

Slam against the door again, wood cracking, shouts on the other side.

Conner peeled the backing off one of the explosive charges, slapped it against the center of the window, flipped the switch.

The man on the other side of the door screamed pure rage, threw himself against the door again. The top hinge popped, clanged on the tile floor. Conner put his back against the door, braced his feet against the bathtub. It was like trying to hold back an avalanche.

The window exploded, glass shattering outward, raining the sidewalk with glittering shards twelve stories below. Wind gusted and whistled through the bathroom. Conner grabbed the attaché case, bolted for the window.

Conner had seen Bruce Willis do something like this in *Die Hard*. Conner would have paid a million dollars for a stuntman to take his place. He took a deep breath and jumped headfirst through the window.

A sensation of wind, clothes flapping, eyes crunched to slits. For a split second, Conner swore he was floating upward, arms and legs outstretched, the lights of Pensacola sprawling and tumbling in the night. Then the nylon line jerked tight, almost snapping his back, like God yanking his leash in midair. The city lights blurred, the line flinging him into the glass two floors down. His head smacked. Bells. He struggled for breath, grabbed the line with his free hand, and righted himself. It was a long way down. Conner decided not to look. Anyway, there wasn't time.

He slapped the last explosive disk against the window, flipped the switch, and kicked out as hard as he could. He swung out and away from the window, then a slight pause before the return swing. Conner flew toward the window, and the charge detonated, the glass window exploding inward a split second before he swung through into the hotel room.

The woman within began screaming immediately.

Suddenly the line connected to Conner's utility belt went slack. A porcelain streak sped past the window. The pedestal sink. An image of the sink pulling him out the window flashed through Conner's brain. He yelped, fumbled at his belt, unhooking the line just as it was ripped out of his hands.

The woman still screamed. She threw a lamp. Conner ducked, ran for the door, worked the locks, and escaped into the hall. He ran for the elevators, but saw the stairs and took those instead. He flew down them three at a time, an iron grip on the metal attaché case. He slipped on the last flight, slid down the stairs on his back. He groaned to his feet, hobbled out the exit, into the parking garage.

There were another dozen people, half-dressed, rushing for cars.

Outside, the beginnings of a madhouse. An ambulance in front of the hotel's main entrance, a fire truck just pulling up, EMS swarming among panicked hotel guests. A bellboy gesticulating at a policeman. Red and blue flashing and high-pitched sirens a few blocks away signaled more cops on the way.

Conner didn't know if it was possible to look inconspicuous, didn't know if it was worth trying. He threaded his way through the Chicken Little frenzy of running people, found Fat Otis's Lincoln, and climbed in the passenger side. He sat low, willing himself invisible, and clutched the attaché case, Joe DiMaggio, the American icon he'd just repossessed.

He watched the entrance of the hotel, eyes darted between the front doors and the parking garage. *Come on, Otis, buddy. Come on. Where are you? Let's get the fuck out of here—oh please will you just hurry your fucking ass up and come on come on come on!*

Conner knew, in the way people always seem to know the worst, some kind of tragic clairvoyance, that Otis wasn't coming. He thumbed the throat microphone. "Becker, if you can hear me, I'm out of here. Okay? Time to go."

He waited.

Only the static hiss of dead air in his earpiece.

Conner scooted into the driver's seat, ducked under the steering column. It was easier with the old cars. Some of the new models couldn't be hot-wired. The repo business was getting tougher. His hands shook, but soon he had the wires out and spliced, started the engine on the first try. He sat up in the seat.

About a billion more police had arrived, they were fanning out, widening the perimeter around the hotel entrance. Conner wouldn't be able to hang out any longer. He looked once more for Otis, but when the SWAT van arrived, Conner figured that was it. Time to go.

He pulled out of the parking spot, drove a dozen feet when a uniformed cop stood in front of him, held up a hand.

Oh shit oh shit oh shit oh shit oh shit.

Conner rolled down the window, all smiles. His heart beat like it was trying to escape from his chest. "What is it, Officer? A fire?"

The cop ignored the question. "Not through here. Turn it around."

Conner made a three-point turn, tried to keep it smooth. He pulled away, resisted the urge to stomp on the gas. Soon he was away from the hotel, the flashing lights, the racket of sirens, and the jabbering crowd. Conner felt light-headed, stomach woozy. Had he lost too much blood, or was he just exhausted, nerve-fried?

He thought of Otis and felt numb. Was the big guy still alive? Conner's gut told him no. He made no plans to avenge his friend's death. He didn't even want to know, didn't care about the details. He would claim not to know Fat Otis if the police ever came asking.

Conner hoped Otis would understand.

THE LAST PART

In which Conner Samson
is Joe DiMaggio.

45

Ahira Kurisaka stood naked in his hotel bathroom, the wind on his sweaty skin raising goose bumps. He'd exerted himself almost to the point of collapse. Knocking down the door, ripping the pedestal sink from the floor, and heaving it out the window was all more exercise than he'd had in a long time. He stood at the windowsill, sucking air and looking at the gathering police vehicles below.

Someone cleared his throat. Kurisaka turned, looked down at Toshi standing in the bathroom's ruined doorway. The Yakuza killer looked bruised and bloodied. His jacket was torn. But the man stood at attention, waited for Kurisaka to speak.

"Tell me what's happened," Kurisaka said.

"An attempt on your life, Cousin," Toshi said. "I personally dispatched two of the killers, which is why I was not at your side when the third man broke into your suite. I apologize for the dereliction."

"No," Kurisaka said. "Not an assassination attempt, not this time. They took the DiMaggio card. Your killers were a diversion."

Toshi's stoic expression wavered in obvious disbelief. He composed himself quickly. "We might have a more immediate problem, I'm afraid. The local authorities will be here soon."

"We'll use the diplomatic credentials," Kurisaka said. "Why else would I have two ambassadors and the deputy minister of the foreign office on the payroll?"

Toshi doubted it would be that simple but said nothing.

Kurisaka turned back to the open window, gazed at the cityscape. "I don't know what to think, Toshi." He'd believed his DiMaggio card a prize to be envied. Then Hito Hyatta had yanked the rug out from under him, had made him feel naïve, idiotic. He'd called the card *cute*. And then, in the middle of the night, someone had felt the card worth a daring raid on Kurisaka's heavily guarded hotel suite. Kurisaka no longer understood his world.

Toshi cleared his throat. "Cousin?"

"Yes?"

"Do Yakuza generally suffer such an attack unanswered?"

Kurisaka thought for long seconds, understanding dawning in his eyes. "No," he said. "No, we do not."

Kurisaka did not see Toshi's wide, wicked smile.

"Gather the men," ordered Kurisaka.

Toshi's smile fell. "They are dead, Cousin. Every last one of them."

Tyranny Jones's insomnia had led her to the blank canvas in the breakfast nook. She did much of her painting late at night, her mind racing, unable to find sleep amid the lace and satin in her bedroom, a separate bedroom from Professor Dan's. She'd begun by painting the canvas, ended up painting herself. First, black toenail polish, then the fingernails black too. She liked it, found a tube of black lipstick, and did the lips.

In the bathroom's full-length mirror, she stripped naked and looked at herself. Tyranny was too tan to go gothic, so she resolved to stay out of the sun until she was nice and pale. She would buy a

long, lacey black dress and a pair of combat boots. Yes, a good deci-
sion. It felt right, a timely reinvention of herself. Shake things up a
bit. What would Dr. Goldblatt say?

She went upstairs, looked at Dan while he slept. His mouth
hung open, a little drool on the chin. He appeared comatose and
oblivious. She envied him. She went down the hall to her bedroom,
took all the black clothing out of her closet, laid it out on the bed.
She understood as a matter of course that she was inventing a project for herself, trying to trick her mind into paying attention to
trivia, sorting clothes into piles, slacks and blouses and underwear
and pajamas.

She put on the black pajamas.

In her bathroom mirror, she studied herself. She looked like a
Marilyn Manson fan at a slumber party.

Her image makeover was interesting but not fully distracting.
So Tyranny did something she almost never did. She went downstairs and flipped on the television. Maybe an old movie. Or music
videos. It had been ages and ages since she'd zoned out in front of
music videos.

Instead, a windblown news reporter told Pensacola that all hell
had broken loose downtown.

"—have responded with fire trucks and ambulances. All off-duty
police are asked to report in. The slaughter follows on the heels of a
similar incident that happened only a few hours earlier at a downtown gentlemen's club." The reporter paused, touched his earpiece,
a wire hanging past his shoulder. "I'm being told authorities have
not ruled out the possibility of a terrorist attack. Apparently there is
a contingent of Japanese dignitaries staying at the hotel. It hasn't
been determined yet if—"

Tyranny flipped the channel, trying to find better pictures of the
calamity. The Channel 2 news copter circled the Intercontinental
Hotel, but without flames or smoke billowing from hotel windows it
was a fairly boring view. Another channel showed the remains of a
pedestal sink embedded in the smashed roof of an SUV. More interesting. She watched awhile longer, hoping to see some bodies.

The doorbell chimed.

At this hour?

She went to the front door, looked through the peephole. It was too dark to see anything more than a vague shape. Instead of reaching for the light switch, she said, "Who is it?"

"Tyranny, it's me. Please open the door."

"Conner?" She glanced up at the ceiling, wondered if Dan had heard the doorbell. It was a big house, and Dan was a sound sleeper. She'd told Conner to stay away. Was he here to cause trouble, pick another fight with Dan? He was such a fucking fucking fucking stubborn, stupid— "Conner, what are you doing here?"

"Jesus, Tyranny, just open the damn door."

She opened her mouth, wanted to tell him to fuck off. Go away. She didn't want to see him, couldn't endure any more of his pleas or professions of love. Couldn't stand breaking his heart, didn't have the energy to figure out how their lives would fit together or even if they could. It was all too much, and all Tyranny wanted was to hide in her room and try on black clothes and listen to a Duran Duran CD over and over again and pretend she wasn't a fucked-up head case. But no, here was Conner fucking Samson throwing reality in her face in the middle of the night like a selfish goddamn asshole, and yet part of her brain wondered if he'd like the new look, the black lipstick, and she wanted to kill him and kiss him and why wouldn't he just *fuck off*?

He pounded on the door. "Tyranny!"

"Shit!" She opened the door. "Fine. Get your ass in here. But stop yelling or you'll wake— Oh my God!"

Conner fell into the light, sprawled facedown in the foyer. He looked like hell, blood-smeared and pale as death. He clutched a metal attaché case.

"Oh, Conner, oh Jesus, what happened?" She knelt next to him, gently turned him over, pulled his head into her lap.

"It's been a long night," Conner said. "I think . . . if it's okay maybe . . . I'll just close my eyes for a minute." He passed out.

"Conner!"

Professor Dan walked in, rubbing his eyes. He spotted Tyranny holding Conner's head in her lap. "This is just typical. In my own house." He took a closer look, saw the blood. "Oh, man. He doesn't look so good."

46

Conner awoke on cool, clean sheets. His shirt and shoes off, gauze and surgical tape on his slashed forearm. He lifted his head, looked around the room. The Kevlar vest and Batman utility belt sat on the chair in the corner, the metal attaché case leaned against a leg of the chair. His entire body ached.

He remembered. Tyranny's house. It must be a guest room. Conner took in his surroundings, dark wood paneling, plaid bed-covers. A wooden duck on the nightstand. Some kind of L.L. Bean nightmare.

The hazy early-morning light seeped in through the open drapes. Barely after dawn. Clouds on the horizon, thunderstorms later in the afternoon, Conner predicted. Good. Maybe they'd cool things off.

Tyranny entered the room, sat on the side of the bed, put a hand on Conner's good arm. "Thank you."

"For what?"

"For not dying in my lap, you asshole. I really didn't need a funeral with me all sobbing and snotty and red-eyed. Anyway, you were mostly just shocked and exhausted. The cut on your arm isn't very deep. Dan wanted to call an ambulance. Or the police."

"You stopped him?"

She nodded.

"Thanks." Conner looked at her fingernails, her lips. "It wasn't a dream then."

"Huh?"

"I dreamed you were a zombie," Conner said. "Like in *Dawn of the Dead*."

"Fuck you." But there wasn't much venom in it. She lightly stroked his bandage. "Conner, what happened? I saw something about terrorists on TV."

He shook his head. "I don't have anything to do with terrorists. I . . . well, I was in on this deal. The details aren't important." He sat up in bed, winced at his protesting muscles. "I'm going to have some money." Without Rocky or Becker, Conner wasn't sure how he'd go about selling the card. "I need to work out the particulars, but I thought . . . I know you were mad at me before, but—"

"Would you stop acting like money is such a big deal. Just shut up about it."

"Why don't you love me?"

"Idiot!" Tyranny balled her little fists, beat the mattress. "It took you ten seconds to open your mouth and ruin it."

A long silence.

"So I'm just . . . I'm just . . ." Conner's voice shook. He was having trouble keeping it together. "I'm just another one of your . . ."

She shook her head, closed her eyes so tight. "It wasn't supposed to be like that. In the pool house, I thought . . ." She exhaled, shoulders and arms going limp, all the coiled anger in her leaking out in a sad puff of defeat. "Did I tell you about when I went to the Louvre in Paris?"

"With Dan?"

"No," she snapped. "I mean yes, we went together, but that's not the point. Will you listen and shut the fuck up?"

Conner shut the fuck up.

"I went to see *The Mona Lisa*. Have you seen it? I mean on television or in a book, how they have it displayed?" She knew he hadn't traveled.

"I know the picture. Not anything else."

"It's behind glass," Tyranny said. "And you have to stand way back behind a velvet rope to see it. I mean, here I am, this artist, right? And there's a giant museum full of a million different paintings, no velvet rope, no glass. I could get right up close and check out the brushstrokes. But all I want to do is stand twenty feet away and look at *The Mona Lisa*. I stood there for over an hour, just thinking, Wow that's the famous painting.

"That's how you were to me, Conner," Tyranny said. "Special. Behind the protective glass. If I just kept our relationship at a certain level, then it wouldn't be ruined. That's what I thought. Funny, isn't it? You were my longest-running act of restraint, and I blew it. I didn't want to fuck you and make you part of my sickness. I wanted you separate from that. I messed it up."

"You didn't mess it up," Conner said. "It's okay."

"It's not okay. In my mind, it's all messed up and ruined, and my mind is where the problem is. No, Conner, we're broken. I broke us. And the only thing that can fix us—if we can be fixed—is time and distance. I have to put you back behind the glass and the velvet rope. And that's the best I can explain it. If you still can't understand or won't understand, then I can only say please please please trust that I know what's best for myself."

"Tell me what Dan does. I'll do the same thing. I won't ask questions. I'll stay out of your business."

"No. You'll end up hating me. Or you'll drive me crazy, and I'll kill you."

Conner shook his head, eyes fogging. "Then that's it. I'm just supposed to understand. I'm just supposed to go away."

Tyranny nodded once slowly, watching with big, deep eyes. "You're just supposed to go away."

Conner stood, reached for his clothes. "I have to get out of here."

"Are you okay? Your arm."

"I don't even feel it," Conner said. He put on his shirt, grabbed the vest and the belt, looked around the room for anything else. He didn't want to leave anything behind. He resolved in that instant to sail away on the *Jenny*, become a wandering boat bum, port to port, hugging the coast around the Gulf and down to the Keys, tie up at some island and become a hermit.

Or Mexico. Isn't that where rogues went to start over? Maybe Conner would grow a moustache, take up with a sixteen-year-old Mexican girl. Drink tequila and brood, and the locals would know him as the crazy gringo with secrets. There was a whole world of tragic possibilities to choose from, and Conner wanted to get started.

I'm so goddamned dramatic.

Conner opened the attaché case, took out the DiMaggio card, and put it in his pocket. It fit snugly, the plastic case making an awkward bulge. He dropped the attaché case. "I'll leave that here, if you don't mind. I'm tired of lugging it around."

Tyranny didn't say anything, looked at her toes.

Conner left the bedroom without another word. She followed him down the stairs, out the front door to the yellow Lincoln.

"Conner."

He ignored her, opened the car door, threw the vest and belt into the backseat.

"Conner, don't be angry." She put her hand on his back.

He flinched from her. "Don't touch me. I hate you. You suck, and you're ugly."

"Okay," Tyranny said. "You can say that if you need to."

"Go to hell." He got behind the wheel, cranked the engine.

It was sinking in now, everything she'd said. Conner could not do anything, say anything, be anything that would make any difference. That he could have so little control over something so important to him hit him harder than anything else that had happened. Even Otis's death. Conner felt feeble and stupid and small. Nothing he'd done had changed anything about him.

He looked at Tyranny, then over her shoulder at the house. The blinds pried apart in an upstairs window, Professor Dan watching the big breakup scene.

"I love you," Tyranny said. "I just want you to know that. You have to go away, but I love you."

Conner pulled the door closed, drove away. Just like Joe DiMaggio, Conner thought, the ballplayer in love with the mysterious woman. He tried to convince himself that somewhere inside Tyranny was a persona it was okay for him to love. Or maybe he only loved the woman he *thought* she was. But he couldn't convince himself, knew it simply wasn't true. He was in love with all of her, the warped and wretched parts too, the funny little buttons in her brain that needed pressing over and over again so she could feel whatever it was she needed to feel. And anyway, Conner made for a pretty cheap DiMaggio.

The long curves of Scenic Highway unfolded before him, the morning sun muted by the rolling gray, the sky promising a trademark Florida thunderstorm. It would build and build until the sky opened and drowned everything, not out of malice, not spite, but only because the sky would be too full to hold it all.

But Conner didn't see the sky. His eyes felt so hot. He sniffed, wiped his nose on the bottom of his shirt. What in God's ugly world would make the pain in his chest go away?

47

It took three hours for Conner to flag down a boat willing to tie onto one of the *Jenny*'s stern cleats and pull her off the sandbar. With the sky growing blacker by the hour, there weren't many boats on the river.

The *Boston Whaler*, which had pulled Conner off the sandbar, was captained by an ex–navy chief with a Papa Hemingway beard and fading tattoos. "Better find some cover," he told Conner. "Weather service says a bad one is coming."

"I hear you." Conner thanked him, made sure the *Jenny* was secure, and cranked the inboards.

It had taken a few hours to find an appropriate marina and get organized. He figured another three hours for the trip. Downstream, under the swing-out bridge to the mouth of the river where it emptied into the Gulf. Then west along the coast to Paradise Marina almost in Alabama, the closest place to take on fuel and outfit the *Jenny* for Conner's escape. After leaving Tyranny, he'd parked Otis's Lincoln at the marina, the trunk full of expensive goods Conner planned to pawn. He thought about selling the Lincoln too but didn't want to invest the time and money in finding the right people to forge a registration and fence the vehicle.

Then Conner found the leather doctor's bag in the backseat.

He'd opened the bag slowly, afraid the money would vanish in a poof of bad karma. Conner couldn't really feel like the money was his, but who else could claim it? He counted it. Enough. More than enough to get him and the *Jenny* to a faraway place where he could forget who he was, decide who he wanted to be.

Conner had then taken an expensive cab ride from the marina back to the sailboat. He kept checking his pocket for the DiMaggio card. He didn't plan to let it out of his sight anytime soon. Somewhere there had to be a buyer for the damn thing.

At the wheel, he eased the throttle forward, eyed the sky. He might just be able to reach the marina before nightfall. If he were lucky.

The weather restrained itself as Conner made it past the swing-out bridge. The guy in the bridge keeper's house leaned out the little window and gave him a wave. At the mouth of the river, the rain started coming heavier, the water a rough, foamy chop, the prow of the *Jenny* slamming into big waves as it motored forward. Conner was in the Gulf now, and the spray stinging his face was salty and cold. Between the rain and the waves the cockpit filled shin deep with water. He hit the switch for the pumps. They chugged to life below the deck, just keeping ahead of the water coming in.

The sky was completely black with storm clouds now, the Gulf a steel blue. Lightning crisscrossed the sky. Conner kept the coastline within a half mile. He flipped on the running lights. He was getting worried. The storm had slowed his progress, the sailboat's engine struggling against the severe chop. Conner was a decent sailor, but all of his experience had been pleasure boating on calm seas.

And then the engines sputtered and died.

Oh . . . shit.

Conner thumbed the ignition. It wouldn't turn over. He checked the fuel gauge. The tanks were bone dry.

Oh, no. No, no, no . . . He hadn't calculated the rough seas, the extra fuel consumption.

Without forward momentum, the boat would flounder. He left the cockpit, pulled himself forward so he could get the sails up. A wave almost washed him over. He threw himself at the mast, hung on as the *Jenny* listed badly, pitched the deck almost ninety degrees. The rain pounded him now in driving sheets. He could no longer see the prow. Water coming over the transom.

Conner fought his way back to the cockpit, threw open one of the bench seats, and grabbed a life jacket. The wind howled, and the *Jenny* threatened to roll. Conner turned his head side to side. He'd lost track of the land. It was totally black now. He was going to drown. He was going to die in the ocean.

In a flash of lightning, Conner glimpsed a twelve-foot wave coming hard. It collided in the darkness. Conner was thrown, blind. Then he was underwater. He struggled, kicked, hit the surface, and gulped air.

The sea churned around him. Fifty yards distant, he thought he saw the *Jenny*'s white fiberglass bottom. The boat had rolled.

Another wave drove him under, and when he came back up again he no longer saw the boat. He didn't know where the coast lay. The heaving black ocean gaped in all directions, immense swells briefly visible in the lightning.

To come all this way. To die like this. Nobody even knew where he was. Nobody would ever know. *Typical,* thought Conner. *Just fucking typical.*

48

The side of Conner's face burned. Bright and hot, the morning sun beat down on Conner as he lay in the sand. He rolled over, groaned.

He'd fought the sea for an eternity, stroking in what he'd prayed was the direction toward shore. And just when he'd been about to give up, exhausted, ready to surrender to watery doom, his feet had hit the sandy bottom. Ahead of him, through rain, lights. He'd found the beach and collapsed.

Now he sat up, found himself in front of a row of condominiums. An old couple sat on their veranda, the old woman bringing her old man a glass of orange juice. The old man waved at Conner. Conner waved back.

He stood, brushed the sand off his pants and shirt, and scanned the Gulf for any sign of the *Jenny*. Nothing. Not even debris. The *Electric Jenny* wasn't Folger's anymore, nor Conner's either. It belonged to Davy Jones. And somewhere on the sandy bottom was Rocky Big's doctor bag full of money. God's final joke on Conner

Samson, cut off his escape route. *It's biblical, the old Job gag. Torment the little guy. What's next? Boils?*

In a sudden panic, Conner checked his pockets. The DiMaggio card was still there, safe and secure in its plastic case. He also still had the cell phone Rocky had given him. Who was there to call?

He grasped the phone tightly, reared back, arm way behind him, gathering the strength to hurl it into the Gulf of Mexico. He'd throw it over the horizon if he could.

It rang.

Conner froze, unsure if he'd heard what he thought he'd heard. It rang again. He unfolded it slowly, pressed the TALK button. "Hello?"

"Conner, thank God you're there." Tyranny. He'd forgotten he'd given her the cell number, had desperately hoped she'd call.

"If you called to apologize, it's too late. I've moved on. I'm actually having a lovely time at the beach right now. Getting a suntan."

"Conner, this is very important." Something in her voice. Strangely calm, unnerving.

"What's wrong?" Conner asked.

"There are some men here," Tyranny said. "They say you have something that belongs to them. They told me to call you."

Conner's chest tightened. "Asians?"

"Yes, that's right. They're very serious. They said it could be bad for me if you don't cooperate."

"What am I supposed to do?"

"They want you to come here immediately. I'm at home. Bring what they want and nobody gets hurt. Dan's not here right now. I'd like, if possible, to resolve this situation before he gets home." She said it like she was ordering a pizza, no tears, no panic, but Conner detected a hint of strain in her voice. She was trying to maintain, not show how terrified she was for herself and for Dan should he come home and walk into the middle of things.

Conner looked up and down the beach, tried to estimate where he was. The marina might be within walking distance. The Lincoln was there. "I need some time. I'm sort of stuck. But I'll be there."

"Don't dawdle."

"Tell them to wait," Conner said. "I'm coming. I have to get to the car, but tell them I'm coming."

"I'll tell them."

Conner hung up, jogged up the beach, through the condo com-plex, and found the main road. He recognized where he was now. The marina was only three or four miles away.

God wasn't punishing him, Conner thought. *He's just letting me know I have unfinished business. Responsibilities.*

Conner ran, every sore muscle screaming for him to stop. He ran and ran and told his muscles to shut the hell up.

49

Conner parked the Lincoln in Tyranny's driveway right next to a long, black limousine. The driver sat low in the front seat, hat pulled over his eyes, apparently napping. Escambia County plates. Both limo and driver were probably rentals.

Conner got out of the Lincoln, walked toward the front door, and tried to get his nerves under control. His plan was simple. Give them what they want, hand over the DiMaggio card. Nothing funny. No shenanigans. It wasn't worth Tyranny's life.

But these guys were dangerous. They'd already killed a bunch of people. So Conner did have one trick up his sleeve. Not a very good trick. Nothing fancy. Just a little insurance in case things got out of hand.

He rang the doorbell.

It opened immediately, Tyranny standing there with a blank look on her face. Half of her was still behind the door, and Conner figured she had a gun in her ribs.

"Are you okay?" he asked.

She nodded.

Somebody mumbled out of sight. Tyranny stepped back from the door. "He said to come in."

Conner went in, and the door slammed shut behind him. A Japanese man stood with a pistol. He was small, but his eyes were hard. He had a lean, tough face. He frisked Conner, didn't find any weapons. He motioned Tyranny and Conner down the hall.

"Don't worry," Conner whispered. "It'll be okay."

Tyranny said nothing, but her hand found his, held tight.

They went to Professor Dan's office, where Conner had taken booze from the big globe during the Dybek party. Behind Dan's desk sat the huge man from the hotel, the one who'd tried to bust down the bathroom door and kill him. Kurisaka. He wasn't naked anymore, but Conner would recognize him anywhere. On the desk next to him sat the metal attaché case that had formerly contained the DiMaggio card. Their eyes met, and they held each other's gaze for a moment.

Finally, the man said, "I am Ahira Kurisaka." His English was good. "You don't know me. We haven't been formally introduced, but we encountered one another briefly."

"I remember."

"You may also recall you took something that does not belong to you."

"It doesn't belong to you either," Conner said.

Kurisaka's smile didn't reach his eyes. "Yes, possession can be a tricky concept. I would like to submit that my claim of ownership is the stronger by virtue of the fact my cousin Toshi is currently pointing a large-caliber pistol at your head."

Conner cleared his throat, shifted nervously. "I choose not to dispute your claim."

"You're a practical man, Mr. Samson."

"How did you find me?"

Kurisaka explained the homing beacon in the specially made attaché case.

Conner shook his head. Unbelievable. "Why?" He'd merely been wondering out loud, but Kurisaka chose to answer.

"What sort of explanation would satisfy you?" Kurisaka said. "Would you like the Sydney Greenstreet speech from *The Maltese Falcon*? The stuff dreams are made of?"

Conner had no idea what the fat man was talking about.

"No," Kurisaka said. "I won't bore you. I'm too tired. You helped tire me, Mr. Samson. This whole business has worn me down, rattled my belief in who I am." He rubbed his eyes, suddenly looked ten years older. "They used to make religious paintings, little golden icons of saints. Many no bigger than a baseball card. People kept them in their homes, built little altars. It seems the icons have changed. Perhaps it's a mistake when we build altars to them."

The billionaire sighed. "Never mind. Let us conclude our business. I want only to return to Tokyo as soon as possible. Mr. Samson, you will now hand over the DiMaggio card."

Conner nodded at Tyranny. "Let her go first."

"I don't think so," Kurisaka said. "How about I have my cousin shoot you both in the head, then I'll take the card from your dead body?"

"I just had a great idea," Conner said. "How about I just give you the card without all that trouble?" As he pulled the DiMaggio card out of his pocket and set it on the desk, Conner thought how cool it would have been if he'd hidden the card somewhere instead of making it so easy for Kurisaka to take it. He really was pretty bad at this sort of thing.

Gently, Kurisaka picked up the card, examined it. His face was unreadable. He placed it within the special attaché case.

Conner cleared his throat. "We're square now, right? You got the card. Now let Tyranny go. That was the deal." He hooked his thumbs behind his gigantic silver belt buckle, shifted his weight as if standing casually.

"I have a new deal," Kurisaka said. "You've caused me a lot of trouble. You and your associates were responsible for the deaths of several of my men. This cannot go unpunished."

Conner tensed, readied himself to grab the belt buckle.

"So, I've decided my cousin Toshi here will shoot you both in the head after all," Kurisaka said. "Toshi, kill the woman first, so Samson can watch. I think that's only fitting since—"

The office door swung open. "Hey, guys, if it's going to be much longer, I can run the limousine though the car wash." It was the chauffeur, the one Conner had seen napping on his way into Tyranny's house. He still had his hat pulled down over his eyes.

"Dammit, driver," Kurisaka snapped. "Wait outside. We're in the middle of some very important business."

The chauffeur's hands moved like a blur, went into his jacket, and came out with a pistol. He put the pistol into Toshi's back. "Drop it."

Toshi tensed but dropped his gun.

The driver took off his hat, stepped out from behind Toshi.

Toshi's eyes popped.

Kurisaka's mouth fell open. "Billy Moto!"

"That's right," Moto said. "Back from the dead and very pissed."

50

When Billy Moto had flipped over the balcony during his battle with Toshi, the world had blurred. Moto had braced himself for the crunching impact that he would surely not survive. But then the slapping palm fronds. He'd bounced off branches, little cuts on his face and hands.

He hit canvas. It ripped but held. He'd slid to the bottom, went over the side, and landed with a thud on the sidewalk. A pair of women sipping umbrella drinks at a small table screamed. More people rushed to him, crowded around. He gasped for breath, pushed himself up.

"Jesus, buddy, you okay?" someone asked.

He didn't answer, looked up at the palm trees, the canvas tarp stretched tight over the poolside bar. He grabbed an umbrella drink from one of the women. "Pardon, but I think I need this." He tossed back the drink.

A miracle. Or at least very good luck.

"Sure," said the woman. "You scared the crap out of me."

Billy Moto pushed his way through the crowd. He already knew what he would do. He would watch and wait and have his revenge.

"You guys seem like you have things to talk about," Conner said. "We'll just run along and get out of your way."

"Don't move, Mr. Samson," Moto said. "This will all be sorted out soon enough."

Tyranny tried to hold Conner's hand. She was scared. He brushed her away. He needed his hands free.

"This is a mistake, Billy." Kurisaka stood, spread his hands. "I feel only relief to see you alive and well. I owe you an apology. And an explanation. Put down that gun, and let's talk about what's troubling you."

"I think you know exactly what's troubling me," Moto said. "You ordered your lapdog here to kill me. Why? I wasn't fetching your collectible nonsense quickly enough. You are a spoiled, evil, fat man. I officially give my notice."

He looked at Toshi. "As for you, I believe I owe you this."

Moto put the pistol further into Toshi's back and pulled the trigger twice. The shots shook the room, blood erupting from Toshi's chest. Tyranny screamed. Toshi's body hit the floor, piled on top of itself, arms and legs folded awkwardly under him, butt sticking in the air, eyes rolled back.

Moto turned the gun on Kurisaka.

"Billy, I can see you're upset," Kurisaka said. "But I know you. You are an intelligent, reasonable man. And I am a very rich and powerful man. Name your price. How much do you believe yourself wronged? We'll call it severance pay."

"It's too late for that."

"Then you'll just have to kill me, Billy." Kurisaka stood straight, put his hands in his jacket pockets, and puffed out his enormous chest. "Go ahead. I suppose I deserve it. I'm a big enough target. You won't miss."

Moto held his arm out straight, the pistol pointed at Kurisaka's heart. He sucked in breath, held it.

"Well?" Kurisaka said.

The fat man sounded cool, but Conner saw a glistening sheen of sweat on his forehead. Everyone in the room held their breath. The moment stretched an eternity, and in the dead silence they all heard a sudden *snick*.

Moto glanced down, saw Toshi's hand rise and fall. He drove the switchblade into Moto's foot. Moto screamed, pointed the pistol at Toshi's head, and pulled the trigger three times. The bullets shattered skull. Moto grimaced, hopped on one foot, turned the pistol back to Kurisaka.

Too late.

Kurisaka had drawn his hand from his jacket pocket, a silver revolver in his fist. He squeezed the trigger, shot Moto in the chest. Kurisaka shot twice more, the chest again and the belly. Moto convulsed, spit blood, and pitched forward on top of Toshi.

Kurisaka spun, took aim at Conner.

But Conner had already sprung the latch on the belt buckle, held the tiny single-shot derringer. He shoved Tyranny to the ground, aimed fast, and pulled the trigger. The *pop* sounded small and comical. Kurisaka stood up straight, eyes crossed. A little trickle of blood down his nose from the neat hole in the center of his forehead.

A perfect shot.

The giant billionaire fell across the desk, scattered papers, the telephone, bottles of cheap booze.

Silence. Smoke hung in the air.

Conner helped Tyranny to her feet. She trembled, held on to him. She looked pale, eyes wide.

"Are you okay?" Conner asked. "Are you hurt?"

"I'm okay, I think." She checked herself. "Yes."

Conner said, "I need to kiss you."

"Okay."

They pressed into each other with desperate zeal and relief, kissing hard, teeth mashing against lips. Finally, Tyranny pushed away, color in her cheeks, tears down her face, breath coming short and sharp. She said, "Conner?"

"Yes."

"I need a favor."

"Yes. Of course. What is it?"

"Can you help me get rid of these bodies before Dan gets home?"

Epilogue

3 WEEKS LATER

"No, not a Dodge Dart," Conner said into the phone. "Like I told the other guy, a Plymouth Fury. Oh, forget it." He hung up the phone hard, crossed through the garage's number in the Yellow Pages with a red pen.

"No luck?" Sid put another draft beer in front of Conner.

"I called everyplace. I don't think I'm going to see my car again." Conner glanced at the TV over the bar, saw the score, and winced. The Marlins were getting shellacked.

"Buy a new car with the insurance money," suggested Sid. "The Plymouth was falling apart anyway."

"It was a vintage automobile."

Sid shook his head. "Whatever you say."

"Besides," Conner said, "I need to make that money stretch. I'm not exactly working right now." Conner still wasn't quite sure what had happened, who the buyer was supposed to be or how to find out, so he'd ended up taking the Joe DiMaggio card to Teddy Folger's insurance company. They'd wanted to know how he ended up in possession of the card. Conner had resorted to the truth. It had been aboard the *Electric Jenny* when he'd repossessed her. Fortunately, nobody had asked him about the boat.

The insurance company had paid him a recovery fee of ten grand. Some of the money had gone to get Conner back on good terms with his apartment complex. He caught up on his other bills too. He even had a little left over. Still, in his gut, Conner didn't exactly feel he'd come out ahead. He was more or less back at square one, minus a Plymouth Fury.

"Where's your girlfriend?" Sid asked. "I never seen nobody get their skull cracked with a cricket bat before."

Tyranny had called once a few days after the globe-room shootout. She was fine and had started seeing Dr. Goldblatt three times a week. She didn't say anything about her and Conner getting together. And when Conner made hints in that direction, Tyranny squashed them in a hurry. The message was clear. She needed space.

Conner wanted to change the subject. "Who's the new girl?" He pointed at the pretty blonde rinsing glasses at the far end of the bar.

"I decided I needed some help around here," Sid said. "It would be nice to take a night off once in a while, see the grandkids."

"You've got grandkids? I never knew."

"You never asked. What, you think you're the only one around here with a life?"

Right.

Conner watched the ball game. The Marlins' relief pitcher started serving up grapefruits. Conner couldn't watch anymore, grabbed the remote, and turned it to ESPN.

The blonde finally made it to his end of the bar. "Another draft?"

"Sure. What's your name?"

"Misty." A smile like sunshine.

"I'm Conner. Sid said you used to work at one of the beach places."

She nodded. "The tips were good, but too many tourists. Creeps.

Some of them think you're there to serve more than drinks. I like it here. Quiet."

Conner said, "Anyone ever mention you look almost exactly like Marilyn Monroe?"

The smile vanished. Her eyes narrowed to ferocious slits. "Did somebody put you up to saying that? Is that some kind of joke?"

"Whoa. Hey, I was just saying—"

"Well, watch it, buddy."

"Hey, fine. Whatever." He took out a cigar, struck a match.

"Don't light that in here," Misty snapped. "Are you trying to kill everybody?" She stormed away, nose in the air.

Conner sulked. He took out a pad of paper, started calculating what he might do with his leftover insurance money, but he lost interest and sank into his beer. He didn't have enough cash. There was never enough. The thought of calling Ed Odeski for repo work made Conner's heart sink.

A tall guy walked into the bar, big hook of a nose, pale. Khakis and a red polo shirt. He grabbed a stool next to Conner. "You're Samson?"

Conner froze. "Who's asking?"

"My name is Devon Haywood. You're Conner Samson, right?"

"Yeah, that's me."

"I'm a friend of Jasper Dybek's. Jasper told me you . . . uh . . . helped him with a little problem a short while back."

Conner raised an eyebrow. "Oh, yeah?"

"Look, I'm going to be straight with you," Haywood said. "My last sculpture sold for six figures. But that was *two years ago*. The bank's going to repossess my house. Frankly, I was hoping you could do for me what you did for Jasper."

The world had gone crazy. "I'm not sure that's a good idea."

"The sculptures are insured." He pulled out a business card, put it on the bar next to Conner. "Just say you'll think about it and call me."

Conner said he would think about it, and Haywood left, looking panicked and desperate.

Conner's thoughts drifted again to Tyranny. He couldn't help it.

He unfolded a letter he'd been carrying around the last few days. He'd found it jammed into the depths of his pants pocket when he'd finally broken down to do a load of laundry. The letter from Marilyn Monroe to Teddy Folger had a dozen new folds and wrinkles from being smashed into his pocket, but the plastic bag had protected it when he'd been tossed into the Gulf of Mexico. The insurance company hadn't asked about it.

He read again the part he liked best.

People are funny. They all want us and expect us to be a certain way. Sometimes people never know the real us.

Just maybe, in a letter to a fourteen-year-old kid she barely knew, Norma Jean had shown herself, had won out over her starlet persona and was just a regular girl with fears and loves and worries like everyone else. Had DiMaggio loved Norma Jean or Marilyn?

Well, Conner knew the Tyranny he loved, every inch, the good and the bad. He'd wait her out, win her over. He didn't know how. He might even fail. But he was sure about one thing. Conner Samson would not go away.

In the meantime, Conner considered Devon Haywood's business card. He reached across the bar, grabbed the phone, hesitated only a moment, and dialed.

About the Author

Victor Gischler lives in the wilds of Skiatook, Oklahoma—a long, long way from a Starbucks. His wife, Jackie, thinks he is a silly individual. He drinks black, black coffee all day long and sleeps about seven minutes a night. Victor's first novel, *Gun Monkeys*, was nominated for the Edgar Award.